Peter Jinks has been a journ███████████████████ of the Year award), a playwright (shortlisted for the STV/ Traverse comedy theatre award) and a screenplay writer (his script is in development with the BBC). He is thiry-one and lives in Sicily. *Hallam Foe* is his first novel.

Praise for *Hallam Foe*:

Quirky and hugely entertaining . . . wonderfully orchestrated slice of Gothic farce'
                                                                    The Times

Quite an achievement . . . quirky and charming'
                                                    Independent on Sunday

'A gripping and unsettling portrait of disturbed youth which is also very funny. The most assured first novel I've read all year.'
                                                            Mail on Sunday

'An old-fashioned story of wicked stepmothers manipulating sex-blind fathers, wronged children, revenge and happy endings . . . I would recommend it'
                                                                    Spectator

'An impressive debut'   *Glasgow Herald*

'This ambitious first novel cleverly shows that voyeurism is not always motivated by desire'   *Times Literary Supplement*

'Peppered with strong characters, an outrageously dysfunctional family, breakneck banter dialogue and a knowing dark humour, Hallam Foe is an excellent and absorbing read . . . Well-structured, fast-paced and assured, Hallam Foe is a highly promising debut from a confident and stylish writer'
                                                                    The List

'A dark, powerful debut'   *Outline*

HALLAM FOE

Peter Jinks

review

First Published in 2001
by REVIEW

An imprint of Headline Book Publishing

First published in paperback in 2002

10 9 8 7 6 5 4 3 2 1

ISBN 0 7472 6748 0

Printed and bound in Great Britain by
Clays Ltd, St Ives plc

HEADLINE BOOK PUBLISHING
A division of Hodder Headline
338 Euston Road
LONDON NW1 3BH

www.reviewbooks.co.uk
www.hodderheadline.com

Thanks to Lucia, Bella Bathurst, Stewart Hennessey, Ruaridh Nicoll and the other friends who have given me help. Thank you also Natasha Fairweather and Charlotte Mendelson.

one

Up in the oak tree, below the angled roof of the treehouse, the telescope swung smoothly before returning to its original position. Behind the long fingers guiding the telescope's shaft, soft breathing was just audible, alongside the clatter of leaves and the slap of some loose plastic sheeting.

Sunshine emerged from behind a white cloud and cast a long rectangle of light over the hunched figure from whose coathanger shoulders a camouflage jacket sagged. A large ring of keys and several rumpled handkerchiefs poked out of one of the bulging pockets. The intimate fug of bark and sap made the wooden cabin's interior seem stuffy, despite the choppy breeze.

With one eye pressed to the telescope's viewing lens Hallam Foe's face was mostly hidden behind twin curtains of thick brown hair, although the other eye, open but temporarily unseeing, was caught in the leaf-filtered light and shown to be grey. His plimsolled feet were muscular like a ballet dancer's and scuffed brown along the instep. They shifted with the mounting excitement.

He let out a harsh little cough, more like a hiccup, and pulled back. Pale bristles on the chin of his long white face confirmed that he was well past the age generally associated with playing in treehouses. But Hallam wasn't playing, he was observing.

The place was Leicestershire, in the geographical belly of England. The precise location Chanby Hall, up at the Back Lake, in the centre of a network of lookouts and listening posts. Platform One. Lower Point. South-West Traverse. Gatewatch. The lookouts spread across thirty acres of trees, lawns, obscured paths and patches of meadow. The lens of the telescope blinked once against the sky. Hallam mashed his nose with the palm of his hand, a nervous gesture that caused the cartilage to click moistly. Then he reached out, without needing to look, for a curly yellow logbook that sat upon a pile of hardbacks, the top one entitled *British Birds and How to Identify Them*. In the logbook he marked the time down, and began to scratch an entry in a swaying, mildly jaundiced hand.

3:32 It looks like they are beginning courtship. Mating expected soon. Not before time, this being midsummer.

A loud, urgent bird cry came up through the trees. The warning was unnecessary; Hallam had already been marking their progress, guided by the quietness and occasional twittering disturbances in the canopy that preceded someone's walk through the lakeland. He put aside his logbook and went back to the telescope. Through it he saw Carl's head appear over the grassy bank. Carl was the gardener, a muscular man in his early twenties with cropped sandy hair. He paused at the top of the incline and looked back. Into sight came a girl. It was Jenny.

Hallam did not need to check his logbook. She was from 36 Bosworth Avenue, which backed onto a stand of conifers at the east edge of the Hall grounds, in the modern part of the village over the hill. On weekdays she would retire to her bedroom at around eleven forty-five, usually undress with the curtains open and, having turned out the light, open the window and lean out to smoke a cigarette. At the end of her smoke she performed a private custom that still impressed even a seasoned observer of unwatched behaviour like Hallam. She would turn round on her bed, arch her back to face the stars and vertically propel a chunk of phlegm into the air with the aim of catching it again in her mouth. Even in daylight it was a feat. To Hallam's mute applause, she often succeeded, and he would mark it down with a tick in the margin of his logbook.

Hallam's records also confirmed more salacious but, to him, less interesting phenomena; for instance that Jenny had slept with four men from the village in the last two months, with a couple of other possibilities in the nearby village of Seaby. Because she lived with her parents, her preferred location, along with several other of the village's teenagers, was a spot off a little-used public right of way in a meadow which flanked the far borders of the grounds. The little condom-strewn nest was sheltered by brambles but was observable from Lower Point. Pairings would often visit around half an hour before the nearby pub's closing time, presumably to avoid the encouragement of drinkers piling home.

Carl, it seemed, was making a bid to be number five. Hallam's grimace of concentration widened into a grin, but only for a second. He pushed his head out of the slit, arranged his bony fingers in his mouth and drew breath to make the answering call that would declare his presence. But then he paused and withdrew his head without a sound. Not bothering to return to the telescope just yet, Hallam saw Carl wait for Jenny to catch up; she must have stepped in something and was wiping a stack heel with a wad of grass. Carl offered her a hand which she accepted and then together they walked to the edge of the lake. Hallam jumped up and in one surprisingly feline move slipped out of the window and onto the roof.

He trotted along a thick bough with a bandy-legged gait that seemed to leave his upper body immobile. He held an arm loosely above him, where a rope was slung. His feet, aimed outwards, curled unerringly round the branch and seemed to have their own knowledge of the precarious route ahead, because Hallam's eyes were mostly fixed on the couple. He gripped the rope with both hands then heaved his legs up and hooked his ankles round. Swinging easily under the rope, hand over hand, he swiftly crossed the gap between the oak and a horse chestnut that stood at the top of the lake.

Safe on the other tree he took out and held ready a pair of cheap and lamentably weak binoculars, but concentrated first on listening. He was perfectly positioned. From this transmission point he could hear almost everything the two distant figures said, as their voices bounced off the slick water's surface.

'It's ten years since I've been here,' said Jenny.

'Notice any changes?'

With an earnest expression she surveyed the trees flickering in the wind and the shifting crops beyond. 'Not really, but I remember it being more interesting on glue.'

He laughed – hur hur – with affectionate sarcasm. 'Bostik nostalgia. Spare me, please.'

Jenny frowned and looked at her feet. 'I shouldn't have worn these shoes. I wish you'd said.'

'Don't you like it up here?' he asked, anxious.

'That depends.' Jenny swung a leg languidly and waited. Flirtation wasn't Carl's strong point. He stood there uncertainly then fired a nervous glance over her face, looking for guidance, but by then she was smiling out over the lake, carefully unconcerned.

Having attempted to decipher these worrying messages, Carl, it seemed, made an executive decision and courageously ducked in for a kiss, but he did so clumsily and their foreheads bumped. She cracked up laughing and he had to step back with a sheepish grin.

'What was the head butt for?' she asked, rubbing the spot.

'Nothing. I didn't hurt you, did I?' asked Carl, very embarrassed. Shyness knocked about ten years off his body language. He looked at his feet and began to tamp down a piece of turf with his heel. 'Sorry,' he said reproachfully. He did not look up, sensing perhaps that she was enjoying his discomfort. She dipped her head, searching for his eyes, and on seeing her sad clown expression he submitted to a grin.

'Yeay, that's better,' she said.

Hallam shook his head and wondered what women saw in these pitiful displays of gaucheness – especially in someone of Carl's (admittedly camouflaged) intelligence. This was the first time that Hallam had seen Carl meaningfully in the company of a woman, and it was perhaps no coincidence that his chosen mate was the person who had been awarded the monicker of Village Slapper, with only mild affection. Carl really ought to get out more, Hallam reflected loftily, enjoying the observer's freedom from equal judgement.

However Hallam did concede that Carl brought out reserves of tenderness in Jenny that he had not noticed in her other couplings outdoors or inwindows. Taking pity on Carl, Jenny hooked her arm in his and pulled him close to her side, and together they looked over the sadly unromantic green-brown surface of the lake. In silence. It seemed that Carl had become tongue-tied.

Jenny sighed. Then she sighed again, louder this time, displaying what might have been impatience or longing. Either way, Carl took the hint. Attempting a slower and no doubt even more agonising lunge than the first time, he leant over and their lips met. And locked. They stayed that way for a long time. It was too far away to be sure, but with the aid of the binoculars Hallam could just see the shadow of Carl's amateur tongue shifting inside her cheek. Hallam took a moment to make an entry.

3:44 Doing the busy maggot.

The two lovers disengaged – after one minute and twenty-five seconds according to Hallam's measurement – and started to walk, with Carl leading her by the hand. Hallam returned to Centre Point, only a light shaking of leaves betraying his passage from outside the canopy. From the side window Hallam saw Carl come all the way up the side of the lake. Jenny liked the look of the beech tree, which anchored the higher reaches of the oak with a taut stretch of thick wire. The wire was looped round the beech's base and rose at about thirty-five degrees from the horizontal, the bark protected by a wad of synthetic padding. Carl was less keen. 'Further up,' he suggested.

'I like it here,' she said a mite petulantly, and sat down on the thick gráss, knowing that he was unlikely to argue. Carl took the opportunity to shoot a glance up at the treehouse, but Hallam had already anticipated him and was standing at the back of the cabin, out of sight. It was a clear betrayal of trust, but what the hell.

'What's that wire for then?' asked Jenny.

'It's to keep up the oak. See the cracks at the base?' Carl settled himself next to her and threw an arm over her shoulder, satisfied that Hallam was not up there.

'Where?'

'I'll show you later.'

Recovering his confidence, Carl reached across and grabbed Jenny's left buttock, then swivelled her round and laid her down. Her giggle was quickly muffled as, lips slipping and sliding, they rolled away from the base of the beech and down onto the thick bed of windblown wild grass, the long green blades silvery pale underneath.

Almost immediately Carl's hand rose up inside her top. This she allowed without protest, but slowly Hallam saw her eyes open and look up towards the oak. Jenny continued to stare as Carl gingerly held her left breast with a degree of curiosity that strongly suggested his previous refusal to talk about women had less to do with honour than raw inexperience. Hallam was unfazed by Jenny's direct upward gaze; he was used to invisibility and was already acquainted with most of the tricks. From her perspective, with the sun in her eyes, he knew all you could see of Centre Point through the foliage was a large black blob clinging to the trunk, more like an enormous growth than something manmade. Carl began to rub himself against her hip with movements reminiscent of the neighbour's beagle, Raymond, until Jenny spoke again. 'What's that up there?'

'What?'

'That big thing on the tree.'

'Eh?' Carl was irritated by the interruption. 'Oh that. An old treehouse.'

'Does anyone use it?'

'Nah, it's shot through with rot.'

Hallam's eyebrows rose. Carl had lied with uncharacteristic fluency; sex seemed to bring out the brigand in everyone.

'It was the son's to play in when he was younger. His father built it, old Foe's an architect. He even put a shower in at one point, made from an old Victorian toilet cistern. Hung it on the next-door branch, till the gale broke it off.'

'He's strange, that young one.'

'Hallam? He's all right.' Jenny gave Carl a look of superstitious mistrust. Carl laughed. 'OK, so maybe he is a bit peculiar.' Up in the dark, stock still, Hallam gave out a minute puff of exasperation. Carl pulled Jenny close to him but she sat up and plucked at her bra, unsettled by the mere idea of being watched, and reached into her handbag for cigarettes. She smiled at Carl's frustrated expression.

'Put a knot in it, you'll last longer.'

Jenny sparked up with a lighter – Hallam heard the electric click of it – and blew out smoke. She looked around her while Carl grumpily adjusted himself.

'Still got a funny atmosphere, this place.'

'It's old.'

'We used to come here on dares after dark when we were kids. You always felt you were being watched. Trish said it was haunted.'

Carl wearily turned back to conversation mode. 'These lakes were dug during the plague, Jen, that's why.'

'What a drag.' This glib remark was a mistake on Jenny's part, as it gave Carl a prompt to plunge into village history, an opportunity he rarely passed over, even at a time like this.

'Well, back in the thirteen hundreds whole villages were getting wiped out by the plague and they thought it was poisoned water spreading the illness. The truth was, nobody had a clue. But the landowners – it was a religious order back then, the Knights Templar, a bit like masons – had to do something or they'd look powerless. So they organised the digging on the lookout for a clean water supply, led by the old owner of the Hall whose tomb's in the church. See, you can see the church spire, all lined up with the lake.'

Jenny exhaled smoke heavily and leaned forward to take a look, betraying only mild interest, clutching her knees. Hallam, too, gazed up at the spire, set on crumbling sandstone masonry, as he must have done a thousand times before. Sure enough the spire was perfectly aligned, poking up over the shrubs one quarter of a mile away. If it could be called a spire. It was levelled off halfway up, truncated, with a weather vane stuck in the top like a comic afterthought.

Carl continued with gathering enthusiasm, fired as always by the distant past. 'So they dug this lake, and kept breathing the virus over each other. That's why the spire's so short – most of the able-bodied men died off. There was no one to finish it. Meanwhile the lake got used to breed trout for the Hall table. Just imagine it, the whole village fading away, except for a few terrified peasants, people like you and me, praying and digging away into their own graves.'

'Shurrup you!' Jenny landed Carl a surprisingly hard punch in the ribs and he rolled over, groaning and laughing. 'I hate ghost stories.'

'Come on, you must have heard this stuff before.'

'I'm not interested in that old crap. Look to the future, that's what I say.'

Carl suppressed a squawk of indignation because even he realised that now was not the time to argue about the relevance or otherwise of medieval history. He risked moving back closer and having a squeeze of her shoulder. She didn't shrug him off but she was not ready to lie back down just yet.

'So it's your job to keep louts like us out of the grounds, is it?'

'I let you in, didn't I?'

She did not seem impressed, so Carl took his hand off her and lay back, staring up at the sky, playing it patient. Jen took another drag, eyes half closed, looking straight ahead now but nowhere in particular. And sure enough she softened after a few quiet seconds, giving him a little dry, sideways look. 'So is abduction off the menu now?' Her gaze moved down to between his legs and Hallam felt a little burst of excitement in the pit of his stomach.

Carl patted the grass next to him. 'Come here.'

Jenny smiled coaxingly and lifted her hand to flick the fag butt away over the water.

'No!' Suddenly Carl was grabbing for her arm, but he was too late. The half-smoked butt fluttered out ten feet or so over the water before dropping with a damp sizzle. Small ripples marked the spot. A muscle in Hallam's jaw shifted slightly.

Jenny was taken aback. 'What's got into you?'

'You shouldn't have done that.'

'What?'

'Thrown your fag in the lake.'

'Why not?'

'He doesn't like it.'

'Who doesn't like it?'

Carl knew he had to lie. 'My boss.'

'The boss didn't see it though, did he? He's not here, is he?' Jenny's scowl intensified when Carl failed to reply. She began to collect herself together. 'Prick,' she said, with conviction.

'Come on, Jen, I'm sorry. It's just he's got a thing about cigarette butts floating on the lake. You weren't to know. I didn't mean to snap. Don't go.'

Jenny was getting up, straightening her skirt. She humphed, still put out, but Carl smiled hopefully, and tentatively reached up a hand to tug her little finger. Damage limitation. Hallam could see the affectionate gesture doing its work. Carl got onto his knees and gently kissed her on the hand – quite the gallant medieval knight – then firmly pulled her back down into the grass.

She was slow at first but soon they were kissing deeply, pressed close.

Then suddenly Jenny sat up and tucked her hair back matter-of-factly. She's going! thought Hallam. But no, instead she began deftly to unbuckle Carl's jeans, which reminded Hallam that she was training to be a nurse. Carl only had to lift his buttocks for her to pull down his pants and jeans in one swoop, causing his erect penis to bounce up. Jenny pulled off her top and bra, then shuffled round on her knees and presented her back to

Hallam. He observed that Carl's face appeared awed by the sight of her large bust. To Hallam, however, Jenny's breasts were about as erotic as a truck's headlamps, vulgarly designed to attract male attention.

He much preferred her back, the long white stretches of muscle bisected by the indented spine – the gentle curve of it suggesting unexpected defensiveness. What particularly drew him was the pale brown birthmark that ran down alongside the spine on the right-hand side. It was not ugly or even obvious, but Hallam could sense in the hunch of Jenny's shoulder and the way she kept Carl's attention elsewhere as she undressed that she was self-conscious about it. These were the things that Hallam liked to know about his subjects. He was excited by what people desired to hide, not what they displayed. His breathing had thickened, less with arousal than enthusiasm for the idea forming in his head. He knew Jenny had not violated the lake on purpose but it could not be overlooked. He turned away from the couple and rubbed his viewing eye, but decided in favour of a second look and returned to the viewing lens, just in time to see Jen lift her skirt up about her waist. Her usual position, Hallam noted. She cocked a leg over Carl and planted herself onto him.

Satisfied that everything was going ahead smoothly, Hallam shrugged off his camo jacket and began to unbutton his shirt, keeping only half an eye on the couple below. He reached across to a King Edward cigar box. The inside of the lid had a mirror on it. Hallam sorted through some ancient-looking make-up. He selected lipstick, dried but still usable. He screwed the base until the greasy red block rose about half an inch, then paused to shrug off his shirt. Carefully he drew a lurid red circle round each of his nipples, and then another larger one to make a bull's-eye of each. He added three arrows for each, pointing inwards round the circumference, evenly spaced.

Having checked his handiwork in the mirror, Hallam pinched his nipples tightly to heighten their colour. He glanced down at the couple again, now fully immersed in sex, faraway moans coming out of them. Hallam rubbed some foundation into his face, which left his skin glossily white and artificial, and thickly applied some eyeliner. He took up an old badger pelt from the floor with the head still attached – a gift from Carl, who skinned animals in his spare time – and secured it on his head with a piece of leather that served as a chin strap. The dried snout of the badger hung over his forehead, its black and white stripes arching over his skull. Then he rose to a crouch in the confines of the treehouse and waited, peering down.

Carl was grunting faster. Her rhythm shifted up a gear and became more jerky. Hallam recognised the sign. He went out of the window and onto the gnarled junction of the oak's main branches. He reached up above his head to where the thick wire supported the trunk. A roller was attached to the wire with a large butcher's hook hanging off it, slung over a branch. The sharp end had been hammered blunt and rags had been wrapped round the hook for a more comfortable grip.

Hallam detached the hook from the branch and gripped it firmly with both hands, interlacing his fingers. He flexed his long, thin biceps. The circles round his nipples elongated slightly as he put his weight on the hook and shifted the roller forwards and back on the wire. The moans beneath were louder. Hallam reminded himself of the distance and likely speed of descent. At which point he found himself distracted. His gaze had not moved from Jenny's smooth white back and splayed buttocks. She was moving gently, instinctively. Her plump body, usually so clumsy and graceless in clothes, had somehow acquired a classic beauty. He saw Carl raise his hands and put them reverently on her, then throw back his head in abandon.

Jenny speeded up her movements, up and down, and it was that noise, the accelerating clap of skin on skin, that brought back to Hallam the obscene comedy of the physical act. He was able to relocate his anger and with it the need to admonish her for sullying the lake. He gathered himself together again.

Carl pulled Jenny over and onto her back, thighs spread wide now, before resuming his inexpert prodding. Hallam checked his grip one last time, pursed his lips with resolve, took a brisk dive and was gone, launched into thirty feet of air. A nearby set of twigs vibrated briefly to mark his passing.

The roller buzzed loudly on the descent. It must have reverberated above her head where the wire was attached because her eyes half opened. Hallam let rip a high-pitched Tarzan warble. Over Carl's heaving shoulders her eyes were now wide in horror at the anaemic figure plunging towards her. She barely had time to let out a scream but her involuntary muscle-tightening caused Carl to climax inside her just as Hallam made impact.

Jenny struggled for a moment under the combined inert weight of Carl and Hallam, one post-coital, both winded. The hook swung drunkenly at the bottom of the wire, clattering against the beech. She wriggled out and scrambled to her knees.

'You dirty lying piece of shit!' she screamed at Carl. She swung a kick into his side. He grunted softly, lacking the breath for anything more expressive. She stepped over him and raised her foot, about to ram the heel between's Hallam's legs, but something stopped her, maybe the awareness that she was on his land, maybe even some residual barrier of class. In that moment's hesitation she realised he could see up her rumpled skirt. She stepped back and tugged it down in a belated attempt at modesty. Tears of anger and humiliation appeared in her eyes as she confronted Hallam's masked face.

'What . . . who the fuck do you think you are? You're a fucking disgrace.' She turned to leave and stamped heavily on Carl's stomach as she went, causing him to double up.

Hallam lifted himself onto an elbow and watched as Jenny jogged away down the slope, ugly and commonplace again in her department-store clothing. She paused after a few hundred yards, kicked off a shoe, and pulled up her knickers which were hooked round one ankle. She wobbled unsteadily on her feet.

Carl at last got his breath back. 'Jen!' he cried. 'Come back here, Jen, I didn't know . . .'

But she was gone. Carl hitched up his trousers and scrambled to his knees to face Hallam, who had flopped onto his back again, looking up at the sky and laughing soundlessly.

'I tried to stop her,' said Carl. 'You saw it, didn't you?'

Hallam sat up effortfully and frowned at Carl. 'I'm terribly sorry, did I interrupt something?' He slowly grinned.

Carl looked relieved, but that swiftly turned to anger. He batted Hallam quite hard around the head.

'Hey,' said Hallam mildly.

'You've ruined that for me now.'

Hallam's smile faded, he could see his friend was upset. 'Aren't you impressed? That was a precision landing.'

The beginnings of a smile moved across Carl's lips, but he dislodged it with an irritated movement of his knuckles.

'You call that a joke, you little pervert? What were you doing spying on me?'

Hallam shrugged and inspected a graze on his elbow.

'Get your own bloody thrills,' shouted Carl. 'What are you, nearly eighteen?'

'Seventeen. Carl . . .'

Carl got up and walked away, buckling his jeans as he went. 'That'll be right round the village, within the day.'

'She won't talk, Carl. She'll sound like a right slapper if she does.'

Carl swung round, then struggled to contain himself. 'She's not a slapper. Well, not to you. Get it?'

'Not really,' said Hallam, with inappropriate honesty.

Carl was going to retort but instead scowled and turned away to hitch up his zipper. Hallam watched him go down the slope then sighed and thoughtfully put his hand on the warm silvery shadow of flattened grass that the couple had left. He felt an unusual pang of loneliness, and decided to return to the treehouse.

He climbed up the rope ladder on the far side of the trunk. Back inside, he heard the mini tractor engine start up. Soon, from his elevation, he saw Carl moving away towards the back drive. The trailer, which Carl was supposed to have been emptying of grass cuttings, left behind it a residual scattering of green confetti. The rattle of its metal hinges could be heard, even at this distance, as it bumped over the rough ground.

Hallam leant his chin on the lip of the treehouse's slit, glum but content. He enjoyed the reassuring dusty smell of old wood baking in the heat. Beneath him stretched an expanse of hip-high wild grass, several fruitless fruit trees and a collapsed line of fence, grey from age and rot. At a higher elevation the upper branches of a great many trees could be seen – chestnuts, silver birches, more oaks – and among them, just visible, the white balustrade of the Hall. The rest was obscured by a long redbrick stable block.

His reverie was interrupted by the whine of a highly revved car from down the slope. Then he saw confirmation, the red stripe of a car cruising up the rear entrance track. Lucy, his sister. Hallam noted his clocking off time, 4:02, snapped shut the logbook and dropped it along with the other books into a sealable plastic bag. He rubbed at his face with make-up remover and put on his shirt again. He slipped a cover

over the telescope and replaced it in a chest kept in the darkened corner of the cabin. The books and binoculars went on top, along with the badger pelt. He locked the chest with a separate key, slid back the window slats and bolted them, and stepped outside, snapping the padlock shut behind him.

two

Hallam walked into the kitchen and found Lucy standing at the stove, stirring the contents of a pan while impatiently smoking a cigarette. 'Hello,' he said, in the drained voice he tended to use after a day in the trees.

Lucy jumped, turned and rolled her eyes. 'You're a sneaky one.'

Hallam flicked through an interiors magazine that was on the table while she scraped the contents of the pan with a spatula, not hiding her disregard for the contents within.

'What's that you're cooking?' asked Hallam, sloping over and taking a cautious sniff of the honey-coloured, viscous substance. 'You've outdone yourself there, Lucy, it smells quite unlike food at all.'

'That's because it's wax, O Dense One,' she replied, and took a deep drag of her cigarette. 'What, you're doing your legs?' asked Hallam, with mild surprise.

Lucy's voice acquired a hard edge. 'Not mine. Hers.' And she nodded up at the ceiling, indicating the master bedroom. Hallam nodded with studious lack of curiosity, and lifted his backside onto the work surface, then proceeded to bang a cupboard door irritatingly with his heel. Lucy shot him a dry look, gave the wax one last stir, passed the remains of her cigarette to Hallam and turned off the gas.

'Where's Julius?' he asked. The door to his father's offices were open and he had seen only the secretary Nicola through the window on his way in.

'He's away at a meeting. We're seeing them at the restaurant later. You'd better make yourself beautiful,' she added sarcastically, 'for the big occasion.'

Her tone was noted. It might suggest that a campaign of passive resistance against their stepmother had been re-declared after a long recess. Hallam narrowed his eyes and took a puff of her stub before tossing it into the sink. He thought Lucy would approve of the inconsiderate gesture.

'She'll blame me for that,' she said. She took the lightly steaming pan out towards the door. 'I don't know why she asks me to do this, it's disgusting. Too personal.'

'Why can't she do it?' asked Hallam, retrieving the butt with a roll of the eyes. He followed her over the wooden floorboards of the corridor, skirting the stepladders and dustsheets.

'She can't inflict pain on herself, she says, but my guess is she thinks I enjoy these intimate moments together.' Lucy's voice dropped as they went up the stairs. 'She's wallowing in her bath at the moment, hippo-like. I feel like her fucking skivvy.'

Hallam remembered, once upon a time not so long ago, when Lucy had indeed enjoyed spending time with their evil stepmother; so much, in fact, that Verity would visit her in Cambridge while Julius buried himself in work. But Hallam did not question this outbreak of resentment. They were stepchildren; conflicts came and went.

They reached the top of the broad main staircase and turned left on the long landing, moving past peeling strips of brownish wallpaper that had been their real mother's admittedly suspect but calming choice. It was now in the process of being steamed off in preparation for the New Start, which was pronounced according to Verity in the slightly arch, over-emphatic manner of a country-house dweller. At the end of the landing they came to four more steps where a shut door led off to the right – the master bedroom. Hallam paused here, at the invisible barrier, and Lucy carried on, shouldering the door wide open but pausing briefly in the doorway.

'I won't be long.'

Hallam turned as if to return the way he had come, but when he was sure that Lucy had entered the bathroom he stopped, and softly climbed the steps. He could hear a murmured voice and the slop of bathwater. Lucy had left the door agape and Hallam popped his head through far enough to confirm that the full-length mirror at the end of the room did indeed give him a limited view into the bathroom. This was not fortuitous; he regularly toured the Hall checking his viewing points, making small adjustments where needed, although this one was seldom used.

He was assisted in his view by the mirror-doored cupboards in the bathroom that faced each other, one of which was half open and provided a collision of slightly steam-spoilt images. Lucy was on her knees scraping the edge of the spatula on the rim of the pan, while in front of her a long pink leg emerged from a white towelling robe, twinkling its immaculate toes. A series of reflected pink legs criss-crossed into infinity. Verity's upper body and face were not visible as she was leaning back Cleopatra-like on the chair while Lucy applied the hot wax to her flesh. In the brief silence Hallam could hear the gurgle of bathwater on its piped descent. The hall of mirrors, he thought.

'You must be getting excited about the move,' said Verity, her voice fuzzy with pleasure. Lucy was leaving for South Africa at the end of the week for an ethically questionable job at De Beers.

'Do you want a hand with the packing?'

'No thanks,' said Lucy, shuffling across on her knees to the next leg that swung into view. 'It's mostly disposal anyway.'

'I admire you travelling light. I always end up with loads.' A pause as the spatula made its honey-coloured trail up towards the knee. 'I expect you'll miss your friends,' she added.

Lucy grunted. 'Not as much as you think.'

'Have you heard anything from Alex?'

Alex, Hallam vaguely recalled, was a friend of Lucy's from university, though he'd not heard the name mentioned for a while.

'No,' Lucy replied, then paused, and dropped the spatula back in the pan with a clatter. 'Have you?' There was a hint of suppressed aggression in her voice.

'Not really.'

Another silence as the legs moved out of sight and the towelling robe was pulled down off the shoulders to the waist, as far as Hallam could tell. Lucy pursed her lips and stood up. The bathroom door creaked forward a few inches, perhaps closed slightly to reduce a draught; it destroyed Hallam's view, so he made himself more comfortable on the floor and concentrated on listening.

'Has Hallam shown any kind of interest in a career?' asked Verity. 'I was thinking, now that we've got you set up, we could arrange some work experience for him during the university holidays.'

Hallam cringed, and resisted an urge to steal away. He hated hearing conversations about himself. They always talked about a Hallam that was weak and quiet and going through adolescent difficulty. He only endured hearing about his public persona because it served as advanced warning against threats to his private and currently bucolic world. Verity's question caused his skin to tingle with fright, as did any suggestion that aimed to lever him out of the grounds.

'Well actually,' began Lucy, 'I've got a feeling he might follow in Julius's footsteps and become an architect. In fact,' she continued breezily, as Hallam choked on the outrageous fabrication, 'after a few years in diamonds I might get involved too, on the business side of course. I quite enjoyed looking after things when you were away.' She was referring to the months after their mother had killed herself, when Julius sank into depression and Verity – technically working in the office as an accountant/PA – had taken an extended leave of absence.

There was a silence, broken only by the soft scrape of the spatula on the rim of the pan.

'Is that a good idea?' Verity asked quietly, but with a voice that had refocused.

'Why not?'

'I saw what went missing from those accounts, even if your father didn't.'

'What?'

'I also know what you spent it on.'

'There's stuff I know too.'

'I know, but I don't think you really want to do that, not when you've got a lovely job to go to, and plenty of help with the bills if you're good. Do you think it's dried yet?' A pause.

'A few more minutes,' said Lucy, humbled.

The time passed in silence.

'Now do it quickly. And remember,' said Verity at last, her voice already tightening in anticipation, 'it's the pain speaking.' He heard two long and vicious rips, so close together they almost combined. A ferociously nipped intake of breath. 'You did that slowly on purpose, you little whore.'

A lopsided grin of disbelief formed on Hallam's face. There was a silence, followed by soft measured pants.

'Now the rest,' Verity said in a husky reproachful voice.

Another, shorter, dual-ripping sound was heard, and the lack of even a yelp caused Hallam's knuckles to flex white, then red. At last there was a deep laugh of utter abandonment. 'You have shown yourself to be highly ungrateful, Lucy. I won't forget it.'

He winced, and peered back through the door into the mirror. He saw Lucy chucking something into a plastic bag, grabbing the pan and getting up. Hallam quickly trotted back down the corridor but was close enough to hear Verity, her normal tone restored, calling out. 'Lucy, please, come back . . .' But Lucy was out through the door, tears rimming her eyes, as Hallam pretended to be emerging from his bedroom.

'That's the last time, so help me God,' she declared fervently. She paused at the top of the stairs, breathed deeply, then with a gesture of irritation shoved the plastic bag and pan into Hallam's hands before stamping downstairs.

Hallam peered into the bag and saw long curled strips of leg-wax, with short black hairs stuck to them. He started to follow Lucy down the stairs, fishing in the bag and pulling out one of two smaller strips with a different pattern of longer hairs. They reminded him strangely of pork scratchings.

'Hold on,' he said, a look of wonder on his face. 'What about these ones?'

She glanced back. 'Bikini line.'

Hallam affected a look of horror and dropped them back into the bag before wiping his hands on his trousers.

Lucy did that?

Lucy laughed, sniffed, and pushed open the green baize door that led back through to the kitchen. 'Her armpits, you dolt.'

There was time to kill before their date with Julius and Verity. Lucy and Hallam headed for the army surplus shop in Leicester city centre. They strolled past a group of teenagers gathered round a glass case, bewitched by the combat knives displayed within. Hallam regarded them with curiosity as he and Lucy went to the counter, where a large round man sat precariously on a high stool.

'Excuse me, do you have any mosquito netting?' asked Lucy.

The man pointed up at the ceiling, from where various nets hung.

'Water purifying tablets?'

'Lucy,' Hallam interrupted, 'you're going to live in Johannesburg. Verity said you'd be better off taking a mobile phone and a machine-gun.'

'What does that silly bitch know? She probably never stuck her nose out of the five star hotel.' She looked at the man again. 'That reminds me, do you have garrottes?'

'Cheesewire? At the back.'

'I don't think she was being rude,' Hallam remarked, for the sake of accuracy.

They made their way through the deodorised smog of Saturday shoppers in the city centre. Lucy carried a bulging green duffel bag of tropical travelling unnecessaries. Her mood seemed to have lifted.

'Will you miss me when I'm gone?' She smiled and looked at her little brother, taking his confused expression, Hallam knew, as shyness. In fact it was a more difficult question than she realised, because he missed her already. He had noted with growing reproach her long absences since her graduation, her distantness when she was around, but the pangs of impending abandonment did nothing to reduce the orchestral love that he felt for her.

He was trying to think of an answer that would be honest without sounding hurtful, when she peered closer.

'Is that make-up on your face? Did you borrow some?'

Actually it was their mother's, salvaged from her personal effects shortly after her death. This was a sensitive matter; one that he did not wish to talk about. He wiped his cheeks rapidly: he had tried to get most of the foundation off earlier but his cheeks were still glossy.

'You look very glamorous.'

'Shut up,' said Hallam.

They walked in silence for a while, and as the crowds began to clear, Hallam's mind hovered around the conversation he had heard in the bathroom, most of which he had not properly understood. All he really knew was that over the course of the past four years both he and Lucy, despite the many reasons to hate their stepmother, had fallen for her instead. Until now. Now it seemed that Lucy was beginning to hate, in the mature way of adults. Hallam had not yet graduated from sporadic personal resentment.

Part of the difficulty was Verity's selective thoughtfulness. She had, for instance, arranged the De Beers job for Lucy. What's more, she seemed to respect solitary nature. All she asked in return was acceptance of her irksome if seemingly well-meaning attempts to slot him into the sloanier end of the county circuit.

It was different with Lucy. Verity had seemed determined to force intimacy on her. Confused and vaguely flattered by being taken into this older woman's confidence – there was fifteen years between them – Lucy responded either with strained cordiality when Hallam was around or, he suspected, gushing confessions of her own when he was not. On the whole he tried not to spy on Lucy, partly out of respect, but also because he liked to think that it wasn't necessary: he and his sister were close, he told himself, at least in a roundabout way.

Lucy gamely booted a tincan off the pavement to break the silence, and cleared her throat. 'Is there something you want to talk about? I'm very open-minded.'

'Lucy,' he said patiently, realising that she must still be thinking about the make-up, 'I am not gay.'

'Oh.' She went for option two. 'Your exam results are due soon aren't they. Worried?'

'Mm.' He had not even thought about them.

'You'll be fine won't you?' said Lucy, trying to reassure him. 'You'll love university, it will get you out of the Hall anyway, away from the hag.'

Hallam's face and mind went blank. The future held no allure for him, and his exam results were the least of his worries, his teachers having assured him of straight As. In practical terms, however, he was comprehensively ignorant of the adult world outside the grounds, and he wished desperately to preserve this state of affairs for as long as he could. He could sense a growing threat to the territory that he guarded on his mother's behalf – she had loved the grounds to distraction – and it frightened him so much that he found elaborate ways not to think about it.

He stepped carefully round a dogturd on the pavement. Up ahead was a litterbin piled high with empty cans and styrofoam chip containers, haloed by circling wasps. In the sunshine it gave off a smell of sweetened orange juice and chipshop vinegar. Lucy stretched her arms and moved onto a happier subject. 'I've got a feeling that I'm not going to see Verity ever again,' she said, but then a small responsible frown appeared. 'Although if she dies I may come back for the formalities. Read an exorcism, place a stake through her heart, etcetera.'

'What's the matter with you two anyway?'

'Never you mind.'

'No, what is it?'

'Girlie things. Wombs.'

Hallam grunted and looked up as they turned the corner. Ahead a group of four teenaged young men in assorted tracksuits and baggy buttockless jeans lounged on a bench, smoking cigarettes. They were also conducting a gobbing contest, the aim of which was to send phlegm through the legs of passing pedestrians. One of them, a short one with an aspiring moustache, received a muted cheer as his yellow missile flashed handsomely between the shins of a schoolboy. Then he noticed Lucy. Faces pointed in their direction. Leers followed and a few whispered comments as they approached. Hallam, in Marks and Spencer's tweed and uncomfortably hot grey flannels, stared downwards: the pavement ahead was speckled with saliva; it made him think of the cuckoo spit he sometimes found on the hedgerows at the Hall.

'But I'm determined to enjoy myself this evening,' Lucy said in reckless sing-song tones, swinging her ragged green duffel bag from one shoulder to the other, 'whatever they're celebrating.' The corner of her bag clipped the tip of one of the group's cigarettes and sparks fluttered to the ground. The moustachioed young man looked down in disbelief at the embers of his cigarette, smoking like a tiny earthed comet on the pavement slab. A few shreds of tobacco were still attached.

'Watch it, you silly cow,' he said in a tone of righteous annoyance.

'Oh, sod off,' she sighed, not turning her head. Then to Hallam, casually, 'I've had enough of being insulted today. Is my bag on fire?'

'What did she say?' Hallam heard the moustache say to his friends. Then the stranger raised his voice to Lucy. 'What was that you said?'

Hallam felt the unfamiliar role of masculine protector fall across his skinny shoulders. He took Lucy's elbow to guide her onwards and felt a sharp desire to be up a tree. 'Sorry,' he said gruffly over his shoulder, on her behalf.

'Come here and say that,' one of them said. There was laughter and they seemed to lose interest.

Hallam felt Lucy slowing down. 'Lucy, we haven't got time for a fight,' he said quickly.

'Thanks for the advice, Hallam,' she said, then stopped, smiled helpfully towards the moustache and raised her voice. 'He said sorry, I said sod off. Is everything clear now? Good day.'

The moustache frowned at the cheek of it but was unable to think of an immediate response. His nearest companion, wearing a tight seventies-style T-shirt and shaggy hair, suppressed a grin; he had a small gap between his front teeth. Then the moustache peered at Hallam. 'Wait, is that make-up? Come here.'

Hallam turned back and the young man approached. Now it was Lucy dragging Hallam away. 'Hallam, don't bother.'

But it was no use. In the heat of confrontation Hallam had discovered a hidden talent for unthinking obedience. It was not cowardice, he later told himself, but something more primordially stupid. The moustache came up to him, wafting aftershave, and peered closer at Hallam's face.

'Leave it, Si,' said the gap-toothed one behind him, sounding bored.

Hallam rubbed furiously at the residual foundation on his cheeks and continued rubbing until he found himself, magically, lying on his back on the pavement, looking up the nostrils of his adversary. Si, it seemed, had hit him. How strange.

In the ladies' toilet of the Barkham Hotel Lucy dabbed Hallam's cut lip with some damp cotton wool and wiped up the blood that had dribbled down his chin and dried.

'You're lucky he just clipped you,' she murmured solicitously. 'There, it's not swelling too much. If I were you I'd get the rest of that make-up off. Here's some remover.'

'Thank you so much,' said Hallam, with what he felt was an appropriate level of sarcasm. He glanced nervously towards the door, worried that more females might come in and offer group sympathy. He felt exposed in this forbidden zone of female privacy, having been accorded temporary eunuch status by the sympathetic lady at reception.

'Now don't be grumpy.' Lucy turned to address her own face as Hallam took some cotton wool and started rubbing his face with make-up remover. Even in the ugly light of the bathroom mirror Lucy's skin looked smooth and unblemished, its light tan softening the lines of her small nose and slightly slanted brown eyes. Hallam paused and looked at his own reflection — not something he enjoyed doing at the best of times. His lip was puffing and it gave him a mild pout; concrete evidence that any attempt to participate in the world outside the grounds was bound for humiliation. He had evolved in a highly specialised environment; outside it he was a runt.

Lucy opened her duffel bag and pulled out first some lipstick and then a rolled-up black dress. 'There's a little surprise in the right-hand pocket.' She unravelled the dress and, with a smile at Hallam, waltzed into one of the cubicles. Her T-shirt, white with a red heart in the centre, flopped over the cubicle door. Hallam searched the duffel bag. Inside was a mini joint, daintily rolled.

'Go in next door and light it up,' she said through the door. Her trousers swung over next. He could see her bare feet and gold ankle bracelet underneath the door, the toenails painted green. In the same pocket he found a lighter. Hallam stepped into the cubicle beside her and lit the joint. The tobacco crackled slightly, and had a sharp taste. With a slight shudder he took a second drag. Over the top of the partition he saw the black dress pass over bare white arms. Hallam reached up to give Lucy the joint.

She took it and a cloud of smoke began to creep along the low ceiling then leak out over the top of the cubicle. There was a short hiss as the joint was dropped in the toilet and the smoke's curiously fascinating effect was destroyed as the door opened and Lucy emerged. Hallam did also. She critically assessed herself in the mirror. She applied lip gloss. Hallam could feel hot blood circulating in his ears. Lucy briefly appeared two-dimensional.

'All done.' She smiled, tossing the lipstick into the bag.

'We're early.'

'Then we must build up the tab for Julius.'

Lucy had recently begun to call their father by his first name. Hallam wondered whether it was a statement of equality now that she had a job, or just a snub, placing him in the same category as Verity, as if by marrying the woman he had lost the privileges of fatherhood. Hallam felt too self-conscious to follow Lucy's suit except when they were alone together, so had compromised by not calling his father anything at all, which had its own practical difficulties.

Lucy took one last glance in the mirror, rolled her lips and, with the air of someone trying out a new mouth, spoke one bright word. 'Cocktails.'

Hallam and Lucy were into their second round of margaritas by the time they heard the sound, emerging from the lobby, of purchasing power passing through an English hotel: it whispered, it burbled ingratiatingly, eventually it rustled. The lady behind the desk smiled in their direction and a porter came through, carrying two ostentatiously small shopping bags.

'Here they come,' muttered Lucy bitterly, 'the happy couple.'

Verity appeared in the doorway, dressed in black. She cradled in her arms a long and elegant cactus, swaddled in florist's paper. Tall, pale, spectacularly correct, she passed the prickly plant to the porter with a curt instruction not to water it, then turned to survey the room. She dropped a hand to her crocheted hip in an artful display of impatience. She straightened a silk-stockinged leg. Enter the hag, thought Hallam.

He tried to pinpoint Verity's nodes of attractiveness – the slight tightness of the skin between her eyes that gave her face an almost oriental intensity, the playful indifference with which she could look at a man. There were more obvious things also; for instance the full-breasted trimness of her figure that made Hallam think of fifties actresses. But more interesting was the way she seemed to hold that arresting figure together, by force of will rather than exercise or diet.

Verity was a consumer. She took undisguised pleasure in food, wine and even, occasionally, Julius's cigars. And yet to Hallam's knowledge she never played sport or went to a gymnasium. He had seen many thirtysomething professional females, and particularly young architects, come through his father's office over the years (although recently the flow had mysteriously abated) and they had physiques variously tanned, toned or starved – all of them worked on. Verity's body gave the different impression of having been attended to. Having witnessed the depilatory episode earlier in the day Hallam now understood the true price of this seeming effortlessness. There was suffering in every curve. Other people's, mostly.

Verity at last contrived to spot them. Seeing their cocktail glasses she raised an eyebrow knowingly and for all their efforts their faces rose with the tide of her conspiratorial charm. But Lucy fought it.

As Verity took the shopping bags from the porter, Lucy whispered to Hallam, 'Wearing that stuffy brooch again, I see. Jane Austen without the knickers.'

Verity arrived at their semicircular seating arrangement. She slipped the bags under the table and looked at Hallam who rose to his feet. Two kisses.

'Hallam, you are becoming handsome.' It was stated as cold fact.

'You should be off shagging girls,' suggested Lucy.

'I'm on holiday,' he parried, feeling himself flush nevertheless.

Verity smiled and leant down to kiss Lucy, although this was a difficult manoeuvre as Lucy did not deign to move. Verity straightened and sat down, followed by Hallam.

The waiter came over. 'A Bloody Mary please,' said Verity, 'and a bottle of Veuve Clicquot, four glasses.'

'Where's Julius?' asked Lucy, careful not to sound as if she gave a toss.

'He is inspecting the car park. Did you see the cactus he gave me?' Verity moved her dark hair from left to right. The movement exposed a long slim throat encircled by a blue ribbon which held the eighteenth-century brooch, one of Julius's bestowals from the Foe inheritance. She always wore it on significant occasions. Hallam's gaze surreptitiously lingered over Verity's hair: it was thick, dark and immaculate.

'Hallam?' There was accusation in Lucy's voice. She had a sixth sense for detecting when Hallam was being lulled by Verity. Hallam quickly wiped the dreamy look off his face, blinked apologetically and stared instead at the Persian rug beneath his feet, willing his shame to seep away into its purple geometry. Shame because this was the power which had hopelessly outclassed and then destroyed their mother. Hallam knew that female mystery was extinct in the modern world, but Verity possessed something that came worryingly close. The timeless twinset of sex and death.

'Here he comes,' said Verity without turning round; she had spotted her husband's arrival in a mirror on the far wall, Hallam noted approvingly.

Julius rambled through the same entrance in a wrinkled dark blue suit, groping in his pockets for some imaginary coins, as he often did when he was bothered by something. He was a tall man in his late forties with grey-flecked hair, but the small nose made him look almost boyish. The impression was reinforced by his neglected appearance and teardrop-shaped brown eyes. They communicated a quality not unlike innocence but which, on surviving into middle age, betrays itself as a highly resourceful form of escapism. So Hallam would conclude several years later.

'Come and sit down,' Verity said.

'I don't know why they build them like that, it's a ridiculous waste of space.'

'Shut up, darling,' she hinted.

Two waiters arrived with the Bloody Mary and an ice bucket containing the champagne. Julius noticed and dragged his mind away from car parks. The architect smiled sheepishly. This was the first test of Lucy's resolution not to indulge in any form of emotional collaboration. There was a silence.

Hallam looked at Lucy, wanting guidance on how to play this. It was the first time they had been invited to celebrate this particular date in the calendar, but four years must have been judged long enough for old sensitivities to heal. Hallam could see Lucy wavering over whether to deploy sarcasm.

'Happy anniversary, Julius.' Irony and grudging affection. Despite herself Lucy had been charming.

'Happy anniversary, Daa . . .' Hallam had his usual problem with the form of address and pretended to cough.

'So,' said Verity, addressing her stepchildren with a look of playful disapproval, 'the pair of you are about to be indulged. But, what with you going away overseas, Lucy, this might be the last time we have a proper family meal together for ages. Right.' She groped for the shopping bags under the table, giving Lucy the opportunity to roll her eyes in a here-we-go manner at Hallam. Out came two gift-wrapped packages. Hallam took his hesitantly, Lucy swept hers up with one indifferent hand.

Hallam's eyes widened as he pulled out of the wrapping a pair of Leica binoculars. The best; they featured prominently in the well-thumbed Spycaptain brochures that he pornographically coveted. He immediately lifted them up to his eyes and swept the room; they were marvellously powerful. He trained them on the blurred images of Verity and Julius, grinned and thought: all the better for watching you with. Unfortunately at this range his subjects were too close for focus. 'They're brilliant. Thanks.' Hallam lowered the binoculars, extremely pleased.

Verity smiled and touched his knee. 'A replacement for that ancient telescope. You'll be able to spot a grebe from a mile off now.'

They all looked then at Lucy. Her head was bowed. Nestled on her lap in a bed of gift wrapping was a mobile telephone. 'You can use it for international calls,' said Verity, 'so you've no excuse not to call and give us your news.'

'You've got to keep it charged up,' said Julius, 'but I've got an adaptor you can use over there.'

Lucy did not look up.

'Don't you like it?' asked Verity. 'For some reason your father preferred buying this to paying for the tattoo you've been going on about, even if it was more expensive. Do you want us to take it back?'

'No,' said Lucy. She looked up at Verity with frank, moist eyes and a smile raw with shame. 'I love it, as you well know.'

Julius grunted with satisfaction and took a swig from his flute of wine. Hallam frowned and weighed the binoculars in his hands. They were reassuringly heavy.

Their table was in the far corner, lodged in the shagpile of the hotel's main dining room. Hallam noticed that things were going from bad to worse by the time food was ordered. Verity, in the presence of Julius, was making her usual effort to be charitable-minded, which she enlivened with the occasional sparkle of claws. The cocktails, too, had helped to make the atmosphere relaxed and enjoyable, and the stress of it all was beginning to show on Lucy. She sat to the right of Hallam, her face a sardonic mask that could not, however, disguise a crawling sense of compromise.

Hallam meanwhile had been displaying his perhaps surprising facility for diverting prattle. He could hardly stop himself, despite the censure he sensed coming from Lucy. Panicking slightly only seemed to make it worse. He mentally blamed it on the spliff.

After a selected update on village affairs, Hallam was discoursing on the rumoured decadence of the local bell-ringing society: beer cans had been discovered in the apse. There was also its association with the new female vicar, who was widely suspected of being a lesbian. 'Hallam, where do you get all this fabulous material?' asked Verity.

'Carl, mainly,' he lied (he tried to gather his own intelligence whenever possible).

'You'd make a tremendous spy,' she said. 'Daniel Defoe's bloodline runs true, it seems.'

Hallam smiled unevenly and took a sip of his wine. Verity kept her gaze on him, the blue eyes bright with assessment, the smile, as ever, affectionate. She put the final touches to the small mound of pâté that she had arranged on a piece of toast and bit it off cleanly, her teeth making a perfect indented crescent in the triangle. She chewed several times.

Then, as she eased the modest mouthful down, something horrible happened. That soft, unlined throat of hers puckered strangely under the brooch's deep-blue ribbon, and Hallam could quite clearly make out the gristly mechanics of the swallowing action. It made him think of a lizard, and the distruption to her beauty – however fleeting – came as a small but shocking moment of enlightenment, as if he had discovered, Dorian Gray-like, where she paid for her beauty. He was amazed he had never noticed it before.

'Julius,' Verity said, as if nothing had happened, 'have you spoken to Carl about pulling up that rose bed? It's playing havoc with my allergy and I must have asked him a thousand times.'

Hallam willed himself not to stare at her throat and drew his mind back to the conversation. He knew that Carl was opposed to the destruction of the roses on a matter of principle – he had put hundreds of hours into that rose bed during his apprenticeship – and Hallam added to the wordless opposition, as he did to any plans that altered the old grounds. Although nothing specific had been mentioned, the front acres were clearly marked down for an assault once the interior of the Hall had been refurbished.

'I want old Mr Hennessey back,' continued Verity, referring to Carl's father. 'I didn't realise gardeners retired; I imagined them slowly turning into compost.'

'I think he wanted to give his son a chance,' observed Julius.

'Is that natural? How sweet.'

'Old Mr Hennessey,' said Lucy, with undisguised relish, 'was a pervert.'

Verity bit her lip with mock excitement. 'Now that sounds controversial, Lucy. What do you mean?'

'Do you know what he did in his last week? I was coming up the drive and he was over by the shrubbery. And he shouted out: "Look what I've found, Lucy. A newborn." I thought, oh dear, what's he got, a half-dead blackbird chick? So I went over. "All on its own, it was," he said, with his hands cupped in front of him. Then when he opened them, what was it? Old Mr Hennessey's dick. Then he squeezed the mushroom bit and his jap's-eye opened and closed like some revolting imitation of a hungry beak.'

Hallam raised his eyebrows and took a sip of champagne. He found Mr Hennessey's actions distasteful certainly. Personally he couldn't think of anything that would give him less pleasure than exposing himself to a young woman. Julius was shocked enough to stop shovelling prawn cocktail. 'Mr Hennessey did that?'

'Do you think I should get some therapy?'

'Why didn't you tell me?'

Lucy shrugged. 'Trauma probably. Mum always said he was creepy. Anyway, too late now, he's dead, isn't he?'

'He's in a nursing home.'

Hallam noted the mention of their mother – a sure sign of the stakes being raised. Julius attempted to take another bite of prawn cocktail, only to abandon it. He put the spoon down on the saucer and wiped his mouth.

'What inspired that little revelation?' asked Verity. Lucy looked mildly perplexed. Verity laughed. 'Your father did have a mouth full of seafood, you know.'

'I'm sorry, Verity. I'll keep any rape attempts to myself in future.'

'Don't be silly, Lucy,' said Julius. 'I'm just amazed you didn't tell us before.'

'Poor man,' said Verity, sighing. 'Perhaps he got the wrong impression.'

Julius straightened his napkin. Lucy scowled. 'So you want to know the purpose of my story?'

'I wonder what the main course will be like,' Julius speculated with quiet desperation.

'It goes to show,' Lucy continued, 'that you, Julius, are blind to certain things that are going on in the Hall.'

'We must all be on our guard,' said Verity, archly.

Hallam felt a strong urge to leave the table. He put down his napkin and stood up.

'Where are you going?' asked Lucy, making it clear that she expected his support. But Hallam wasn't interested; he was the one who would have to live with the fall-out from this, not her.

'I am going to relieve myself,' he informed the table, then inclined his head smartly, and headed out.

Hallam intended to get some fresh air; the joint they had smoked earlier had made him feel slightly sick. Preferring to steer clear of the busy street at the front he found a fire exit ajar at the back of the hotel lobby, which opened onto a small yard next to the car park entrance. Across the yard he saw another door flanked by wheelie bins which led, he guessed from the smell, to the kitchens. A metal ladder led up the brick wall to the hotel roof.

The ladder inspired in Hallam a sudden longing for height. Glancing quickly around him – there was no one about – he obeyed his impulse, strolled over to the ladder's base, and then quickly clambered up. Each rasp of shoe sole on rung was a rising note of exhilaration. He was climbing out of confusion. His face was open and smiling when he hopped onto the roof three storeys up.

He looked around him, past the service lift and ventilator shaft, at the world below. He stepped softly over the birdshit-spattered roof and surveyed the city that was around him. The streets were cooling and quietening under the evening sky. He breathed deep and luxuriated in the horizon's deepening colours. He knew his time was restricted to a few minutes, and this gave the moment a sweet poignancy.

It was abruptly broken by the clatter of the service lift opening up. Out of it stepped a kitchen porter on his break, lighting a cigarette. A puff of smoke rose from his cupped hands, slipped away, and then he looked up and saw Hallam. A gust of wind brushed the hair which looked sweaty from the kitchens and Hallam saw his face in full. He was the one from the street, the one with the gap in his teeth.

The young man recognised Hallam immediately. Then he looked thoughtfully over Hallam's shoulder to the horizon. Hallam turned and looked too. It was turning pink. A brief silence. He heard the young man cough and stroll up.

They stood side by side a few feet away and shared the horizon. The young man offered Hallam a cigarette from his packet. Hallam smiled and shook his head; he contemplated saying something, decided against it. 'Si's a wanker,' said the young man simply.

Hallam nodded, as if he didn't have an opinion on the matter but would take his word for it. Not feeling the need to communicate further, they both returned to making use of their observatory. The sky looked all the more beautiful. Hallam was struck by a sentimental sense of comradeship with the young man. He smiled to himself with a pleasure that was almost conceited. Only a roof could bring this kind of reconciliation, he thought, free from the various stupidities of existence on the ground below. He now recognised the young man as one of his kind, another voiceless dissenter, the one who always hung back. His earlier reluctance to intervene when Hallam got punched was thus entirely understandable and forgivable. Hallam even felt gratitude now for the little 'Leave it, Si' comment he had heard him say before the swing came.

Hallam breathed deeply again. Could it ever be possible, he thought, for a life to be conducted entirely free of association with the ground? Imagining such a state was a regular daydream of his, and one that had always been suffused with solitary romance. But now the horizon filled him with a drowsy sense of possibility. Perhaps, in his dreams at least, he did not necessarily have to be alone. But then he harshly dismissed this last thought as weakness. He looked at his watch and realised he had to go. Noiselessly he returned to the head of the ladder and only paused to regard the porter's back in silhouette, caught briefly against the red sky.

'Ah, here he is,' said Verity as Hallam slipped back into his chair, eyes down. 'We're not going to bother with a naff toast but it might be fun to explain why we chose this venue tonight.'

'Certainly not the food,' muttered Lucy, and Verity chuckled. It seemed that Lucy no longer had the power to irritate.

Lucy reached for her glass. 'Go on then,' she sighed.

'I shall. Because while it is four years to the day since Julius and I got married, this restaurant has a significance all its own. It was where Julius first proposed that I become a partner in the firm. I was just his accountant at the time, and he couldn't believe it when I said no.' Verity smiled at her husband mischievously. Julius bobbed his eyebrows and embarked on his main course. Lucy took an impolitely large mouthful of costly Chablis. Hallam grunted. 'Isn't this the moment then, Julius?' she prompted him gently.

'Ur?' Julius looked up open-mouthed. His mind must have been somewhere else entirely; up a buttress perhaps, or down a foundation.

'The little proclamation.'

'Oh. Yes.' Julius swallowed. 'Verity's going to become a partner in the firm – we agreed it this afternoon.'

Lucy looked utterly crushed. Hallam, while he was not exactly interested in business matters, understood the significance of this: now every single aspect of their father's life was subject to her influence and power.

Even Verity seemed slightly unsettled by the silence. 'So,' she said, 'it's all come full circle, as chance would have it.'

Hallam's heart began to beat a little faster. He straightened up. 'When did Julius first offer you the partnership exactly?' he asked in as offhand a manner as he could. He had asked a question to which he knew the answer: it was when his mother was in the city psychiatric hospital and shortly to kill herself, just as Julius's affair with Verity was getting underway.

'Well, Hallam, let me see,' she said, appearing to think. During that pause Hallam glanced over to Lucy who was waiting with similar attention to Verity's response. Those few moments on the roof had boosted Hallam's self-confidence to the point of recklessness. He wanted to establish whether it was possible for Verity to display any symptoms of conscience. He wanted to demonstrate to Lucy that he had not completely caved in.

Verity knew the question was a challenge, but it seemed to be no problem at all. She looked Hallam straight in the eye. 'It wasn't long before your mother passed away, because I remember, a few months later I had to come back from my break and help out Lucy here. The business needed someone to take care of it while,' she paused here tactfully, 'while everyone sorted themselves out.'

Hallam loathed the way Verity used that term 'passed away', with all its pious delicacy, and the term 'your mother', as if their mother hadn't also been Julius's wife. And yet he almost enjoyed these sensations of disgust, and only partly because he wanted his father to witness the depthless insincerity that his wife was capable of. It was probably a wasted effort in that respect anyway.

Verity continued smoothly, 'And do you know, the funny thing was, that evening someone else rang me up. Randall, his name was . . .'

'Dear old Randall,' muttered Julius.

Verity laughed again. 'Yes, dear, dear Randall. He had a soft spot for me and absolutely insisted on taking me out to dinner that very night and guess what, he took me to the same bloody restaurant. I can't think what the staff thought, me coming here with two different men on the same day.'

'They probably thought you were a whore,' laughed Hallam, then thought, who said that?

Lucy coughed, put a napkin to her mouth, and kept it there. Hallam realised that he might have gone too far. That spliff, the height.

Verity turned her head slowly and looked at him. Her eyes did not narrow when she became angry, they widened, seeming to accentuate the tightness of that white skin between. Her shoulders hiked a few millimetres. Hallam found himself panicking, preparing for all sorts of possibilities. A wine glass on the head? Cursings? A scene? In the past he would have found all of these things impossible to imagine Verity instigating, but now some hormonal flare seemed to have wafted across the table, which communicated a degree of anger that went beyond indignation or outrage, into the realm of the animal, utterly contradicting her posture of artful composure. Hallam realised that all the muscles along his back were painfully tensed. How could he have said it?

The second passed and nothing happened. Or rather, something did happen, but it was a change that Hallam could not identify exactly. Verity was now merely looking at him thoughtfully. Julius shot Hallam a glance from under his eyebrows and then shot another towards his wife. Verity smiled, at last. Relief began to seep over Hallam: had he escaped? Verity's smile did contain mild reproach, but it was a smile, that was the important thing. Then she began to laugh. Now that was slightly worrying, even though a helpless grin crept up on Hallam's lips too, and – a further disturbing development – Verity continued to laugh long enough for

Lucy to feel that she could take away the napkin from her face and openly chortle along.

Eventually even Julius smiled, albeit faintly and briefly. Hallam could still feel Verity's eyes on him. None of the laughter was pleasant. He looked down at his watch in the hope that normal inconsequential behaviour would somehow restore order. It was 8:11.

In a superficial way everything did fall back into normal patterns. The rest of dinner dragged on in a reassuringly dull way after that, and Lucy's expressions of impatience eventually got to the point where she emptied another glass of wine and said, 'I'm meeting some friends in half an hour. Is that all right?'

Verity sipped her coffee and looked at Julius. 'Shall we let them go, Julius?'

'Go on,' he said, puffing on his cigar, 'enjoy yourselves.'

Hallam rose and opened his mouth hesitantly, wondering whether he should apologise. He looked at Verity but she smiled at him forgivingly, and wafted him away.

'Thanks for dinner,' he said to both of them, and then added, for safety's sake, 'Happy anniversary.'

'Come on, Hallam,' said Lucy briskly. 'Don't forget your present.'

Lucy and Hallam walked out together into the warm summer night, gifts in hand. Soon they were motoring out of Leicester and going down an underpass, through the unreality of fluorescent orange. Lucy was normally a fast driver, she steered with the straighter than necessary arms and square shoulders of a car lover, but neither of them were in a hurry to get back, and compared to the drive in, the backbeat from the air vents was slower and more deliberate.

Lucy shook her head and grinned wickedly at him. 'I liked the comment,' she said. 'I could hardly control myself.' The effect of her smile was not comforting: they were now leaving the city limits and her face was greenly lit by the dashboard consoles.

'You could have been a bit more subtle. I thought she was going to kill me for a moment.'

'What was I meant to do?'

'A smirk was all it required.'

She shrugged and went down into fourth. The main road pushed on ahead, over flat fields and among electricity pylons, until it peeled off and began to follow the signs for their village. The land started to bank and roll, while ahead the road wound on, past thickly grassed paddocks and grey spinneys. On the right, a low hill shaped the sky.

'I think she's got it in for me,' said Hallam, doomladen.

'What? Nonsense, I thought you judged it rather well. Mind you, if I'd said it there would have been hell to pay.' Lucy glanced over at him and grinned again. 'She had to dig deep to see the funny side though, didn't she? I'm meeting the girls in the pub at Tur Langton if you want to come.'

'No thanks, just drop me at the turn-off.'

'Are you sure? This is Cold Satchville – it'll take you ages to walk to Chanby from here.'

Hallam smiled. 'Certain. I'll see you tomorrow.'

Lucy shrugged and pulled in at the Cold Satchville junction; she was used to his eccentricities. Hallam stepped out and waved her off from the pavement, then began to walk away from the village lights on the road for Chanby.

It took him under an hour to reach the village. He went past the local pub, the Pankerton Arms, which was emptying slowly. A pickup emerged from the car park and the beams of its headlights swung across Hallam's legs before heading up the hill towards the housing estate. He crossed the road, leaving behind the boozy sounds of the bar, and soon he could make out the tall shadow that was Lower Point to the right. Gatewatch loomed over the mouth of the Hall's long drive. The big iron gates went by on either side of him, beyond which the lines of trees stood, their boughs keeping out the distant neon streetlights. Hallam entered the natural corridor with relief and he ignored the light-switch that could have lit his walk. The darkness would calm his thoughts.

He was perhaps halfway up the drive when the first white lamp blinked and then fully illuminated. The rest came on in sequence, obliterating the protective gloom section by section until the full curve of the drive was lit, and with it him. He turned and saw Verity standing by the light-switch, the left side of her face shining from the lamp beside her. The shadows strangely elongated her face and gave her wonderful bone structure a faintly skull-like appearance.

Hallam stopped and waited uneasily as she came towards him. He wondered what she had been doing there in the dark and mentally reprimanded himself for not having been on his guard to sense her presence.

Even close up he could not interpret the expression on her face. He twitched slightly when she reached out and linked an arm in his. 'Didn't you go with Lucy then?'

'No.'

They continued up the drive together, the inanity of her question unsettling him. When she spoke again she picked her words carefully, in a confidential manner.

'Do you ever think you might take after your mother?'

Hallam frowned but answered honestly. 'I can't really tell. I find it difficult to remember her when she was well. I was a bit young.'

Verity nodded sympathetically. 'I think you do take after her.'

Hallam considered this. 'In what way?'

'Well, in the sense that you both nurse a special resentment towards me, but also, I suppose, because you seem to be going the same way as her.'

'What do you mean?'

'Madness isn't necessarily hereditary of course.'

'She wasn't mad.'

'She did kill herself, Hallam. I do think that's a little eccentric.' Hallam emitted a small puff of laughter out of nervousness. Verity squeezed his arm and smiled at him warmly. 'I'm glad you find it funny, Hallam, because I'm sure you contributed to her final decision. You were a horrible, selfish little boy and there was Lucy too of course.'

'I don't find it funny. She was ill. It was manic depression. Anyway, what do you know?'

They continued to walk. The trees drifted by on either side, the soft white light coating their bark like fungus.

'When I first saw you I thought you looked like her,' said Verity thoughtfully. 'Something furtive and unhappy around the eyes.'

'I didn't resent you,' said Hallam with sudden conviction, and it was true. He vividly remembered when he first saw Verity, and his first impressions were certainly a lot more flattering than hers of him, it seemed. For it was Verity who first opened his eyes to the abstract fascinations of the female body. He was thirteen when she had appeared in the door of his father's office. This striking-looking woman had smiled at him, he recalled, but what really stuck in his mind was a totally novel impulse that drew his eyes down to her midriff as she passed by, and caused him to pay attention to the little valley between her hipbone and belly. Why? He did not know and it was certainly not consciously provoked by Verity. It was a small detail but a significant shift in his life, and Hallam had rather cherished it. Even now, pathetically enough.

'Well, that's nice to know,' said Verity. The Hall came into sight round the side of the last tree. Still holding his arm she stopped to admire the symmetry of its Queen Anne lines, assisted by the moon which hung to the left.

'Now look at that – isn't it beautiful?'

'Yes, it is,' Hallam agreed.

Her voice dropped. 'Enjoy it.'

Hallam's throat contracted and heat coursed through his body, in outrage and excitement.

Verity released his arm and calmly resumed her stroll towards the back door. 'I'm going in,' she said over her shoulder, the softness of her voice reinstalled.

A gentle breeze passed through the leaves overhead. He thought that hate must be the most powerful intimacy, free as it was from the restraints that love imposes. It must be nourishing too. He could not help but admire the swing of Verity's hips as she passed out of sight.

Hallam was dozing in bed, exhausted by the evening's events, when he heard Lucy's drunken footsteps coming up the stairs. There was a tap on the door and she entered. She patted his bed so as not to sit on his legs and then squeezed his knee through the sheets. He could smell the pub on her clothes.

'Sorry to barge in,' she said in a slightly slurred whisper.

'That's OK.'

'Was everything all right in the end then?'

'Yeah. Fine.' There seemed no point in telling her. 'What about you?'

'I've decided I can't face saying goodbye to the cow. I'm off to London now, just got to finish packing. I'll drop the car off at my friend's, it's on permanent loan in exchange for a day's drinking, then it's Heathrow and an air freighted hangover to Johannesburg, followed by a meteoric career in the diamond industry. Or something like that.'

'You're drunk. Wait till tomorrow.'

'Don't be rude. I'll drive carefully.'

'No you won't. Plus you might get a pay-off from Julius. A handy solution to your overdraft.'

She considered this, sighed, and that triggered an enormous yawn. 'Oh fuck, maybe you're right. Night then, sweetie.'

'See you tomorrow.'

She got up and opened the door, then Hallam remembered. 'Lucy, you never told me about Mr Hennessey flashing at you.'

'That's because I made it up. But he did look like a flasher, don't you think?' Lucy blew him a kiss and stepped out into the corridor. With pantomimic exaggeration she checked that the coast was clear before shutting the door behind her.

Hallam dropped his head back onto the pillow, dunking it into sleep. The last fading imprint on his conscious mind was an image of white balustrades and stonework glowing in the night, a skeletal outline of the redbrick Hall.

three

Hallam always woke up to Verity's footsteps. With shoes on, her short, measured gait ticked like a metronome, past his bedroom door and down the corridor at the end, signalling the start of the day. Sometimes he would jerk awake to what he thought were her ticking heels and find he had been fooled by the bedside clock, which showed the time to be three in the morning. Even then he would lie awake and strain his ears listening to the fading echo of what was not there.

But Verity's footsteps went further back. He had the impression that he knew them even before he knew her, in childish dreams made distressing by their formlessness. They were not steps then, but the sensation was the same. It might be a surrounding noise that grew to an almost unbearable volume before fading again. Or once, he recalled, the colour red absorbing the greyness of a space without context, inducing panic as it threatened to engulf him. Verity had always controlled his dreams.

Hallam's eyes opened to the shuttered dark, but soon the shapes of furniture asserted themselves. The steps, it seemed, had stopped. Then the door opened and Hallam saw Verity standing in the morning glare. It exposed the grub-like shape of his legs under the duvet. He wriggled up into a sitting position and squinted, shielding his eyes.

'Hallam, I think your father has some chores for you to do today.' She left the door open and headed downstairs without waiting for a reply. The briskness was not unusual; Verity rarely bothered with the formalities of good morning and goodnight. It was as if she knew she never left him.

He sank back down under the duvet. He put his hands behind his head and thought back to the night before, which, with birdsong outside, seemed to have acquired the status of a paranoid fantasy. Perhaps his conversation with Verity on the drive was not what he thought it had been: namely, a declaration of enmity containing a threat. Perhaps it had simply been a frank emotional discussion between adults; the sort that he would have to get used to now that he was a man.

For Hallam was sure that at some point yesterday he had been initiated into manhood; it could have been about the time when he was punched in the face, or when he smoked pot, or when he made that daringly rude comment about his stepmother. He considered consulting Lucy on the subject but it did not seem right, indeed it did not seem manly, especially now that she was leaving. Nor could he think of a good reason why Lucy's advice should carry any special weight after her botched attempt to outflank Verity. Hallam realised that he would have to rely on his own judgement in deciphering Verity's motives and intent. It felt like a very adult resolution to make — even if his hand had been forced.

Hallam was emerging from his room and buckling up his jeans when Lucy hissed at him from her own bedroom doorway. 'Morning,' she said, then checked both ways before whispering theatrically, 'almost out of here.'

Hallam smiled. 'How does it feel?'

'Bloody marvellous.'

He peered into her room and saw that her suitcases were almost packed. The personal decorations and accumulated knick-knacks that had bedecked her room were now dumped in the bin. It seemed that she had rooted out everything in her life that was superfluous. Hallam wondered if that included him.

'Defy the hag. You'll be gone soon too.' Lucy did a passable imitation of a hunchbacked crone and hobbled back to her packing.

Hallam carried on downstairs and showed his face in the kitchen, where Julius was sitting at the table with a cup of coffee, shirt untucked, not yet shaved. He saw Hallam and stood up. 'Morning,' he said cheerfully. Then he spotted his wife as she passed by behind Hallam on her way to join Carl outside. He coughed gruffly and adopted a sterner attitude. 'Come into the office, would you?'

Hallam followed his father along the corridor, past the study, and into the orangery where Julius and his staff of two, sometimes three, worked amid drapes of vines and pot plants. Computer screens and drawing boards were positioned around the circular glasshouse facing out. A semicircular shade shifted imperceptibly above them with the passage of the sun, to protect the terminals from glare.

Julius's secretary Nicola perched nearby, the new cactus handling security behind her. She smiled neatly at Hallam and carried on tapping at her keyboard. Julius picked up some notes from his desk, which were, most likely, a product of the early morning conference he usually had with Verity while they took tea in bed. Hallam could see that they were fastidiously laid out in Julius's imitation Rennie Mackintosh handwriting. In appearance Julius was sloppy and neglectful, but there were compartments in his life – work and written presentation – that were ruled by unbending codes of discipline.

Julius held the page out to Hallam, then changed his mind and passed it to the secretary. 'Actually, Nicola, could you tidy this up and get a print-out?'

'Certainly, Julius.' Nicola gave the list a curt inspection and started to type with controlled fury, her little smile unmoving. Hallam looked her over. She had short red hair, a delicate complexion, and a sexless sense of order, but she was still fairly young. He wondered how long she would last now that Verity had acquired voting rights.

'Have a read and tell me if you have any questions,' said Julius.

'Right,' said Hallam.

The phone began to ring. Nicola picked up the receiver and lodged it between shoulder and ear; she continued to type, although the downpour of keystrokes abated to a shower. 'The Foe Partnership, how may I help?' Julius was already distracted. Nicola looked up, one finger on the phone's secrecy button. 'It's John Hammersmith from the surveyors.'

'Oh, right. I'd better get that.'

Nicola transferred the call. Julius gratefully dashed to his terminal and started talking into his phone. Hallam stared up at the shade and, as usual, failed to detect its incremental progress. Nicola hit a key. The printer started up and floated a piece of A4 down into the tray.

Nicola turned in her chair and handed it over to Hallam with a smile. 'Here you go, Hallam.'

'Thank you, Nicola.'

Nicola returned to her original task and Hallam looked down at the piece of paper, headed: Hallam Foe – Punishment Duty.

I wasn't terribly impressed by the remark you made yesterday evening, and I think it's time you pulled your weight a bit more round here. So could you help us in the following ways:

1. Dredge the lake, and make an assessment of its viability, with special reference to blanket weed problem and flow of water. Ask Carl for tools.
2. Assist Carl in planting of rhododendron bushes and other landscaping tasks.
3. Brush cellar steps and tidy route to wine cellar.

This should help to form your character and usefully contribute to the Foe premises. Any feedback can be made in the usual way.

Best of luck, Julius Foe (signed in his absence by his PA)

Verity had put him up to it, surely. Hallam looked over at Julius but he was now immersed in his conversation and bringing up various architectural plans on his screen. Arse. Hallam smiled to himself, rather proud of the ease with which these adult judgements were flowing, and headed for the back door, folding the instructions as he went. He climbed the concrete steps towards the redbrick stables and unlocked the tall black doors, whose floor bolt scraped along an ancient groove in the cobbles. He stepped inside, savouring the cool darkness and the whiff of engine oil mingled with sweet grass cuttings. The mini tractor was parked there, surrounded by stacks of his mother's old furniture and other junk.

Hallam looked up at the wooden-planked roof, above which a loft ran the length of the stables. In the gloomy silence, set apart from the world outside, he imagined being watched from up there. There were gaps in the planks and a specially drilled spyhole that had already seen its most fruitful days. Hallam often entertained the notion that some part of him was for ever patrolling the listening posts and observation points in his absence, maintaining the watch while he performed the drudgery of life on the ground. It was an idea that lulled him.

Until he heard a noise. From the loft. Hallam was jolted by a piercing fear that his fantasy might have taken shape. He froze and listened to the beating of his heart. He told himself to think of more sensible possibilities. A rat?

There was another noise, a scuffle, this time for certain. Hallam grabbed a pitchfork – it seemed like the appropriate thing to do – and ran out of the stable down to the end of the block. He shoved open an unlocked door and raced up the wooden steps to the loft, not allowing himself the coward's option of giving the intruder an escape route. He had not even reached the top before there was a panicked clattering of wings and a white dove rose up in front of his face, bisecting the floor with a thin line of black and white shit. The dove settled on a rafter, its white fantail upright and twitching. One eye blinked. Hallam panted with mingled relief and anticlimax. Then he reproved himself for being so jumpy and turned back to the steps with a last sneer at the bird. He hated doves, the way they flounced among the trees with all the wildness bred out of them. The dovecotes had been Verity's idea, naturally.

Hallam manoeuvred the trailer by the side of the lake, turned off the tractor engine, and waited for the natural sounds to return. He looked longingly up at the dark smudge of Centre Point and thought of the smell of dry wood that would be in there now as the morning sun warmed it up. But there was no escape for him today.

He went back to the trailer and banged down the flap. He took out a pair of shears, rusty but newly sharpened, then squatted by the lake edge. Dragonflies jinked across the surface as if wire-guided. He put one foot into the water and coolness gripped his ankle, then flooded into his trainers and between his toes.

He lowered himself in with a gasp. He toes found the slippery roots on the bottom and the water level was up to his ribs, bracing him like a corset. He familiarised himself with the cold, then gingerly turned to face the bank. Wisps of disturbed mud rose from the bottom and spread against the water's surface. He thought of smoke against a windowpane.

The problem, Hallam knew, was that a huge interlacing of blanket weed was clogging the lake, depriving any remaining fish of oxygen and causing the water to stagnate. The underground sluice that fed the two smaller ponds further down was little more than a trickle now, and was barely audible where once, standing on the turf above it, the rumble of shifting gallons could be felt through the feet.

The real task, he surmised, was to demonstrate the futility of clearing the lake by hand, and thereby convince Julius and Verity to buy the expensive poisons that would do the job properly. Hallam grabbed a handful of weed and plunged the shears beneath the water. His ear dabbed the water as he sawed.

Two hours later, with the sun higher in the sky, his face and clothes were stained with muddy brown water and the trailer was draped with stinking green dreadlocks. He had a long strand the thickness of rope in his fists. He tugged but it held firm. He wiped his brow, the cool water dribbling down his face and off his lip. Then, looking closer, he realised it really was a rope.

Furtively he glanced behind him. On unsteady footing he followed the rope until he was up to his chest in the centre of the lake. Then he twisted it over his shoulder and dragged. Something tore. He staggered and turned. What slowly broke the surface was just recognisable as the prow of a rowboat under a thick net of weed. He only saw it for a second before he slipped and the boat was sucked back down.

Hallam sat on the jetty at the head of the lake. The smell of the half-stagnant water rose off him in the dappled shadows. He listened to the wind forcing its way through the trees and gazed over the bushes at the lake's end, towards the church stump.

It was late in the night when she woke him up. He could only have been twelve at the time. It was the middle of the night and he could smell her perfume as she gently shook his shoulder and told him to get up and come outside. It took the promise of a special surprise to rouse him properly.

His mother dressed him and took him by the hand out of the Hall. He remembered the shock of the cold night air and the echoes of their breath as they made their way through the passage between the stables and the cottage. The grass around the lake was shorter then, and Hallam could hear the gurgling of water from the sluices to his right as they approached the head of the lake.

She had told him to take extra care while going down the ramp onto the jetty. It was only then that she informed him of her intention: they were going to undertake a lunar expedition. As she untied the bobbing rowboat, Hallam looked up at the clear night sky and saw the moon, almost full, high above. He thought she was being somewhat over-ambitious and told her so but she would not listen. He asked tactfully whether they should wake up Dad so that he could come along. She told him that it was too late now.

His mother rowed them out a few feet into the lake, by which time he realised what she meant. He saw the moon close up, a huge flashlight trembling on the surface of the water. As they approached, it began to wave signals. She laughed and slowed the boat with one oar and they bobbed around the moon's quivering perimeter. She informed him that the eagle had landed. Hallam reached out a hand and put it in the water, and reported that, contrary to scientists' claims, the moon was wet. She asked him to sprinkle some of the moonwater on his face and hers, telling him that it would keep him young. She told him that he didn't want to get old. He remarked that he wouldn't mind turning seventeen so that he could drive. He remembered that she smiled and touched his hair.

That was when Julius appeared at the side of the lake, unmistakable despite the dark, outraged in his dressing gown. He shouted at Anne to come back to shore. Anne asked him for one good reason. He berated her for getting Hallam up in the middle of the night.

The next day, after a night of wild argument and weeping, Anne was back in hospital. That was when Julius had first spoken out loud the name of Hallam's mother's illness.

Hallam heard Carl's loud chirruping call and replied by arranging his fingers in his mouth and emitting a birdlike morse of his own. A few seconds later Carl appeared at the top of the ramp. 'There you are.' He bounced down the ramp and sat down next to Hallam. Hallam flicked a black bug the size of a pinhead off his lightly steaming jeans.

'You smell like shit,' said Carl and grimaced.

Hallam smiled, relieved that he had been forgiven. 'Why thank you.'

They both sat back and looked over the lake, enjoying the re-confirmation of their friendship.

'There's some surveyors arrived at the Hall,' said Carl eventually. 'They're heading up this way.'

'Surveying for what?'

'Search me.' Carl rubbed some dried mud off his hands. Hallam admired his strong fingers with their brown, cracked nails.

'I'd better look as if I'm doing some work then,' said Hallam.

'Verity says you're to help me with the hedge.'

'Didn't you just put it in?'

'It hasn't grown fast enough, according to her. She wants us to tear it out and put in bigger plants.'

Hallam knew that this would upset Carl; Carl hated Verity's impatience with nature almost as much as her interference, although he never said a word against her, despite constant encouragement and occasional teasing.

'What's it like in there then?' asked Carl, indicating the water.

'Pretty hopeless,' said Hallam. 'I'll try and convince Julius that it needs to be fixed properly. I think the sides are collapsing.'

Carl nodded. They both knew that the prospect of repairs was very dim. Over the years Carl had constantly lobbied Julius: for plantings that would take twenty or thirty years to start bearing fruit; for investments that would guard against problems fifty or one hundred years further down the line. Most of them Julius politely but firmly ignored, and Carl would gracefully withdraw for another couple of months, until a sense of duty brought him to the back door once more. Hallam shared Carl's loyalty to the lakes, the trees, and the life within them. There was something sedimentary and precious here that had to be defended and preserved. All the more because it was less definable than petty frets about budgets and pest control. How could the spirit of nature and man, so rarely and harmoniously combined, be weighed against dredging costs?

'Hallam,' said Carl, 'why do you spend all your time up in those treehouses?'

Hallam did not know what to say.

'Ever since your mother died you've hardly come down.' Carl never asked questions like that. Hallam moved his trainers on the wooden slats of the jetty.

'You watch people, don't you?' Carl persisted.

Hallam was desperately trying to think of a way out of this. He could say birdwatching, but it was too transparent a lie to give Carl, especially after the incident with Jenny. So he shrugged and nodded vaguely. 'Yeah, sometimes.'

'Why?'

'That's such a stupid question.'

'Why?'

'Why not?'

'Because it's not . . .' Carl struggled for the appropriate word, 'polite.'

'I can't explain.'

'It's to do with your mother, isn't it?'

'Look, Carl, I'm sorry for what I did, I won't do it again, but it's none of your business.'

Carl sat up, offended but resigned. Then he stood up and looked away. 'I'll be down along the drive.'

'See you in a bit,' said Hallam. 'I'll do some more here for form's sake.'

Carl went up the ramp, his big, firm footsteps causing the planks to judder. Hallam watched him go with regret, then returned his gaze to the surface of the lake.

Hallam knew why he went up to the treehouses in the first place, that was simple enough. To escape from the useless grief of relatives, unfamiliar ones mostly, who moo-ed sadly about the past and stayed the night, who called up to express their most unctuous sympathies, who popped over with cakes and delicate phrasing, who pitied.

Soon the treehouses became a refuge. An uncle, thinking the lad might be interested in ornithology, bought him a book on the subject, together with an old telescope, and Hallam took them with him up the tree, more to allay the worried looks that on occasion were sent his way. He only wanted to be left alone.

The rest was more complicated, although there was one deceptively small incident that over the years had acquired a talismanic significance in his mind that he himself had never fully addressed until now. It was in the green dampness of early summer – a world thriving, it seemed, on his mother's self-sacrifice – that he had looked down and seen, in the adjoining field, their neighbouring farmer, Mr Cheney, creeping stealthily along the hedgerow with a shotgun. Hallam had watched him, idly at first. Then the farmer had frozen, and remained absolutely still, apparently listening. Presumably he was on the lookout for crows or other vermin. Hallam had experienced the sharp childish pleasure of not being seen for what was perhaps just a few seconds, and then the farmer moved on into the adjoining field. But a mysterious fascination had been activated. Somehow a perfectly everyday rural procedure had been turned into a private, unrepeatable piece of theatre. One moment of tense silence unknowingly shared between watcher and subject was enough to make Hallam want more. Four years on he now firmly believed that he had been born with a predisposition for observation. It was a matter of the soul that could not be explained away by Carl's clumsy Freudian connection-making. It had only been a periscope-view of salvation at first, made fraught by the terror of discovery, but with practice Hallam had gained in confidence and gradually learnt the principles and disciplines of observation. Here was true escape; not withdrawal from the world but entry into a new one. He had discovered what his kind of voyeurism could be: not a lonely vice – the common perception – but a passionate engagement with the lives of others. And a passionate detachment from his own, of course.

He became fascinated enough by the things he saw to want to record them. He plotted out and named this new world in his logbooks, feeling like a pioneering anthropologist. There was self-abnegation in the long hours of discomfort and boredom. And as he crawled through dripping hedgerows or crouched immobile behind gravestones with throbbing, bloodless feet, he knew that he was learning more than physical resilience. It was returning his curiosity in the world when he felt deadened to it. It was providing him with a secret existence. Most importantly it brought him solace, although he did not understand why, exactly. He did not want to know why.

That farmer with his gun. He was protecting his land and beasts the simple way, with direct action. There was something noble about that, Hallam concluded. There was something to be learnt.

Hallam was back in the lake when Julius arrived with two men in suits and wellingtons. Their conversation was muttered and from his position it was difficult to hear. They stopped within view and Julius pointed up at the oak tree, at Centre Point. Then they checked the plans that Julius had with him.

That was when Julius spotted Hallam, who had been forced to swat at the insects that were attempting to gain entry to his nostrils. 'Hallam, could you go and help Carl down the front?'

Hallam waded slowly to the lake edge, hoping the men would continue their conversation, but they did not. They smiled at him instead as he climbed, dripping, from the water.

'You're doing a fine job, lad,' said one of them, 'just don't come near me.'

Yo ho ho, the three of them went, with the gruff jocularity of men on site. Hallam trudged away, strangely depressed by the poor joke. His trainers squelched comically and it made him even more disconsolate. The men waited until he was out of earshot before they went back to their plans.

Hallam was struggling to suppress a sense of impending catastrophe as he walked down beyond the stables, at which point he glimpsed Verity and Lucy walking round to the front of the Hall, deep in conversation.

'It's not that I don't love him,' Verity was saying. 'God knows the sex is amazing. But he seems incapable of controlling his feelings. It scares me sometimes.' And then they were gone round the corner. Hallam was momentarily – and by his own standards, unprofessionally – stunned. But within a few seconds he was dashing round the other side of the Hall, pounding down the back of the walled garden and skirting the drooping branches of the wellingtonia. Leaping over the gravel path so he wouldn't be heard, he reached the cover of thick bushes just as the two women hoved into sight and turned down a path that weaved its way through some silver birches.

Hallam reached his listening post and had time to control his panting as Verity and Lucy came to their customary bench surrounded by a high clipped hedge. For the first time, Hallam was unable to achieve the objective concentration that he had always found so useful as a spy. This was not because he was presumably about to find out about his father's sex life; fucking held no secrets for him any more, and repeated observation had all but extinguished any personal desire for first-hand experience. More exciting was the prospect of having access to the emotional life of his father which hitherto had been little more than unsubstantiated rumour, unless you counted the beige spectrum between bluff and grumpy.

Hallam held his breath as they hovered a foot away from him. Verity was still talking. ' . . . you must have noticed his look yourself, all that possessiveness and hostility. How am I supposed to . . .' But then they moved on, down towards the front lawns proper where they could only be overheard dimly from South-West Traverse, which was too exposed for comfort and difficult to reach without being spotted. Hallam watched despairingly as they lingered in the middle of the lawn. Then Lucy, in the midst of their conversation, lost her temper and shouted, 'Why are you telling me all this?' She turned and strode back up the same path.

Verity followed. 'Because you understand,' she replied soothingly, attempting to take Lucy's hand. 'Because we're friends.'

They were perfectly in position, by the bench, when Lucy turned and pulled her hand away. The suggestion of friendship obviously disgusted her now. 'I can't believe I let you into my life.'

'I have always felt that we could trust each other.'

'I started to believe that. It was my mistake.'

A pause. Hallam could not see their faces and was therefore denied access to their silent communication.

'I wouldn't if I was you,' said Verity. 'I know what you're thinking.'

'What?'

'You're thinking of telling Julius about Alex.'

Lucy's friend Alex? thought Hallam. Verity and Alex? He felt rather letdown. Infidelity no longer had the power to shock him, any more than the sexual act, or so he thought, although the way that Verity appeared to have made Lucy complicit in her affair was quite a development.

'Can't you see the position you've put me in?' Lucy replied, lowering her voice. 'He's my father.'

'You'll grow out of moralising soon enough.' Verity's voice had relaxed carefully. 'It only makes you look stupid in the long run.'

'You were an early developer, I presume,' said Lucy, attempting irony.

'Perhaps I was wrong to confide in you,' Verity said, her voice still conciliatory, 'but didn't you want to talk too? It was only because we felt more like sisters than—'

'You were never going to be that. Your closeness is control. But who cares, I'm leaving now.'

'Julius is happy, Lucy. Don't let me down.'

Lucy replied with a snort of derision.

'Or is that the problem?'

Lucy did not answer the question. Hallam still could not see her expression through the foliage. He shifted and found a fragment of view.

'You won't be able to put him off, although you'll certainly hurt him.'

Lucy stepped closer. 'Do you think I want him?'

Hallam was confused. Who were they talking about now? People's trains of thought in private conversation could be a bewildering maze for the eavesdropper.

'Perhaps not.' Verity sighed then smiled and looked away down the path. 'I wonder where Hallam is. He does worry me sometimes.'

'Hallam?' asked Lucy blankly.

'Presumably you don't care about him either.'

'He's not done anything to you,' said Lucy, her tone colourless.

'I think it's time you went.'

A brief silence and then Lucy's footsteps crunched quickly away. Verity stood there alone for so long that Hallam wondered whether she might have seen him and was waiting for him to stand up and surrender. His knees shook violently and he willed himself not to lose his balance or allow his trainers to squelch, or for her to smell the dankness coming off his clothes. Eventually Verity's footsteps followed Lucy's; they were slower, more measured.

The digging made the main drive look as if it had been bombarded. Around thirty holes had appeared among the shrubs and trees, about two foot square and deep.

'You've been busy,' remarked Hallam to Carl, who had a welly placed on the blade of his spade. His temples were shining with sweat. They both turned and saw Verity coming down the drive. 'We're going to have to shift that dirt in the trailer later on,' said Carl. 'There's fertiliser coming. Rhododendrons. I think the rose bed's due for the chop once we've done the hedge, from what I hear. She says it aggravates her pollen allergy.'

Verity joined them. She looked over at the house that backed onto the drive. A neighbour was peering balefully out of a window. 'Good afternoon, Mrs Hitchens,' called Verity. 'Enjoy the view while it lasts.'

Mrs Hitchens scowled and drew the curtains. Hallam had several entries in his logbook about her stealing through the gates after dusk to take cuttings from some of the more expensive shrubs that had been planted in the past few months.

'I can't bear that woman gawping into the grounds, it makes my skin crawl,' said Verity. 'There's always someone watching what you do in this village.'

Then Verity noticed Hallam's wet clothes covered in green slime and bugs, and started chuckling. 'Oh, Hallam,' she said indulgently.

'He belongs in a handkerchief,' quipped Carl.

She laughed and continued her stroll down the drive, inspecting the holes, plotting fresh devastation. 'By the way, Hallam,' she called over her shoulder casually. 'Come up to the house in an hour so we can all see Lucy off together.'

Once she was a safe distance away, Hallam spat on the ground. 'Bitch.'

Carl sighed and lifted his spade over his shoulder. 'She seems all right to me.'

'Well, I expect she's up for it if you're interested.'

Carl looked horrified by Hallam's interpretation of his comment, but realising that it was one of Hallam's less savoury jokes, gritted his teeth in anger and embarrassment. He went over to the hedge. Hallam felt slightly guilty and followed him.

'Seems a shame to rip them out half-grown,' Hallam said, knowing what was on his friend's mind. For all Carl's loyalty, it was clear to Hallam that he thought Verity suffered from a fundamental misunderstanding of the whole long-term philosophy of gardening. Carl had a respect for rootedness. It was probably why he had such a peculiar fixation with local history.

Carl grunted and inspected the nearest plant. Its leaves were still pale green and the branches had not yet grown out enough to link with its neighbour. Carl ran his hands up either side of it, ruffling the foliage with a last gesture of affection, then dug the spade into the soil.

'Don't come in with those dirty things on, Hallam. Leave them by the washing machine.'

Hallam went over to the utilities room and pulled off his shirt and jeans to reveal a spidery white body streaked with dried lake mud. He stretched the elastic on his underpants and shook a foot, causing small pieces of grit to fall out.

Hoping Verity wouldn't see him, he padded barefoot to the stairs. Unfortunately she just happened to be coming down the corridor with an armful of fabric samples. She paused and brazenly inspected his body. As he slipped past on his way to the shower he glimpsed a charitable smile that caused him to feel pitifully unqualified.

Hallam helped Lucy carry her suitcases to the battered Peugeot. Verity was standing by. 'I'll just lever your father from his computer screen,' she said cheerfully, and disappeared inside. Lucy watched her go and let out a sardonic huff. Hallam slammed the boot and Lucy turned to him with a smile he wanted to avoid.

'Come here.' She gave him a long hug, to which he did not respond. 'It's every man for himself now. Good luck. Make sure you tap him for some cash before term starts. It's all he's good for, and to be frank I think it makes him feel better.' Lucy paused. She inspected his face and her smile dropped away. 'Don't look at me like that. I don't need this.'

'Look at you like what?'

She frowned. 'You know exactly what you're doing. It's not fair, there's nothing I can do.'

'I'm not asking you to do anything.'

Verity emerged again, with Julius in tow. Lucy took a deep breath and turned towards them. She gave her father a cool look. He didn't want to meet her eyes, and instead circled the car, going over it, feigning concern about practicalities.

'Is everything packed? Have you checked the tyre pressure? Oil? Can you see out the back?'

'Julius, please, the car's fine.'

'What about the windscreen wipers? Is there enough water?'

'Dad!' Lucy screamed suddenly and stamped her foot in frustration. He looked at her, startled, then grinned bashfully. Lucy held out a hand to shake. He used it to tow her into an embrace instead. Hallam watched Verity watch Julius as he crushed Lucy to his chest. Hallam counted the seconds – one, two, three – until Lucy at last acknowledged defeat and wearily patted his back.

Julius broke his hold. There were tears in his eyes, Hallam noted with disgust. Lucy looked at her feet and opened the door to the car.

'Don't I get a kiss?' asked Verity and stepped towards her. Bravely she planted one on Lucy's cheek. Lucy brought the car door shut between them.

'Promise you'll come and stay when you feel like it.' Lucy started the engine, revving impatiently, and Verity had to raise her voice to be heard. 'Call us from Johannesburg when you get there. Your father's worried sick.'

Hallam felt a last rush of regret and dipped his head, hoping to receive one last smile from his sister, but Lucy's eyes were already beyond the gates. There was a short squirt of pebbles and she drove away, not returning their waves.

Hallam walked upstairs, pretending to fetch a plaster for the blister on his hand. Instead he went into Lucy's room and stood there. No longer Lucy's: the stripped walls, the overflowing bin. He wanted to cry, but it was not an outlet he had allowed himself access to for years. He wanted to smash up Lucy's things, but it appeared that she had got there before him. He peered into the bin and saw a small bent trophy. How could he forget her pubescent gymkhana triumph when he had cheered her on beside a now absent parent amid the mud and sawdust. And there, the stained plastic Snoopy that he had given her as a childish surrogate gift seven or eight Christmases before (he had not bought it, but he had helped wrap). Lucy had even chucked a silver napkin holder, a christening present. He could see what had happened. Lucy had swept the length of the mantelpiece, deleted the years, including him.

Hallam heard the argument from the kitchen in the early evening as he returned from a tour of the lower observation points. He paused at the back door, surprised because he could plainly hear Julius's raised voice, when normally his style was to maintain surly low-volume resistance.

'I don't blame her,' said Verity. 'What do you expect if you neglect your daughter? I can't be a father for you.'

'She can't have thought that.'

'I'm not sure I don't agree with her. It was as if you wanted her gone.'

'It's not true.'

'Is it because of who she reminds you of?'

'What are you talking about? No.'

'Have you really forgotten her?'

'Yes, of course I have,' he replied, but the tone of weary patience sounded artificial.

'You're lying,' she replied, indifference growing in her voice. 'You still think it was our fault.'

'No.' His voice rose again.

'My fault then.'

'I said no.'

'It's as if this place is still hers. You know I can't stand it.'

'But I've told you to make whatever changes you want, within reason, and you are.'

'Even so, I might go away for a few days.' She sounded languid now, distant.

'The project's about to start, you know that. Where are you going?' A brief pause. 'Please don't.'

Her footsteps clicked down the hall towards the stairs and then went quiet. Hallam heard an odd quack come from the kitchen. It may have been a chairleg snagging on the slate floor.

Hallam was back at Gatewatch, twenty feet or so up the cedar, when he saw, through his beautiful new binoculars, Verity's silver BMW hiss down the drive. She slowed down at the gate then turned hard up towards the village with a solitary blink of the indicator. He wondered if she'd seen him. Verity, he noticed, was the only person who made him wonder that.

four

It was the tedious bond of blood that kept him indoors for the rest of the day. He hovered uncomfortably in the kitchen or clopped unostentatiously through the corridors on the off chance that Julius might want to unburden himself in some unimaginable departure from precedent. There was also, Hallam could more readily admit, morbid curiosity. To remember his father in a similar state Hallam had to scroll back several years to his mother's funeral, at a grey little crematorium, on a blustery spring day.

Even then the sum expression of Julius's emotions during the brief service had been one sharp expulsion of snot into a large handkerchief. Hallam remembered very little of the day, although even then he had been sensitive to the eyes of a fellow observer in the form of an egg-shaped stranger in a black mackintosh who stood back discreetly as they filed out towards the grubby ornamental garden. Now, like then, Hallam felt somehow responsible for his father's suffering.

After Nicola had made a tearful early departure following some persistent and uncharacteristic bullying from Julius, Hallam set about preparing overcooked pasta, accompanied by a neatly divided pork pie on the side. The two place mats set on the kitchen table had an inevitable poignancy which Hallam was agonisingly sensitive to as he walked in, ahead of his father. He feared it might provoke Julius but instead he merely looked at the food without interest then lit a cigar and wandered dreamily down to the lawns, leaving Hallam to eat alone. If nothing else, the dreary afternoon and evening made Hallam feel that he had done his duty.

The next morning Julius threw himself into his work as usual and only emerged to disappear for a meeting. Hallam made his way back up to the lake.

He had barely glimpsed the water through the foliage before he sensed something was wrong. It might have been a different note in the calls of the birds, or shadows of disturbances in the grass that seemed clumsily human. That was why he cast his eyes with special care along the lakeside and found evidence of an incursion: a crushed beer can, half hidden behind a hanging shrub.

On closer inspection of the long grass he found confirmation: cigarette butts, and three more crushed cans of Tiger bitter. Poachers, he thought, although it must have been years since villagers had bothered to come up here and cast a line into the torpid waters, the trout having been missing presumed dead for as long as he could remember. He gathered the trash up in a heap, and was preparing to head down the slope towards the dustbins when the possibility of something far worse occurred to him. He turned and ran to the oak tree, sprang onto the rope ladder and clamberered up to Centre Point. He hadn't even reached the top before he saw the covering of lurid spray-paint graffiti. The most striking message was in dark red capitals across the door: PERVERT.

With shaking hands he checked the padlock; it was intact, as was the door. But the splinters testified that there had been an attempt to force entry, probably by kicking. He silently blessed his father's neurotic insistence on quality materials when he had nailed Centre Point together during the early days of his partnership, building in the trees when business was thin on the ground.

Hallam rapidly drew up the rope ladder behind him and inspected the damage, circling the roof to read the abuse, in vivid colours, which wrapped all four sides of the cabin. PEEPING was scrawled in big letters on one wall, with the G squashed up. TOM BENT had been attempted with some difficulty on the far side (it must have been sprayed from above), and SNOB MONKEY WANKER on the next, in smaller text. Finally Hallam looked under his hands and knees at the most intriguing honorary title of them all, sprayed diagonally on the roof in green: COCKFUCKER. Hallam wondered whether this was a condensation of two insults, or a simple misspelling. Either way, that was the one which stuck in his mind. Cockfucker. Indeed.

He turned the key in the padlock and with some difficulty opened the sliding door, excising E then R then V to leave P ERT. He bent down and crawled through the word into the dark interior. With the window slats pushed aside to allow the light in, Hallam could breathe properly again. One of the slats was battered but had withstood the assault at the price of some cracks and scrapes. Everything was undisturbed. The string hammock was draped on a hook in the corner as before, and his logbooks, telescope and beautiful new binoculars were still snug in the chest.

He sat down cross-legged and giddily imagined the horror that might have been. A break-in. The logbooks! He did not want to contemplate the consequences had they been stolen, with all the records they contained of the movements, al-fresco sexual encounters and other observed or eavesdropped privacies that he had gathered over the past four years from various corners of the grounds, village gardens, hedgerows and the church cemetery.

This had to be the result of the Jenny episode; her brother perhaps. He would have to take extra care from now on.

He passed the rest of the morning cleaning up Centre Point, working fast in case Carl should see what had happened. Initially he tried to sandpaper off the insults, but all it did was leave plainly legible shadows of the words on the old wood, so he settled instead on painting over them in blotches of dark green, which had the added advantage of camouflaging the treehouse. But he realised that this place was no longer secure. He returned the paint pots to the workshop and moved his logbooks to his bedroom.

He spent the rest of the day in the oak tree, dozing through the heat, and even bedded down there for most of the night, as he knew Julius was unlikely to notice, let alone care. It was a pleasure listening to the owls and occasional badger movements below as the stars came out. He saw no further sign of intruders, only distant voices of returning pub-goers. The long thin carving knife that he had procured from the kitchen (feeling slightly foolish) and subsequently strapped to his leg remained unused. But it did confer a kind of ceremonial legitimacy to his watch.

The following morning he was positioned by a small arched window in the stable loft when he spotted his father emerge from the back door and disappear down one of the paths that ran past the church. Hallam decided to make a covert pursuit.

A quick scan of the ornamental pond at the bottom of the lawns indicated that Julius had not taken an indirect route to his favourite smoking spot. So Hallam followed a hunch and made his way cautiously down the path towards the gate that opened into the churchyard. He opened the little iron gate, overgrown with ivy, as quietly as he could, and trotted down the stepping-stone path round to the church entrance. Inside, the church was cool and empty, the pews bare. He glanced over towards the occupants of a previous Hall destroyed by fire; they were laid out on their tomb, shrimp-sized, in full medieval regalia. At their feet were what looked like masonic symbols. Hallam went to the back of the church and stepped round the hanging bell ropes. He climbed a metal ladder attached to the wall at the back and emerged through a trap door and into the bell chamber. He squeezed through the window and pulled himself up over the low crenellated wall at the top of the tower, where he found himself on the ledge beside the stump of the spire. The lead roofing was warm under his hands. He crawled round the stump with its absurd weather vane, keeping his head down, and passed one of four badly eroded gargoyles whose secular purpose was to spew rainwater.

Squeezing up beside a heavily eyebrowed griffin with a stone beak, he spotted his father, on the far side of the churchyard, puffing on a panatella. Julius skirted the old gravestones, pretending to read their barely decipherable inscriptions, but hovered near the family plot all the while, where the church authorities had generously allowed a small plaque to be placed in memory of his wife. Hallam knew that Julius would be understandably paranoid about visiting her memorial, for fear that somehow the information might get back to Verity. Hallam was not the only spy in the village.

He watched his father for some time, but learnt nothing. Only when a person under observation felt entirely secure in their privacy did Hallam feel that he could gain furtive access to what lay at their centre. Julius was too self-conscious for that. Hallam sighed. If he could not burgle intimacy from his father, then he would be forced to try a more conventional approach.

Hallam was back in the grounds and sitting on the bench by the hedge when he heard the gate squeak and the approaching footsteps of Julius. Hallam pretended to be a little surprised when he came into sight. 'Oh, hi.'

Julius seemed distantly to detect his son's presence in front of him. 'Hallam. What are you up to?'

'Not much. You?'

'Not much either.' Julius started to walk away.

'Where's Verity gone?' Hallam asked, more stridently than he intended. Her absence had not yet been remarked upon by either of them.

Julius paused but kept his back to his son. 'She's away for a few days. Nothing to worry about.' He walked back to his office.

Later Julius went into the kitchen and found Hallam making a sandwich. Hallam, as usual, felt vaguely guilty about being there.

'Hallam, I was just wondering,' Julius paused and looked pained. He jingled the absent change in his pockets, then fixed Hallam with an earnest gaze. 'Would you like a driving lesson?'

Hallam's mouth dropped. He shut it again. An unwelcome rite of passage was being forced upon him; what did cars have to do with him?

'Why? I mean, no. I don't think so,' he blurted. Panic fluttered between them. 'I didn't know you let anyone drive your car,' he added.

'I don't.' Julius was crestfallen.

'Besides, I don't have a provisional licence.'

Julius's eyes lit up with hope and he pointed at the binoculars which were hanging round Hallam's neck. 'Why don't we go birdwatching?'

That was when it dawned on Hallam. 'Is this an attempt at bonding?'

Julius scratched the back of his neck and flushed slightly. Hallam had patronised his father for the first time. It felt like a significant moment. Julius let out a long sigh of admission and the embarrassment began to lift. 'Yes,' he confessed. 'I suppose it is.'

'OK, let's take a drive. We don't have to go on the road.'

Father and son sat side by side in the front of the dark blue Jaguar. Despite his good intentions, Julius was proving to be an outstandingly bad teacher. Hallam's hands hung self-consciously from the steering wheel at ten to two, as recommended by the Highway Code manual, while Julius testily explained the controls, addressing him like a moron.

'Now remember, the pedal on your left is the brake. That's the most important one. If you're worried you're out of control, that's the one to hit, don't worry about the rest. OK?'

'OK.'

'So step on it.'

'Cool.' Hallam reached for the ignition.

'No, step on the brake.'

Hallam sighed and did so.

'Good. Now do you want to go through the rest again?'

'I wouldn't mind turning on the engine, if that's all right with you.'

'All in good time. Now don't forget what I told you about an automatic.'

'I've driven the tractor, I think I can handle it.'

At this point Carl walked past them carrying a petrol can. He stopped to stare briefly at this unusual sight, before gathering himself together and continuing on his way. Hallam decided to ambush Julius. 'Did you and Verity fall out for some reason?'

'Not that I know of. Now turn the key to the right to start the ignition.'

'I got the feeling that something was going on.'

'Just pay attention to what you're doing,' Julius snapped. 'Hurry up, I've got a meeting in twenty minutes.'

'Who with?'

'Concentrate on what you're doing.'

Hallam grunted. He wanted to know what Julius was cooking up but his father was obsessive about security and the office was always locked if he went out. He started the engine. Then, without waiting for instructions, he let off the handbrake and shoved the gear lever into drive, pressing on the accelerator as he did so. The big car plunged forward.

Julius screamed, 'Wait!'

Startled, Hallam had to drag the steering wheel left to take it onto the main drive, but he oversteered, aiming the car instead towards a low stone mushroom.

'Stop!' shouted Julius, groping for the handbrake.

Hallam attempted to stamp both feet on the brake, but he caught the accelerator as well, and the bonnet reared up to the sound of screeching metal.

That evening Hallam kept himself hidden in Centre Point and dwelled gloomily on his situation and the seemingly intractable failings of his personality, to which the only reliable solution, so Verity had seemed to suggest on their walk up the drive, was suicide. His contemplation of self-slaughter lacked serious conviction, but out of that reckless spiritual curiosity particular to his age group he had, earlier in the day, climbed out onto the roof and tested the strong breeze, stepping right up to the edge and leaning fractionally beyond what was safe; just to experience how it might feel, out there, on the margins. But the wind had pushed him back like an unappetising meal. What was more, the prospect of a violent impact just hadn't seemed that appealing.

His initial refusal to kill himself was not, of course, definitive; he wondered if momentary madness required mental preparation. But he did not think he was mad, or even vaguely capable of what was called an 'episode' in the loathsome quack-talk of the psychiatrists and other buffoons who had failed to help his mother. Still, there was always the possibility that Verity was partly right and that he had inherited some strand of instability. It was perhaps even likely that he would grow into a dangerous pervert, at the very least. Then who knew what expression the bad seed would find for itself?

For now, however, he decided that suicide was not on the agenda and he turned his mind to the more bracing fantasy of Verity and Julius's accidental death. He got as far as choosing the coffins (pale pine, he thought, in consideration of the rainforests) before his pleasure was destroyed by the suspicion that, as fantasies went, parental death was actually rather pedestrian, adolescent even. Perversion, he resolved, should henceforth be a point of pride; he determined to be exacting in its cultivation. It held the promise of originality. His mood lifted and he stretched with satisfaction. Whatever traumas his father was going through, Verity's absence was a boon for him. His mind had cleared. Perhaps if he understood himself better then he would find the way ahead in his life.

He considered the lake below and strove to understand the reverence it inspired in him. Its construction, he saw now, had been a labour of hope. In the face of extermination from plague, the villagers had tried something to save themselves; a futile attempt, as it turned out, and an act of desperation, but the digging had served a purpose, and not just to give the ruling aristocracy a semblance of control in helpless circumstances. Their suffering and hope had created something beautiful that would endure. It had become somewhere to commune with the past. It was a genuine memorial, not a dumpy pompous block of stone with soldiers' names on it, like in the churchyard beyond, or a weather-smudged plaque in the family plot.

Perhaps the lake offered hope to him, too. It had already offered him a memory of his mother. With obsessive repetition he had revisited every image and sensation associated with it – the smell of his mother's perfume, the water's slap on the hull – to the point where he feared that over-use might warp the memory somehow. He wanted more of his past back, but he was unable to summon it on his own. What had he done with it? Tonight, though, he felt as if contact might be possible. The night was cool, as it had been with his mother, the moon was just as high if not, this time, so full. Hallam took up his badger pelt and the cigar box and made his way down the rope ladder. He walked to the side of the lake and took off his clothes. He tied the pelt round his head. He applied some of his mother's old make-up, the lipstick on his mouth this time, and the foundation across his chest as well as his cheeks. He was familiar with the sensations of the lake now and he moved with greater ease into the water, the whiteness of the foundation on his skin echoing the shattered reflection of the moon. He attempted to summon a spiritual frame of mind. He trawled his way out into the centre of the lake, flapped briefly when he lost his footing, then found what felt like the side of the submerged boat. Holding his arms out wide for stability, he waited for what might come. It did not look promising. The wind thrust harshly through the trees and a bank of cloud absorbed the moon.

It got chilly. He let himself float on his back. He tried this with his eyes closed and then open. He tried to think of some appropriate incantation that might cause something to happen. But his feeble attempts sounded absurd. Our father? Art he in heaven? I don't think so. He discovered how little spiritual equipment the modern world possessed – no more jujus or prayers – and he began to accept, as the cold numbed his feet and hands, that he was not going to be transported in any way whatsoever, and that she wasn't there. This had been a mistake.

Hallam was wading back to the grassy bank thinking of hot tea when he heard the crack of a branch and the twang of a fence wire being jumped over. By the time he had pulled himself out of the lake the dark figure that he might or might not have seen was away over the fields and the clouds did not help him pick out which way they were going. Hallam stood there exposed and helpless, one hand cupping his balls. He peeled a strip of rotten weed off his thigh. There was nothing he could do. So, rubbing his meatless ribcage to restore some circulation, Hallam went to find his clothes.

The silver BMW scraped to a halt in the pebbles in the late morning. Verity emerged and took some supermarket shopping bags out of the boot, as if she had only popped into town for a couple of hours. Julius was undignified in his rejoicing. He rushed out of the back door and they hugged and laughed and immediately went up to their bedroom where Hallam saw them, through the binoculars from South-West Traverse, pinballing around the room and attempting to undress without interrupting their passionate kissing. Hallam caught a brief flash of his father's white buttocks pressed bawdily against the windowpane before he quickly turned away, appalled, and concentrated instead on the more wholesome sight of the Hitchens' beagle Raymond shitting on the front lawn, its actions no doubt heartily endorsed by the owners. Hallam was not pleased to see Verity again. But when he came in that evening, after giving the reunited couple sufficient time to rut themselves to exhaustion, he was greeted with smiles of forgiveness. Even, with certain reservations, from Julius.

Verity kissed Hallam with moist sincerity, declared, 'Let's open a bottle of some good stuff,' and Julius hummed his way down the cellar steps, exhibiting a shamelessly post-coital bounce as he went. Hallam decided to go with the flow. Open hostility was a drag compared to superficial reconciliation, and vintage champagne would certainly help ease away the compromise that seemed to coat his gullet.

They were eating supper in the dining room and Hallam had taken a mouthful of peas when Julius made his announcement about the plans for developing the lake. Hallam's intake of breath caused one of the peas to attempt entry into his lungs and his coughing fit prevented Julius, for a moment, from presenting the details.

When Hallam had finally spluttered to a wet-eyed conclusion, Julius impatiently sought permission to go on and received a stunned nod of assent. Verity caught Hallam's attention with a smile and discreetly tapped her chin, mouthing the word 'drool'.

Hallam wiped the spittle with his napkin and dropped his eyes apologetically.

'The plan,' Julius started, 'is to transform the wasteland around the lakeland and turn it into an ultra-modern residential development. In short, bungalows.'

'Bungalows?' gasped Hallam weakly, failing utterly to disguise his horror.

'Not bungalows the way you're thinking,' laughed Julius with the hearty enthusiasm he reserved for work alone. 'They'll be underground. Let me show you.' He reached round to the serving table and unrolled a large plan of the lake area.

'Julius, can't this wait until we've finished eating?' asked Verity tiredly.

'Come on, it was your idea in the first place.'

'Underground bungalows,' said Hallam, staring at but not assimilating the plan spread out over the table's polished mahogany.

Julius began to explain. 'Now if you see here, the new village will take the form of a hexagon. We'll plant saplings along here, and where the main lake is now we'll have a long gentle stretch of lawn for recreational use. It will be an environmental village, partly submerged to preserve heat and maintain the unspoilt appearance of the area. We'll have all the latest techniques for supplementing conventional energy supplies, computers too.'

'Where are the lakes on this plan?' asked Hallam.

'They will be filled in,' answered Julius briskly. 'You've seen for yourself, Hallam, that they're stagnant and on the point of collapsing. A health risk. Young families with kids won't want it.'

Hallam saw the plans for what they were: a map of desecration. 'You can't do it,' he said simply.

'Yes we can,' replied Julius. 'What's more it will help pay you through university, not to mention the other improvements in the grounds. There's no point being sentimental.'

'Sentimental?' Verity sounded amazed. 'How can either of you feel sentimental about the lake? Do we want anyone else drowning in there?'

'I take it one was enough,' snapped Hallam.

There was a short silence and Verity looked down demurely at her plate. Hallam could see that she was gaining in confidence. Once, just a mention of death was avoided. Now, short of explicit reference to suicide, the tidemark of acceptability was creeping forwards. Julius looked startled.

'Filling them in won't make any difference,' said Hallam quietly.

Julius breezed on. 'I'm glad we're agreed then. The oak will have to go too of course, and a couple of the other trees with it. And that, I am afraid, will include the treehouse. Still, you're growing out of that now anyway, aren't you, Hallam? Graduated to wrecking cars.'

Hallam blinked stupidly. He knew he was helpless. 'The trees?'

Julius sighed, scratched his head. 'Although there might be ways round that. Temporarily.'

Verity straightened up. 'Surely, Julius, you're not going to risk the oak falling down and flattening someone. It wouldn't be professional. You heard what the tree surgeons said. Either it's coming down in a controlled way or one day it will just keel over.'

Julius grunted, and wrapped up the plans with a scowl, annoyed that his enthusiasm for the project had not met with the unanimous rapture that he was hoping for. 'You're probably right. But Hallam does spend half his life up there, doing his,' he paused diplomatically, 'birdwatching.'

'Well, once the oak tree is down I think it will be a brilliant site,' said Verity. 'I'm sure Mr Cheney will be pleased. Overgrown land harbours all sorts of vermin, doesn't it?'

'We won't risk publicity until we've got the project through the planning application, so keep it quiet.'

Verity filled up her wine glass and Julius went back to eating the roast pork. Hallam felt sick. He excused himself and went upstairs to his bedroom. His logbooks had gone missing.

The phone call came the next day. Nicola picked it up, and after a brief panicked discussion while the journalist waited on the line, Julius decided to take it, with the full intention of putting the man off. In fact he said slightly more than he intended because he was vaguely familiar with the journalist, and he found himself letting off steam while he tried to persuade the journalist to tell him how he had come by the plans for the development. But the journalist was unable to say.

The rest of the day was chaotic. There were manic phone calls downstairs as Julius tried to establish who might have leaked the story. Upstairs, Hallam ransacked his room for the missing logbooks which, he could only conclude after three ruthless searches, had been taken from where he was certain he had left them, at the back of a cupboard. He sat down on his bed, surrounded by upturned drawers and scattered clothing and papers. He decided against confronting Verity and demanding his property back, mainly because he suspected it would not work, but also because he lacked the courage. He needed to know what she wanted from the logbooks before deciding on his strategy; this would at least keep his options open. Was it to blackmail him into leaving? Was it simple curiosity to know what he did up in the treehouses, and did she now plan to use the material she had stumbled on as ammunition against her enemies in the village?

The theft of the logbooks was not simply an invasion of his privacy. They were not confessional diaries. It was bigger than that; the private lives of the whole village were in those volumes and stood to be compromised. Hallam felt guilty of professional negligence. It was an adult sensation that he did not savour.

As a result of Julius's elaborated No Comment, the *Leicester Argos* was able to run a story of villagers reacting in fury to plans by a defiant local squire to flatten a historic medieval site and build an ugly New Age housing estate on the top of it – or rather, underneath it. 'No To Hobbitland' was the headline.

The villager quoted was Mr Hitchens, determined to protect the village beauty spot from 'developers prepared to flatten our heritage for a trouserful of cash'.

Julius let the newspaper drop. 'What about the ugly little estates they live in? And what the hell is it to do with them? And since when have any of them given a toss about the precious heritage of an overgrown swamp? All I've ever got is complaints from that bloody farmer.'

'But how did the paper get to hear about it?' asked Verity.

'How do I know?'

'Could it have been someone in the planning office?'

'It can't have been them because the plan wasn't submitted until late in the afternoon. They wouldn't have even looked at it until the next day.'

'Who else knew?'

'The surveyors, I suppose, but I can't believe they would do it. There's no reason, I've worked with them for years.'

'The tree surgeon?'

'All he knew was that a dangerous tree needed to be cut down.'

'The office?'

'I have complete trust in Nicola, and the rest of the team.'

'Then who's left? Carl?'

'I may have mentioned something . . . but I can't believe it.'

Verity smiled at Hallam, who looked sullenly back. 'Well, that only leaves family. Hallam, you didn't speak to a journalist or anyone else about this?'

'I wish I'd thought of it,' said Hallam.

'Get out of my sight,' said Julius.

Hallam walked out of the kitchen. He had a pretty good idea who Lucy must have used her new mobile phone to call. Julius must have told her about the lakeland plans. But whoever was responsible, Hallam already suspected that he was going to pay for it in one way or another.

In the early evening Verity called for Hallam from the top of the broad stone steps at the front of the Hall. Julius was with her. Hallam had already seen them, of course. He could almost read their lips from South-West Traverse with his new binoculars. She and Julius descended the steps and strolled down the path, arm in arm. She had a large handbag slung over her shoulder.

The couple were admiring the full frontal view of their property from the bench in front of the ornamental pond by the time Hallam hit the ground. He shambled towards them, long arms hanging self-consciously, feeling exposed amid the open expanse of lawn.

'I don't mean to be a pain, Hallam,' said Verity, 'but did you get round to tidying the cellar?'

Hallam had forgotten. 'I'll do that now.'

'Just the steps and around the wine cellar.'

Hallam made his way up to the house, noticing that Verity was patiently waiting for him to move out of earshot. He wondered if she had chosen that bench on purpose because it was so difficult to be eavesdropped upon. Creeping along behind the high hedge that divided the grounds from the meadow and public path was almost the only option, and even then you could hardly hear a thing unless they raised their voices. He suspected that this chore was just a way of ensuring that he was well out of the way.

If so, she underestimated him. Once he was out of sight, Hallam raced upstairs and into his bedroom. Slowly, he opened the window which looked down on the lawns. Verity and Julius were no more than the size of toy soldiers until he brought up his binoculars. There he saw her lift one of his logbooks out of her bag and place it on Julius's lap. Hallam's chest contracted.

As Julius began to leaf through it, Hallam let his binoculars drop and concentrated instead on hearing. Verity's voice was just audible. Her consonants bounced off the water of the pond and up to the Hall window fairly intact, but Julius's bass tones seemed to fall to pieces, and arrived as no more than a low grumbling.

Hallam snatched up a scrap of paper and a pen and started to transcribe the words, regardless of their sense, according to how they sounded. When he was unsure he made dashes for vowels and dots for consonants. In this way he was free to focus on the evidence of his ears and not be distracted by attempting simultaneously to understand the larger meaning which could be pieced together later. His pencil moved busily across the page, with the urgent concentration of a codebreaker. Locking himself into this familiar procedure helped control the surge of panic. Eventually, scribbling frantically, he saw out of the corner of his eye that Julius had risen and was making his way back towards the Hall. Verity got up to follow him, and his transcript came to a sudden halt as she stepped away from the pond.

With shaking hands he looked over what he had written, annotating and correcting where he could. The first pertinent line was not, on first sight, very promising: 'ENO JUPEE PIN HE SIT. AIR HUMMING SERIOUSLY ONGEEM.'

He thought he could make sense of it: 'It's not just peeping, it's sick. There's something seriously wrong with him.' Then came Julius's answer, but it had been beyond hearing, and was very short. The notes returned to Verity, and Hallam continued to interpret where necessary, but the next section was remarkably clear, as she had raised her voice: 'I'm suggesting that he needs help. Psychiatry (SYKO TREE). He was seen trying to drown himself in the lake, in make-up. It's around the whole village. I won't be held responsible.'

Hallam's notes had become wobbly after that, for all his concentration. Julius had responded, but he had had his head down and again he was incomprehensible. Verity came back onstream, but fuzzily. 'You ignored the signs with Anne. Do you want your son to go the same way?'

Then the one line of Julius's that Hallam heard because it was shouted: 'He's not like her.'

She raised her voice back at him and the rest was clear again, even though Julius had got up and moved out of range: 'Who could possibly have tipped the papers off if not Hallam? Lucy didn't know, did she?' She paused. 'There's no way we can change the plans (CHAIN THE PANS) now. The lakes are a deathtrap (DEBT RAT).'

The notes came to an end as Verity, too, had moved out of range. Hallam stared at what he had written and tried to assimilate the information, but the garbled phrases circled meaninglessly.

With a jolt he remembered that he was supposed to be cleaning the cellar. He rumbled downstairs with the notepaper safe in his pocket and opened the cellar door just as he heard Verity and Julius come inside the Hall. He picked up a stiff broom that was leaning in the corner and began to sweep coal dust from the top step down onto the next, slowly descending into the cellar's darkness. Chain the pans, he thought, sweeping left to right, right to left. Chain the pans.

Hallam lay in the hammock of Centre Point and stared up at the wooden roof. One long leg swung him forwards and back into the bright rectangle of morning sunshine. He listened to the skitter of a bird's feet on the roof, and continued to rock.

He knew for certain that the end was coming. Julius had confirmed that the tree surgeons were coming tomorrow to cut this oak down, and no village protest would stop it, even if Julius had to stand there by himself and fight them off (or so he claimed). He had never seen his father so impassioned, or so determined.

Hallam did not have to overhear any conversation to be aware of the suspicion that hung about him. Neither Julius nor Verity were being openly hostile, as there was no evidence linking him with the leak, but even Nicola failed to give him so much as a perfunctory smile when he popped his head into the office. So Hallam kept himself scarce, savouring the last hours in his condemned refuge.

He decided to take a second look at the scrap of paper that was still tucked into the pocket of his jeans. He asked himself whether it was conceivable that he might have got it wrong; there was inevitably a margin of error in what he did.

He frowned. THERE SNOW WAY WEAKEN CHAIN THE PANS could as easily have been framed as a question, 'Is there no way we can change the plans?' as opposed to 'There is . . .' which radically changed it from a death sentence to a plea for clemency.

He entertained doubt. Had he been wrong about everything? Was Verity not the monster he and Lucy thought she was? Was it his fault? Was he just emulating Lucy thoughtlessly and causing all this trouble for himself? Was he drunk on paranoia?

'Hallam!'

His leg stiffened and the hammock jerked to a halt. Was that Verity's voice?

'Hallam, could you answer me, please.' Her tone was polite, weary; she knew he was there. He got up and stuck his head out of the treehouse. She was alone, staring up, mouth open, shading her eyes.

'Hello?'

'Can I come up?' she asked.

'I'll come down.'

'Please, I've never been up there before. This is my last chance.' He frowned but dropped the ladder down to her. She began to climb up, taking her time, grinning tight-lipped with the effort. Hallam cast his eyes nervously around the treehouse, suddenly conscious of potentially incriminating evidence. He swiftly bundled his fresh logbook into the chest along with the cigar box and the carving knife. He picked up a ragged porn magazine that he had found in the cemetery but had barely looked at and tucked it under the bird reference books which were laid ostentatiously by the telescope. He still felt a strong sentimental attachment to the instrument, despite its obsolescence.

Verity reached the top and scrambled uncertainly along the bough on all fours. She was, he was pleasantly surprised to find, at a disadvantage up here. With ironic treetop gallantry, he gave her his hand and helped her inside Centre Point.

'Thank God for that,' she gasped with a little laugh as she crawled in on her knees. 'I don't even want to think about going down again.' She looked up to him, panting softly, and smiled. He motioned for her to sit in the hammock. She looked at it, back at him with a faint smile, then stood up and banged her head on the roof.

'Careful,' said Hallam, still concerned about the roof's welfare, even if it was about to be torn down. Half crouching, she went over and lowered herself into the hammock.

'Thank you. There's enough room for two if we squeeze up.'

'That's OK,' said Hallam cautiously, and sat down on the floor cross-legged.

'It will be a pity to see this go. Peaceful, isn't it?'

He was not in the mood for small talk. She sighed and pressed her knees together, assembling the stepmotherly charade.

'I want us to have a talk, Hallam.'

'Do go on,' he replied, 'Verity.'

'I only want what's best for your father and, you may be surprised to hear—'

'I want them back.' It came out of him unplanned.

She put aside her unfinished sentence and looked at her nails. 'Yes, I expect you do. I'm curious, did Lucy put you up to this?'

'No. Are you disappointed that Julius isn't packing me off to a secure unit?'

She glanced up. 'What are you talking about?'

He smiled. 'You must be disappointed that Julius won't throw me out.' Outside, the wind rose, causing the leaves to ripple.

Appearing bored, she glanced around her. 'I hope I'm not keeping you from your birdwatching.'

She leant over and uncovered the porn magazine. Hallam contemplated snatching it out of her hands, then thought better of it. She raised her eyebrows with faint surprise.

'Girls. I was beginning to wonder.'

In fact the pictures were not at all to his taste. They were posed and therefore false. Their sexual conventions were strange and bore no relation to the lives he had watched. Also, the way the model on the cover leered so knowingly into the camera made him feel visible and unerotically sordid. But what was there to say?

'Why don't you join me on the hammock? You don't look very comfortable.'

It was mockery but a suggestion all the same and it caused Hallam's throat to dry up. He opened his mouth to speak but at first nothing came out.

Amusement suggested itself around her mouth. 'Are we a virgin?'

Receiving no response, she rocked herself softly. 'Those notebooks of yours make for fascinating reading in their own way. You must have been very intrepid, gathering all that information. Lots of sneaky little thrills, you communicate that wonderfully.'

'Showing Julius didn't work though, did it?' Hallam managed to inject a bit of triumph into his voice. He was so massively exposed it felt almost liberating.

'Do I scare you, Hallam?'

'No, you physically repel me.'

This was a lie, but to Hallam's surprise it sent a shiver through her composure. Was vanity her weak spot? He attacked it, with all the violent instinct of the playground. 'You're my father's fuckbag, what did you expect? With your horrible fat arse cheeks and thick ankles.' Hallam saw Verity's anger exposed. This time the expression went out of her eyes and into her mouth. It caused her upper lip to protrude. She looked comically neurotic. For a brief second Hallam really didn't fear her; he was too fascinated by this transformation. How stupidly hate animated the face, he thought. Unfortunately, however, the moment of Olympian observation did not last very long before it was replaced by something bigger and more biblical in proportion: dread.

'I know what your mother must have told you about me; Lucy too no doubt,' she said, those eyes widened now, the upper lip curled, 'and that's why you hate me and think I'm a whore. I expect you think that I had a part in her dying. Well, your mother was a lying fucking bitch, she was destroying your father and she couldn't bear the possibility of him being happy with me. So that's when the lies about me started, the persecution complex, trying to poison everything that Julius and I might have together. Do you know, I wish I had held your mother under, drowned the lying bitch myself. But she did it for me, she killed herself, like the selfish jealous bitch she always was. It was her last attempt to get me out, the sickest and most despicable of them all. And it failed. And there's nothing anyone can prove, nothing.'

Hallam felt the whole treehouse sway, but the breeze was gentle outside. What was she saying? His mother hadn't told him anything, and neither had Lucy. He could barely focus; his mind swung violently, rebounding from the force of her assault. Verity was panting slightly, putting her ardour back under control.

'What do you think they told me about you?' he at last asked, trying to control the tremor in his voice. He had never been the subject of such open and unadulterated adult loathing.

But Verity's face had slowly reconfigured. She had thrust the hatred back inside. She was wary again, perhaps regretting, behind that mask of indifference and mild amusement, her outburst. She was not going to give anything more away. And, shamefully, Hallam felt an enormous surge of relief. He did not want to know. He belonged in the trees.

'Well now,' she said and glanced at her small gold wristwatch. 'You need to pack this place up.'

A surge of incoherent emotion passed through Hallam. Perhaps it was naivety, it was strong enough. 'Please, I understand that you hate me, and my dead mother, and my sister, but why do you have to destroy this, and the lakes, and the land? It's done nothing, it's got nothing to do with this.'

Verity smiled and shrugged. 'Perhaps I'm not as bad as you think. Perhaps, in a funny way, I'm on your side. I'll prove it to you.'

Hallam was baffled, suspicious, unsure what to say. She slipped the magazine back under the book with ostentatious care, then got up, remembering the low roof in time. Making her way out of the treehouse sideways, she turned round to face him, reversing into position above the rope ladder. She gingerly set her foot on the first rung, grabbing a nearby branch more for reassurance than practical safety, as it was too slender to save her if she slipped. Then she cautiously lowered herself, squatting awkwardly. Hallam watched her vulnerability and felt himself swing back towards loathing and violence; it tautened his muscles, and caused saliva with a metallic taste to flush his mouth. One firm kick in the face and it might all be over. Verity looked up at him warily. But the moment passed, and she was on her way down to the ground below.

In the morning Hallam saw from Gatewatch the tree surgeons arrive in their van. First they had to pass a truculent gathering of eight local people at the gates. Mr and Mrs Hitchens had even knocked up a couple of placards: 'Save Our Lakes'. There was jeering and a young man slick with hair gel, Jenny's brother Gav whom Hallam recognised, half-heartedly blocked the van's path up the drive. Standing slightly apart and lately arrived was an egg-shaped man with a notebook who looked vaguely familiar. Gav moved to the side after a couple of angry hoots on the van's horn and a loud rev of intent. Toff-baiting didn't extend as far as personal injury.

Hallam climbed down from Gatewatch and was spotted by one of them. 'Look, it's the Peeping Tom!'

Hallam did not condescend to pay any attention to the hostile laughter, nor to the waves of the journalist who was attempting to draw him over to talk.

'Nobody told us this job was controversial,' said one of the surgeons as they unpacked their chainsaws.

'You're all right,' said Carl. 'It's just locals with nothing better to do.'

Carl clearly felt guilty about having to play a part in this. He avoided Hallam's eye when all Hallam wanted to do was give him a smile of reassurance. Julius was fetched and together the men went up to the lake. Hallam was not invited and did not want to go. He went up to his bedroom instead.

The chest was on the floor of his bedroom, the badger pelt flopped on top of it. His equipment suddenly looked quaint and childish out of its proper setting. He sat down on his bed and tried to wait, but it was no use. He had to see what was being done.

He was jogging up towards the passageway between the stables and the cottage, worried that he might miss the felling altogether, when he heard an ambulance siren and the high rev of its engine as it negotiated the back drive at speed. He pounded through the passageway, his panting amplified and echoing around him until he burst out, meeting the crowd of former demonstrators now running towards the base of the oak tree. His father, Carl and a tree surgeon were kneeling around a prone body.

The ambulance screeched to a halt on the drive, blocking Hallam's view.

Paramedics climbed out and headed up towards the crowd. Hallam followed. It was the other tree surgeon. His right arm had been neatly removed at the shoulder. The saw was just a few feet away, its chain broken and spattered with blood.

Hallam went up to the base of the tree where the chainsaw had bitten into the trunk; two bent six-inch nails, still shiny new, protruded from the wound. Only on close inspection did Hallam see that the rest of the trunk was full of them also; the nailheads had been blackened to camouflage the glint of metal.

They lifted the shuddering man onto the stretcher. The egg-shaped journalist asked the paramedics which hospital they were going to. The hushed crowd began to disperse back down the drive, shooed away by Carl.

Then the other tree surgeon stopped and screamed at them, 'Whichever one of you bastards spiked this tree, are you happy now? An innocent man doing his job!'

Julius and Hallam entered the passage on their way back towards the Hall. By the time they emerged on the other side, Hallam was convinced.

'Dad, it was Verity.'

Julius stopped and looked at him closely.

'I know she's been trying to tell you I'm mad. But I'm not. She is.'

'I know you're not.' Julius took him gently by the arm and walked him back into the Hall. 'Come on into the office, Nicola's not in today.' Hallam followed, reassured by his father's calmness.

'Sit down,' said Julius. Hallam did so and Julius sat opposite. He opened a drawer and took out a chequebook. He wrote four thousand pounds on it then offered it to Hallam. Hallam didn't understand, although of course he took it.

'What's this for?'

'Hallam, this is to discharge my obligations. You're not ill and that's why I hold you fully responsible for your actions. Now listen carefully. You are moving out of the Hall. Please don't come back or contact us again, although I don't mind if you send a forwarding address for mail.'

'Dad, I didn't do it.'

'I appreciate there is no firm evidence. However, I'm calling a taxi. It will arrive in twenty minutes and take you wherever you want. You've got some change, have you?'

Julius picked up the phone and dialled and did not look at Hallam again. Hallam stood up groggily. Four thousand pounds? Why on earth four? Zero he could understand. Fifty thousand maybe. He reflected upon the ineffable mystery of his father's thought processes. He could hear a phone ringing in a distant office. He turned to go.

'And don't think this will stop the development,' Julius called after him. 'In fact, quite the contrary.'

The taxi pulled away down the drive with the chest and a suitcase in the back. Hallam, sitting in the back, had not said goodbye to Verity. She was nowhere to be seen, until they were sweeping past the main door and he glanced up at the bay window above it and glimpsed her face looking down at him. She wore a faint smile and raised her palm, in benediction or mocking farewell he could no longer guess, and anyway the Hall was now a guttering image of redbrick in the wing mirror. All Hallam could do was stare out at the green lawn flickering through the line of trees and then the taxi went out through the gates and he left the grounds, he assumed, for ever.

five

Hallam kept his head low as he trotted along the roof, making sure that he could not be seen from the tenement windows of the neighbours across the yard. Pitched rooftops on either side kept him largely obscured for the length of the valley gutter until he hopped over a bolted trap door above the block's communal stairwell, and nimbly ascended the steep lead-lined join between two stretches of slate. There was no avoiding exposure here on the ridge so he paused a moment, shading his eyes in an innocent pose, to admire the view over Edinburgh's medieval Old Town.

The castle squatted in the distance, visible over the tall buildings flanking the Royal Mile. He could, theoretically, be seen by hundreds of people up here but he knew that in his boilersuit he would not attract a second glance. Mass exposure conferred its own kind of anonymity. The rooftops of the city were constantly populated by repairmen, drunken students, window-cleaners, satellite dish installers, not to mention burglars; a ragged community living among the pigeon shit and pollution, and all of them, in their own small way, like him.

The five years since he had left Chanby Hall had altered his appearance. A light wind ruffled his now short hair. His long arms had acquired more sinuous strength, his fingers, too, had thickened, and the pads on his palms had roughened like those of a gymnast. His skin had lost the milkiness of its acne-resistant teenage years and the light of the early evening sky showed that his face had filled out a little. As he squinted towards the dropping sun, a frown mark shaped like the Greek letter pi appeared between his eyes – another new addition. But some things never change.

He pattered softly down the other side of the double-pitched roof with fast tiny steps and the same bandy-legged gait of old. He paused behind a large ten-pot chimney stack, kneeled on his haunches and looked over to where her bathroom window had been left open a few inches. Steam drooled out of the thin aperture, carrying with it the scent of sweet almond oil as it was sucked away over the roof tiles. He felt a familiar twinge in his stomach, savoured it, and crept forward, every step measured, soundless. He brought himself right up by the window frame, mindful not to cast a shadow within. Tenderly he curved his body round the frame, slowly relaxing his muscles and resting the underside of his arm along the metal lintel. They were made for each other, the window and him. They fitted.

Hallam closed his eyes and listened to the gentle slop of warm water just those short few feet below him. He felt the warmth of the steam leaking up over the side of his face, and he locked its memory away, helplessly in love with this moment. He opened his eyes again, puppyish with ardour, and moved back down into a crouch to bring his eyes level with the sill. Steam streamed over his ears as he peered below the misted pane.

She was there, lying in her bath below him, rosy and inert. Her head was out of sight but he could still see her whole body from the neck down: white simple breasts and carved hips amid the soapy water. He was moved to compassion by her vulnerability.

He smiled sadly at this situation, him hustled by the cool Edinburgh wind out here, her safe and secure within. At this moment the barrier between them, voyeur and subject, seemed so cruel. And yet, he had to remind himself, it was insuperable. After all, voyeurism had its responsibilities.

Hallam did not regard what he was doing as sleazy. Until he had come upon the graffiti over Centre Point in his previous life he had never even associated the comically dated term 'Peeping Tom' with what he did. Where was the 'peeping' in his almost scientific dedication to observation and recording – a close-packed notepad always primed in his back pocket – not to mention his cultivated sense of levity in sexual matters?

It was not necessarily sex or human drama that interested Hallam in his subjects. Usually it was the quiet moments that appealed to him; hearing the steady breathing of their sleep, or the sounds of their restlessness, or just following the pottering domestic activities that somehow managed to encapsulate the flavour of their private existence. He felt no more arousal watching a couple making love through a skylight, he had convinced himself, than a primatologist, say, watching two gibbons mate. Neither possessed much dignity when dispassionately observed.

There was more to it than that though. Once he had tried to read all sorts of possible meanings into these body letters, body words, but the frustration eventually put him off to the point where he shirked observation of it altogether. In reality the sexual act was a crossword he could not solve, in a language he did not understand. Kate, however, was a special case. He felt drawn to her in an unusually compelling way, and this was precisely what the Rules of Distance were for. Hallam thought of the rules as a professional code of conduct. They allowed him to pursue his calling without harming or disturbing others, and it provided a coherent framework that helped curb the perils of obsession. Besides psychological protection they also reduced the risk of brushes with the police, although the law was strangely impotent in matters relating to voyeurism, even including its distant and, in Hallam's view, utterly repulsive cousin, stalking. The rules, formulated by himself, were as follows.

Firstly, they forbade him any sexual contact with his subjects (not that this was even conceivable). Secondly, they decreed that there be no social interaction with a subject beyond that which was practically necessary. Thirdly, the voyeur should not use his privileged knowledge and information to interfere in the life of the subject, even if did appear to be in their best interests. Lastly, but sacred among all the rules, was that the voyeur should never make his activities known to a subject, under any circumstances.

There were certain amendments of course. Hallam did allow himself to use the things he learnt from his subjects for his own personal gain, so long as they did not harm the subject. Theoretically one could break the rules to intervene in a subject's life if that life was in immediate danger, although this was not a moral imperative. Hallam believed that the voyeur, being dedicated to the observation of life and being by necessity invisible, operated outside the normal scheme of things and consequently did not bear the same responsibilities as other people.

Hallam had no doubt that many people would find this code, and the whole voyeuristic calling, disgusting and parasitic. Perhaps they would be horrified that he did not report occasional cases of domestic violence that he witnessed or heard going on within homes he passed over. But what could he do? And besides, he was not alone. The twentieth century had brought the voyeuristic impulse well into the cultural mainstream, in many ways for the better, and the twenty-first only promised to elevate it even higher in the lives and experiences of the people.

Hallam saw himself as the product of a wider cultural movement, although of course he belonged to a different league entirely from the slack-mouthed telly-watchers and internet-browsers below. He took note of the times of all his subjects' favourite television programmes and organised his own viewing schedules to avoid them. Aside from the boredom of watching someone gaping at some supposedly 'real life' soap like *Big Brother*, or whatever else was popular at the time, there was repulsion too. The few times that Hallam had stuck around to watch, he had been haunted afterwards by his subjects' seemingly lifeless bodies and faces, eyes glittering in the television's glow. It made him feel as if he was looking at himself.

Occasionally, Hallam wondered if he might be slightly mad. But he knew that he was not, chiefly because he possessed doubts. What, he had asked himself a hundred times, if these rules were merely the intellectual dressing to help him feel more comfortable about his vice? But, he answered himself, at least it was a victimless vice. It was not invasive; besides, he paid for his pleasure with risk, although of course this soon became part of the pleasure itself.

Hallam never needed to ask himself whether the danger was worth it as he prepared to jump across a thirty-foot plunge between tenements to check on the daily rituals of the occupant of Top Flat, 2 Urquhart's Close. That would have been missing the point. He cared for his subjects; he forgave them their unspeakable table manners when they ate alone; he was, in a sense, their guardian angel. The tragedy was that they would never know he was there.

The girl jolted upright in her bath, causing the water to splash over the sides and onto the terracotta floor of the bathroom. Hallam instinctively ducked, and his reverie was blown away across the grey city stacks. Had she somehow sixth-sensed his presence? Of course not, he reassured himself, and concentrated on regulating his breathing. He of all people knew the myth of the itchy neck or burning sensation that fiction writers gave their characters when they felt they were being watched. It did not exist, or if it did then it had been bred out of the modern city dweller.

People were constantly under watch, they even wanted to be watched, by security cameras at the very least. It gave them peace of mind.

Cautiously Hallam brought an eye to bear again, just in time to see her rise out of the bath and reach over for a towel, a little stream of water pouring off her pudenda. Then he heard the telephone ring twice, until it was picked up by the answering machine. She paused, wrapping the towel round herself. Together she and Hallam listened to the recording: 'Messages, please, for Kate Breck.' A bleep. He smiled dotingly at her brevity. Then on came the voice that Hallam loathed: smug, East Coast, with an inexcusable drawl. 'Yeah, hi, Kate, it's Alasdair here . . .'

She was already racing across the hallway to the bedroom to pick up the phone, so keen, with that childish absence of shame that he had observed so many times in people who are alone. Huffing his disapproval, Hallam pattered back up the join, over the angled loft and across to an inward-pivoting skylight. It, too, was partially open, one of the blessings of the warm weather. He put his ear close and heard her voice. It was calmer and more casual than her indecorous sprint to the phone, but still it failed to disguise her excitement and flirtatious inclinations.

'You just caught me in the bath, Al, I'm dripping all over the carpet . . . oh no, don't worry, I'm fine. So, er, do you still want to meet tonight?'

For God's sake have some dignity, Hallam thought, he's no good for you.

'Oh,' she said, pathetically disappointed. 'So the weekend's out as well. Really? Um, I suppose so.'

What a surprise. So that's the second time he's cancelled.

'OK, tomorrow then. No, that's OK. See you.'

She put down the phone and sat on the bed, thinking. Her black hair hung limply round her beautiful flushed cheeks and ended just below her sharply drawn jaw. Hallam loved the harshness in her face – the downward curve of her mouth and arched eyebrows; he thought he could see what lay beneath. A bead of water slid down between her shoulder blades. She ran her fingers up the nape of her neck and shook the damp locks. Her sigh caused Hallam to rise up and move away; watching was never easy.

It was getting dark by the time he returned to his part of the Old Town and put his key in the outside padlock. He lifted the rooftop skylight, perched on the edge and dangled his legs inside. Then, with a lithe twisting motion, he turned and dropped out of sight – except for his fingers which had snapped shut on the skylight's sill. They flexed once, twice as his body swung gently beneath, then let go. Hallam fell between two wooden rafters and landed feet first on his mattress. He bounced gamely on it then hopped off onto the beams that supported the loft, brushing his hands with satisfaction. Home. He lifted up a pole with a metal hook on the end and used it to shut the skylight above him and push home the lock. The skylight's blind was down, as always; he did not like to wake up to the morning light, and just the idea of being observable from above was enough to stop him falling asleep.

The journey from Kate's place to his over the rooftops was relatively short and simple; it was part of his flat's appeal. Besides that, it suited him perfectly. Small enough to be affordable for a young man with a reasonable job in the charity sector and some money from a will, a loft above it big enough to put in a mattress, and neighbours – students and young professionals mostly – who took no interest in him whatsoever. And, of course, the skylight.

He turned on the loft's lightbulb, which he had softened with a burgundy shade, and disappeared down the stepladder to the flat below. The dim light revealed that the loft was almost completely bare. A fridge door opened and closed, then Hallam climbed back up again, holding a bag containing a carton of orange juice and a Cornish pasty purchased at a petrol station up the road. He lay back on the thin mattress, which was supported by some plywood laid over the beams. He took a bite out of the pasty and helped it down with the juice. It had been a good day, by his standards. Chewing idly, he listened to the rising wind as it washed over the roof.

It was fairly quiet tonight, but when the gusts picked up he could feel the whole loft shudder and the wooden rafters creak. He closed his eyes and allowed the smell of dust and dry wood to bring him relaxation and escape. He would fill in his logbook later. With a heavy arm he plonked down the carton and shoved the pasty away, curling up fully clothed, already willing himself to dream about the trees.

Hallam said good morning to his boss as he walked into the offices of Cancer Action, and went to his desk.

'Morning, Hallam,' replied Kate, without looking up. She was sipping at a mug of coffee and perusing the latest issue of a newish Scottish society magazine, *North Britain*, which was aimed at the nation's rich and glamorous but sold mainly to Americans of Scottish ancestry.

'Get up to anything last night?' he called over casually, turning on his computer terminal.

'Pretty boring,' she replied, then looked up at him and smiled. 'Couldn't be arsed going out. Stayed in for a soak. Rather pleasant actually.'

'Sounds nice,' replied Hallam. He felt affection for the small lies and half-truths that buffered his subjects' public and private lives. Men: would she never learn? 'They're not worth it,' he said.

She smiled ruefully in agreement then suddenly frowned. 'What aren't worth it?'

'Evenings out midweek. They're draining.'

'Oh,' replied Kate, slowly going back to her magazine. 'Yes.'

Hallam knew he shouldn't play these stupid little games. It was hardly healthy for someone who intended to observe the rules of distance for ever. Still, how could Kate ever guess that she was his prime subject?

'Come over here for a second, would you?'

Hallam shrugged off his jacket, hung it on the back of his chair and went across to Kate's desk. He leant over to look at an article that she had circled in the magazine's gossip column. 'Have a quick read of this.'

Hallam quickly scanned the story. It mentioned that a certain Dorothy Carter née Mackenzie was returning to live in Perthshire after an absence of over twenty years following the death of her American husband, the New York-based merchandiser, Frank. She was reported to have said that she wanted to be back in her home town, and had recently been treated for cancer in the States. It also mentioned that her son, Gordon, owned an art gallery in Edinburgh.

'Coming home to die maybe?' said Hallam.

'You never know,' replied Kate. 'Her husband's American, which means that it should be simple finding out the details of his will. See what else there is, any family history of illness, donations to charities, you know the sort of thing. Check that we've sent our legacy leaflet to their solicitors. Might be nothing, but still. What about the son?'

'Gordon Carter? He lives in Edinburgh all right. I've heard of him.'

'We should sound him out. It pays to be discreet, so remember the code: softly softly.'

'No direct sales pitch. Their initiative, no pressuring. I know, I know.'

Kate ripped out the page and passed it over, smiling up at him. 'Thanks, Hallam, you're a brick. How are you getting along with the copy for the leaflet?'

'Fine. Photo-wise I thought we could get some cute pensioners with the younger generation; protective hand on the shoulder kind of thing.'

'Yeah, lots of smiles; no references to illness.' Her attention was back on her computer screen. He turned briskly on his heel, still savouring the cool pleasure of their professional relationship, the way she trusted him with this work, the slick efficiency of their discussions, the effortless decision-making. He smiled to himself and tingled in the way a normal person might remember the night before.

At his desk he quickly logged on and brought up the Public Records Office website at the New York State capital, Albany. He tapped in the name Frank Carter. Up rolled the details of the will, it was as simple as that. Hallam sucked in his breath as he scrolled through the document. The man had been rich – and it had all gone to his wife.

By mid-afternoon Hallam had built up a portfolio of information on the Carters, covering the financial state of the family, Frank's death, and discreet press references to the bouts of illness that Dorothy had been suffering from over recent years. Some of the information came from press cuttings but most of the stuff on Gordon from a young gay man, Stewart Campbell, who worked in fundraising at the Edinburgh Festival and obviously considered Hallam a closet case in need of bringing out. This entailed occasional excruciating evenings at gay bars where the clientele were apt to stare at nervously grinning young men. But the information gleaned on rich donors to the arts and general gossip made it worthwhile. Gordon Carter was often mentioned for the decadence of his gallery's private viewing parties and the invariable prettiness of the featured female artists. Both pointed towards considerable independent income. His name had come up in the last couple of weeks, Hallam seemed to recall, while he had been on the case of a degenerate Anglo-Scottish aristocrat, Ian Hamilton, who liked to slum with the artsy crowd and possessed a family tree afflicted with the right cancers. At the bars frequented by this crowd Hallam was the dully-dressed, vaguely defeated-looking young man of no consequence who was jostled or crowded unobtrusively into proximity with other people's conversations.

Gordon, it had to be assumed, would eventually be the beneficiary of the estate in the tragic event of Dorothy's death, as she had no other close relatives still living. As far as was known, her donations to charity had never been substantial and usually only extended to attending the odd society ball.

Hallam bounded over to Kate's desk. 'Hey, Kate. Dorothy Carter is very rich and almost certainly on her way out.'

'What's she dying from?'

'One of the big cancers. She's had several operations, without success, it seems.'

'Any idea of time frame?'

'She's unlikely to last the year is what Gordon told a friend.'

'Is she of sound mind?'

'No senility. Quite sharp still, apparently.'

Kate smiled. 'Well, that sounds promising. Good work, Hallam.'

Hallam smiled back. Only four hours' intensive labour and he had already earned another smile; this was easy. 'I'm just going to pop by the gallery. Won't be long.' He returned to his desk and picked up a Cancer Action collecting tin while humming a tune.

'Hold it, what's that you're humming?'

'The Afro-Cuban Allstars, I'm mad on the album.'

'You are?' Kate laughed. 'So am I! How did you hear about them?'

Through crouching by your window listening to you playing the album, thought Hallam. 'I saw a preview of the documentary and ordered it on the net. Much better than Buena Vista Social Club, in my humble opinion. Actually I'm thinking of doing some Cuban dance lessons.'

'You are?'

'If I could find a partner.' Hallam couldn't believe he'd just said that. He was extending her an invitation, however indirect and unlikely to be taken up, and that was pushing the boundaries of the rules. But he had watched her dancing in her flat and it had been a revelation. Solitary dancing was so much more erotic and unfettered than the self-conscious posturings in nightclubs that he had seen from glimpses of other people's late-night TV sets. He had loved her sweetly narcissistic shimmies in front of the mirror.

Kate frowned. 'You know, I've been trying to convince this guy Alasdair to come and do them with me, but he's so stubborn.'

'Alasdair?' asked Hallam mildly, not wanting to sound intrusive, and noting with ambiguous relief that she had side-stepped his hugely irresponsible invitation. Alasdair? he asked mentally. You mean the one who plucks his nostril hair in your bedroom when you go to the toilet?

'Sort of ex-boyfriend. I'm meeting him this evening.'

'Well, enjoy yourself.'

Kate rubbed the back of her neck. 'Hallam, I hope you don't mind me asking you a favour, but . . . well, this is a bit personal.'

Hallam looked sympathetic. His subjects usually found him understanding because he was already familiar with their private preoccupations. He never went so far as casually to touch on, say, Kate's worrying predilection for gorging on chocolate or masturbating while weeping on the sofa. But he was able to pick up tips like her bedside reading, musical taste and the rest. Seemingly coincidental shared interests could have a magical effect on predisposing a person towards him. Everyone was superstitious at heart about personal chemistry: it was a repressed belief in fate.

'It's just that, whenever I meet him, things tend to get a bit out of control. I know he's no good for me, and I've told him it's all over, but it would help if someone else was there, to keep things at a certain level.'

'You want me to come along?'

'Would you mind? Have you got something on?'

'I can put it off.' Lies, Hallam thought: my social life is a husk. This was amazing luck. He lifted up a hand as she began to protest. 'I wouldn't offer if I didn't want to.'

She smiled and touched his hand. 'Thanks. I would ask a girlfriend but . . . I know this sounds awful. The thing is, he's very good-looking.'

six

Hallam entered the MacIver Gallery fully armed with Edinburgh name-drops and even, if required, some items of gossip – all intended to relay confidence that he was a known and accepted, though not prominent, initiate in the city's bleary social circuit. A pretty young woman at the reception desk sat engrossed in her computer. The doorbell had rung but she only glanced at him for a nano-second before she identified him as a non-threatening nonentity. This was annoying as, for once, Hallam was trying to be visible and attractive.

He approached, casting an eye over the mostly tasteless late-Victorian daubings in gold frames, cleared his throat and asked if Gordon was in, said he was Hallam Foe, a friend of Ian Hamilton. Hamilton's name had been selected because he was a helplessly sociable drunk who forgot names and faces within seconds so Hallam had no risk of being exposed should Gordon check.

Gordon Carter had a small, compact body and a large but moderately handsome face, moulded into an expression of stoic suffering as he entered from the storeroom at the back. The usual beer-and-whisky hangover, Hallam guessed.

He put out his hand. 'Sorry I didn't warn you I was coming. I'm doing the rounds collecting for Cancer Action. You know Ian Hamilton, don't you?'

'I'm afraid I vaguely recall seeing him last night.' Gordon's tone was rueful, with the ghost of an American accent. Hallam smiled sympathetically. Gordon sat on the desk and rubbed his face. 'Sorry about this. So, is he one of your donors then?'

'He's been very generous actually.'

'I don't have any cash on me.'

'That's OK. There are other arrangements – if you're interested in giving, that is. I've got a range of leaflets here, from standing orders that can directly debit your bank account, to legacies should you or, ah, a relative wish to bequeath an amount in their will. I can leave them with you if you like, there's no obligation obviously.'

Gordon looked up, his bloodshot hazel eyes slowly turning suspicious. 'Hold on. Is this anything to do with my mother?'

'I'm sorry?' Hallam felt himself being inspected closely, a deeply unpleasant sensation at the best of times. But his job had trained him to be prepared for relatives who ruthlessly fended off any claims on their prospective inheritance. He counted a second and then put a hand to his mouth, attempting horror. 'Tell me I haven't barged in at a bad time.' Gordon looked at his feet and the secretary shot Hallam a look of hostile confirmation. 'Christ, I'm sorry, Gordon. This happens sometimes and it looks awful, I know . . .'

Gordon raised his head again. 'No, it's all right. As it happens my mother might be interested. I'll take your leaflets and talk it over with her when I get the chance.'

'Are you sure?' Hallam hesitated as if about to apologise further, then handed them over. Gordon tucked them into the inside pocket of his linen jacket.

'I'll study them this evening.'

Hallam left the gallery in turmoil. Normally he felt what he did in his job was justified by the ends. But this situation left him feeling more sordid than usual, doubly so because he was now crippled by fascination. Death, after all, was the greatest privacy of them all; a mother's death, for Hallam, the greatest loss. The promise of Gordon's impending bereavement drew him with dreadful irresistibility. This sudden voyeuristic craving both frightened and excited him. He wanted to see into Gordon's suffering. He wanted to know whether Gordon was sincere. Would he broach the subject of the charity with his mother or would he jealously guard the family money? Hallam knew that he must see Gordon's mother for himself, and not just for professional reasons. It was a compulsion whose urgency he did not question. He absolutely needed to observe this.

Kate and Hallam entered the conveniently close if tacky Irish theme pub and she bought him a drink. They sat down together on green leather seats and remarked on how the decor annoyed them. But Hallam could sense her nervousness. She was fretting about Alasdair's impending arrival, or otherwise.

'Hallam, you've been with us a good three months and I don't even know where you're from,' she said.

'The Midlands.' She wasn't really listening, her eyes scanning the bar in case they'd missed him.

'University?'

'Yes.' Hallam then realised that, since she was addressing the graduate trainee, she was probably inquiring which university. He rapidly tried to remember which one he had put down on his curriculum vitae. 'Newcastle,' he said.

'Newcastle's supposed to be fun, isn't it? And what brought you to Edinburgh?' Kate was focused on the door, on the off chance Alasdair would appear.

'I got on a train out of England. This was the last stop.' This was true. Walking out of Waverley Station directly after his exile, Hallam had been immediately seduced by the grey foreignness of the city, so different from the green undulations of Chanby. He had decided to stay and with his father's cheque had embarked on a life of almost complete non-association with the world. No job, no friends, no talk, no television. He sought invisibility and found it. For uncounted months Hallam lived close to his ideal state. He had got thinner, he had grown paler.

Kate was faintly irritated, it seemed, by his evasively short answer to what was no more than a polite question anyway. They were only having this drink together because he served a purpose. 'And why this line of work?' She was on automatic. But the answer? The money had run out. He had to claim social security and thereby began, officially, to appear. Government training schemes loomed and Hallam bowed to the inevitable. He got a job, and was thereby introduced to estate agency, which had the one virtue of giving him access to tenement keys that opened up most of the city's rooftops. But the job bored him and he decided that he might as well do something worthwhile during working hours. And so turned to the light. Charity. Ha.

'I wanted to prey on the old and dying for a good cause.'

A faint smile. 'You're good at it too.'

'That's what worries me.' Hallam did not feel like lingering much longer on his motivations. 'Who is this Alasdair then?' he asked.

'Jesus, it's all unutterably boring,' replied Kate, suddenly ferociously engaged with the conversation. 'He used to work in the oil industry up in Aberdeen, he was a dive manager on the rigs, quite a senior job, but then ROVs – you know, the little underwater robots – started taking over most of the divers' work and he left. Rented himself a rundown old Victorian place in Perthshire with the redundancy money. He's doing photography now. Arty stuff, illustrations. He's ludicrously precious about it, he won't show me any of his latest work because I dumped him. As if that's some kind of punishment. Typical. Arrogant arse.'

'So why are you seeing him?'

'Masochism? Curiosity? I'm not sure. That's what you're here for.' Kate took a sip of her gin. Hallam glanced up and saw a man with close-cropped prematurely grey hair and an annoyingly handsome profile. About thirty-five, with a long face, straight nose, blue-grey aquiline eyes, but with a mouth too soft and full to be matchingly cruel. It was a droll mouth. Good for a sneer, too, Hallam suspected. The name: Alasdair.

Hallam recognised him immediately from his observations of Kate's flat. As the logbook would attest, Alasdair's average length of coitus, from penetration to orgasm, was roughly three minutes – unless he was drunk, in which case it would sometimes go on interminably. On Sunday mornings he slept in late and usually waited for her to go to the bathroom before he threw aside the sheets and farted, a small gesture of consideration which was, so far as Hallam could see, perhaps the only point in his favour.

Alasdair spotted Kate, who had not yet seen him. He began weaving his way towards them through the after-work crowd. Hallam thought about notifying Kate of his impending arrival, but decided against. He sat forward earnestly and fixed Kate's attention. 'What exactly do you mean by that?'

'Well,' Kate began, 'he's a manipulative bastard behind all his easy-going pose.' Alasdair came within hearing range. 'Imagine going out with someone who spent most of their twenties in a dive bell under the North Sea. The athlete's foot would be enough for most girls.' Hallam couldn't resist glancing up to see the look on Alasdair's face as he was standing directly behind her now. She twisted round. 'Oh, hi, Alasdair, this is Hallam, a colleague of mine.' Kate blushed. Hallam stood up and shook hands with Alasdair, who smiled warmly.

'Kate tells me you're an artist,' said Hallam.

'Of bullshit, I presume,' he replied somewhat pointedly, despite his grin.

Kate smiled weakly then when Alasdair had turned to get drinks, glared at Hallam. 'You could have warned me.'

Hallam opened his arms innocently. 'How was I supposed to know what he looked like?'

Alasdair and Hallam wasted no time in lashing one another with bonhomie. Hallam guessed that his youth made Alasdair consider him as falling in the grey area between being a sexual threat and an amusing object of contempt. Kate, as a woman, appeared oblivious to it, so Hallam went on the offensive. He craned forward in fascination over every word Alasdair uttered and asked probing questions about his photography. Alasdair was very vague about his work but still managed to elaborate on it at length. Hallam offered to pass his name on to a friend of his who was researching a landscape photography exhibition in London. This was untrue, of course, but it secured him one of Alasdair's business cards.

'So, Hallam,' said Alasdair, returning some withering enthusiasm and glancing over to Kate, 'you're a professional philanthropist too.'

'I have that privilege.'

'I bet you earn it with Kate as a boss.'

'He certainly does,' said Kate, ignoring the dig. 'Hallam's my star. I'm nurturing him for greater things.' She touched Hallam's hair in a big sister manner. Hallam smiled and took a sip of his pint, trying to reconcile his irritation at being patronised with the pitiful thrill of being in physical contact with her.

It was now clear to him that he was only here to make Alasdair jealous. The big sister act was coded encouragement for Alasdair. It told him that nothing was going on between Hallam and her – yet. Hallam reflected upon the perversity of normal people's relationships then swiftly forgave Kate, but only after he had selected a small act of retribution to stir things up. All in her best interests of course. He brought the conversation round to a recent episode from the dismal TV soap that he knew Kate watched, where an infidelity had been exposed (he had read about it in a newspaper review).

'Yes, I did see it,' replied Kate to his question, and Hallam immediately detected the tension rise. His hunch was correct; infidelity was involved in their break-up, or at least a strong suspicion of infidelity. Alasdair was playing it completely innocent but Hallam could almost smell the villainy on him.

'What about you, Alasdair?' she asked.

'I don't watch TV much,' said Alasdair.

'Another drink, anyone?' asked Hallam, standing up. By the time he returned to the table with the round he was pleased to see that they were arguing. Alasdair sought to cut it dead when he saw Hallam coming. He received his pint with almost manic relish.

'Excellent, Hallam, thank you. So, what are you up to this evening?'

'Oh, nothing much,' smiled Hallam, not taking the hint to leave. He could see Kate, her eyes reckless with drink (she couldn't take the stuff), glaring at Alasdair's evasions.

'We were talking about sexual fidelity, Hallam,' she said. 'Alasdair here thinks it's overrated—'

'I did not say that,' inserted Alasdair patiently, but Kate continued.

'While I figure it's a fairly important gesture of respect, even if the man in question does suffer from a no doubt genetically-driven urge to screw different girls. What do you think, Hallam?'

Alasdair was silently daring him to play the virtuous card: just you dare. Hallam frowned earnestly, this was the first time he had been bullied into an expression of masculine solidarity. He was, in a way, flattered, because he did not think of himself as a man as such. The word implied sexual experience.

'Actually I don't think sexual fidelity is a virtue in itself. It may suit some people, but I can't see what's intrinsically good about it. And it's not just men who are unfaithful.' Hallam supped his pint, and Alasdair sat back, pleasantly surprised, it seemed, that the pressure was being taken off him. Kate didn't say anything at first. She mastered her temper and took a large swig of her drink.

'You can't just dismiss fidelity like that. You're just pretending a responsibility doesn't exist to suit your own weakness. You can't dismiss the pain of betrayal. Fidelity shouldn't be a restraint, it's a positive choice if the relationship's right.' It was clear that she would never understand what Hallam suspected Alasdair and other men felt but rarely expressed: that it was in men's natures to be unfaithful, and it was their duty to protect their partner from this cruel reality. This meant lying, and the guilt had to be stoically born. As a man, naturally, you had to take it.

'You're confusing fidelity with loyalty,' said Hallam.

'No I'm not.'

'Why argue something you don't really believe?'

'But how do you know I don't believe it? I do believe it.'

At this point Alasdair, it seemed, felt that he should say something, despite his obvious reluctance to prolong the conversation; maybe he didn't like the emotion in her voice, the need in it, directed at someone else.

'I think,' he said carefully, 'you do need to aspire to fidelity in relationships. Both sides. But in real life, people are so often unfaithful that it's probably better seeing it as an ideal. You know, you can say you believe in fidelity, but it's like saying you believe in God. It's a wilful suspension of disbelief.'

Hallam nodded his agreement, although this whole topic was for him purely theoretical as he had never been in a sexual relationship. This did not, however, prevent him from savouring the irony of taking sides with his enemy against his most cherished subject. This was all a game to him, or so he liked to think.

'Ah, come on,' she said, and scowled at Alasdair. 'What's so ideal and unreachable about not shagging someone when you're in a relationship? That's so cynical.'

'I'm just saying—'

'Oh, bullshit,' she said dismissively.

'I'm just saying,' Alasdair repeated, half smiling in mild embarrassment, 'that by observing how things are—'

'That it's a way of accepting you can carry on like that.'

Alasdair opened his mouth to say something, then decided against it.

'So,' said Hallam in diplomatic tones (it was his turn to play the rational male). 'I take it you believe that infidelity is intolerable in a relationship.'

'That's right,' she said.

'And I take it that you've never been unfaithful yourself?'

'Oh yes I have.'

'You have,' said Hallam in measured tones. This is a development, he thought. He longed to glance at Alasdair, but he decided to suppress it.

'As retaliation,' she added, somewhat smugly. 'And it hurts men much more. Especially when you tell them exactly what happened.'

Hallam sneaked a glance at Alasdair who seemed to have gone pale, although his face was expressionless.

Kate gave Alasdair a smile that contained an impressive level of sadism. 'So, Alasdair, in conclusion, having taken this discussion into account, what do you think is more important now, fidelity or loyalty?'

Alasdair didn't say anything. The fruit machine played a happy tune. Hallam admired her bravado, even if she wasn't telling the truth about being unfaithful herself, from what he knew. Kate and Alasdair stared at each other, and he could see, in that silence, Alasdair accommodating this blow and assessing the various possibilities. Someone from work? Hallam? Someone from another network of friends? His face flushed. Kate was watching the various hues of his emotions passing over him and Hallam could tell that she was enjoying this proof, in his pain, of the emotional hold that she still had on him. And all three of them knew, as Alasdair's face returned to its normal colour and he formed a smile, that he wanted Kate back.

'Hallam,' said Alasdair, not taking his eyes off Kate. 'Don't get me wrong, you're a lovely guy, but do you think you could fuck off?'

To Hallam's horror Kate smiled, as if he had said something rather daring and witty, and stared at her drink, then gave Hallam an apologetic look from under her eyebrows. It was effectively his dismissal.

Hallam left the bar affecting nonchalance. Of course this outflanking by Alasdair did not matter. As the rules decreed, he was not taking a sexual interest in his subject. He was merely playing. Of course he would like Kate to pay him more attention and that was why he worked so hard at his job. Impressing your subject, he told himself, was still within the letter, if not necessarily the spirit, of the rules. Also, not that it was important of course, he now knew Alasdair's address.

Hallam's head popped up through the trap door and he swiftly pulled himself up onto the roof. Below him was the top of a tenement's communal staircase, above him the neon-polluted night sky. He closed the trap door and put aside the padlock. Gordon Carter's place was just a few streets from Kate's, but a wide road had prevented him from travelling entirely by rooftop. The keys copied from the estate agents had proved their worth again, and Gordon's address had not been difficult to find: it was a well-known party venue.

Mentally reviewing the layout of the building, Hallam soon arrived with a soft thud on top of the apartment that he was looking for. Gordon's flat was off a close at the lower end of the Royal Mile, and the view of Holyrood Palace was very fetching. Construction of the new Scottish parliament building to the left was also underway, but currently all that could be seen were banks of scaffolding and tarpaulin. Like most single people, Gordon had taken a top flat for the views and the lower asking price. Judging by the smell of liver and bacon coming from the ventilator fan, Hallam was just in time for the end of Gordon's dinner.

He heard a chair scrape in the kitchen and footsteps go through into the hallway. A door shut and he heard a second ventilator starting up: most likely the bathroom. Then up floated the sound of whistling: Elgar's cello concerto, unless he was much mistaken, presumably to the accompaniment of a bowel movement.

The toilet flushed and after a brief phone call to a crony Gordon was out the door and off to a bar. Hallam waited until he was safely out on the street below, then he left a few more minutes to caution before crawling to the edge of the roof. He peered down over the stone gable and with the aid of a mirror confirmed that the window had been left open, Lothian-based cat burglars being thin on the ground. Fortunately the building backed onto an old warehouse with a rarely used close running up the side. He was therefore unlikely to be seen. He pulled out a length of thin rope from inside his boilersuit and flipped the noose over the gable's top crenellation. He stepped into his abseiling tackle and clipped the rope through the metal fastener. Then he lowered himself steadily over the edge, hooking his legs into the open window. He twisted under the mullion and landed cleanly on Gordon's polished floorboards.

Hallam underwent his standard tour of a new subject's property, getting a feel for the place, assessing the personal touches, flicking through the correspondence. In Gordon's case the content of the desk drawers indicated the parlous financial state of his gallery and a variety of personal debts. In the wastepaper basket were Cancer Action's crumpled leaflets.

Hallam looked at the telephone on his desk the next morning, sipped from his daily Irn Bru and took a deep breath. Kate had wandered out of the office to get a coffee and now was his opportunity. He picked up the receiver and dialled the MacIver Galleries. It was the girl who picked up. Hallam asked for Gordon and on being asked who was calling said to tell him that it was Cancer Action again. A pause.

'Hello?'

'This is Hallam Foe, Gordon, from Cancer Action, do you remember?'

'Yes I do.' His tone was colder. 'I spoke to my mother and sent her the leaflets, and it's up to her now really.'

'Thanks very much, but I wasn't actually ringing about that. I just thought I might have left an address book there. You've not seen it, have you?'

'No, I'm afraid not.'

'Thanks anyway. Maybe see you around.'

'Sure.'

Hallam put down the phone. The excuse about the address book was just to guard against any possible accusation of harassment. So Gordon was lying. Hallam was in no position to divine his motives but it was clear that access to Mrs Carter was denied. This was not enough to stop him.

His finger dialled another number, lifted from the telephone directory under Strathkeld Lodge, the family residence mentioned in the magazine article. It rang for some time until it was eventually picked up and a small female voice, echoing in what sounded like a vaulted room, answered.

'Hello, this is Dunkeld 2452.'

Hallam cranked up his sunniest voice. 'Good morning, is that Mrs Carter? My name is Hallam Foe. Your son Gordon put me on to you because he thought you might be interested in the charity I work for. In fact I was round at his flat just the other night. A beautiful set of prints he has on the wall . . . For his twenty-first, were they? What a wonderful gift . . .'

Early for the appointment, Hallam went up the potholed private road that wound between two mountains. It was a surprisingly bleak view after the lushness of the Perthshire countryside he had driven through north of Edinburgh. In front of him was Strathkeld Lodge, a former hunting lodge from its appearance, sheltered by a stand of pines on the left and a hill behind. A car was parked outside, presumably that of Mrs Carter or a housekeeper.

Mrs Carter answered the door. Hallam looked hungrily over her face, as closely as politeness would allow. She was a kind-looking woman, despite the puckering around her eyes that arose, he suspected, from long-suffered pain. She had a thin nose, a straight dignified posture and a discreet wig. She might have seemed intimidatingly grand in her pearls and thick tweed skirt, but Hallam was not put off by that. It was not untypical of the moneyed and dying in this part of the world. He introduced himself and she ushered him in, immediately fussing about him, or at least, because she had to move slowly and gingerly, giving that impression. Her time in America had not touched her accent any more than her appearance.

Hallam was taken through to a cosy sitting room, crammed with carpets and sofas, the fire blazing in the grate despite the close weather outside. She sat down with great caution, talking as she did so, to distract attention from her movements.

'I've spent most of my life in the unlucky position of never having to think about money at all. I say unlucky because ever since my husband died it has been rather fascinating discovering all the ins and outs of the family investments. He did put it into some very strange things once he'd sold his business, tobacco and timber and mining. I wouldn't dream of questioning his ethical decisions but I must say I do believe in doing something useful with money if you do have it, don't you? Something that does good.'

'I completely agree.'

'Now, I want you to tell me all about your charity.'

He began to explain the details of the legacy programme. He crouched beside her on one knee and guided her through the leaflet with the point of a sharpened pencil – a no-nonsense yellow number, unchewed, which he had selected from several in his pocket. He was pointing out the easy-to-fill-in instructions to the solicitor when he heard the front door open then close.

It was all going swimmingly; she seemed bright and perfectly amenable. Another door shut beyond the far wall near where he assumed the gun room would be. With practised hands Hallam flipped over the leaflet and pointed again with his pencil. At this point he heard the whistling of Elgar's cello concerto.

Hallam stood up woodenly and returned to his seat opposite Mrs Carter as she burbled appreciatively. 'Well, that all sounds wonderfully easy, and it is such a good cause, close to my heart as you can imagine, I feel sure that I will make some arrangements . . .' Hallam smiled wanly as he heard the flush of the toilet cistern. The cello was reaching its crescendo now, just where its melody is swept up by the rest of the orchestra. Gordon's falsetto strained to interpret the deep yearning of the music and the note broke as he stomped towards the sitting room.

In he came, dressed in thick green corduroys and a frayed brown chequered shirt. He looked unusually healthy. He paused in the doorway and glanced towards Hallam but only for a moment before he spotted the loaded tray and made straight for the pot of tea. He began pouring.

'Gordon, look here, don't gobble up all those scones yourself, what about offering some to our guest?'

Gordon stopped masticating on his scone and took a heavy slurp of his tea. 'Sorry, Mother. Hello there, Hallam, would you care for another scone?'

'No thank you,' said Hallam. 'I'm fine.'

Gordon gave his mother a 'you see?' glance and took another bite. He chewed away, gazing blankly at the coals in the grate. In this country setting, he seemed boyish and content.

'I hope you don't mind Gordon being here, I thought he should be present since this is a family matter, after all. But you think it's a jolly good idea, don't you, dear?'

'Yah, sure.'

Mrs Carter shifted uncomfortably in her seat, pain running along the rivulets around her eyes, and Gordon jumped up. 'Let me help you there, Mother.'

He placed another cushion behind her back and she thanked him. She smiled apologetically to Hallam. 'My son spoils me rotten, as you can see. I am lucky to have a boy who is prepared to help look after his old mother. It gives Mrs Macdonald some much-deserved time off.'

Gordon went and sat back down, the picture of a concerned and affectionate son. And why shouldn't he be?

Perhaps he had been wrong to suspect Gordon of being mercenary, thought Hallam. How could a son not love his mother? He saw the solace that Gordon was providing in his mother's faded smile of gratitude. Hallam looked from one to the other and felt emotion catch him, as usual, unprepared. It was as if impending death could almost be a blessing, a natural bringing together before departure. This was the sort of son that he would have been, he told himself, if he had had the chance; if she had lived long enough for him to prove it to her; if she had given him warning that she was going to go.

His rush of self-pity transposed into sudden anger. His eyes stung, his throat tightened and he stood up briskly. What was he doing? Why was he doing this to himself?

'Thank you so much for the tea, Mrs Carter. I really ought to be going.'

'No, thank you Mr Flow. This really is a most wonderful idea. Show your friend out, Gordon.'

'Really, that won't be necessary.'

But Gordon rose anyway and stood by the door as Hallam shook hands gently with his mother. It was all he could manage not to cry. He felt a pitiful urge to put his head on her lap and be comforted. Then he thought to himself, what brand of selfishness is this, desiring succour from someone who was on their way to death?

She noticed his emotion and smiled. 'You should be used to this by now.'

'Goodbye, Mrs Carter.' He was choking. He stood straight and went stiffly out, through the violence of Gordon's gaze.

He was down the corridor, walking fast, when he heard Gordon say cheerfully, 'Back soon, Mother,' and follow him out.

They stepped out of the front door and Hallam made straight for his car. But Gordon grabbed his arm and swung him round. 'How dare you approach her directly, you fucking vulture? And then have the nerve to snivel over her like you care.'

Hallam pulled himself together. 'Your mother is obviously a very kind and generous woman, and I certainly didn't mean to offend you. But you saw for yourself that she was interested in this charity and if I had left it to you she would never have heard about us.'

'That's not true.' Gordon was about to continue with his denial but he saw the knowledge and contempt in Hallam's face. It made him angrier.

'You should appreciate her more,' said Hallam with great seriousness.

Gordon began to shake. 'How can you . . .' He controlled his voice. 'You don't know the first thing about her. Oh, she looks terribly sweet and pitiful now, but she let my father walk all over me. She was a coward, she never loved me. So yes, I want her money, why not? And why should it go to you?'

Hallam shook his head, his worst suspicions confirmed, and got into the car. Gordon bent down, those hazel eyes now angular and full of desperate conviction. 'You're no better than me.' He was wrong of course. Hallam felt, with a certain pride, that he was capable of a great deal worse. But he did not reply, only waited to see whether Gordon was going to add anything, then he shut the door, turned the car swiftly round, and drove away. Gordon stood and watched him until he passed out of sight behind the shadow of the mountain.

As it was Friday, Hallam phoned the office and told Kate the encouraging news. She told him to take the rest of the afternoon off; after all, it would be late by the time he got back. She sounded a little cool. Did she want to avoid him? However, it was just the opportunity he needed to take a drive across the county, towards where Alasdair kept his studio.

Cruickshank. Alasdair Cruickshank. Hallam negotiated the gentle banking corners on the country road, hedgerows skimming by in the pale summer sunshine. He preferred these green rolling hills and deciduous woodland to the desolate grandeur of the full-blown Highlands further north. The human scale helped him think, while the vast northern glens that he had driven through in the past had only filled him with a sense of emptiness.

According to habit Hallam mentally shifted the letters of Alasdair's name into the special superstitious grid he applied to subjects of curiosity, to see if they augured well. A-L-A-S-D-A-I-R. The first name fitted. Eight letters. This was unusual, though not especially significant. He then applied the surname. Eleven. 8:11. The time when life had changed, all those years ago at the Leicester restaurant. A perfect correlation. Hallam frowned; this augured something, but what? The digits 8 and 11 were indicators of significance in his life, whether he found them in the number of chimney pots on a stack, or in a subject's address. They beckoned him towards Alasdair.

The peeling sign to Athelford Grange came into sight about half a mile after the end of the grey stone-built market town, which was dominated by an ugly and stuffy-looking hotel. However, he did not follow the sign. Instead, he went back into the town centre and parked outside the tourist information kiosk so as not to attract attention. He pulled off his tie and jacket and wriggled into a big brown jersey. Next he took from the boot a haversack, a pair of walking boots and a Goretex windcheater. Shoving the Leica binoculars into his pocket and a camera on a belt round his waist, he completed the picture: tourist.

He popped into the kiosk and picked up some leaflets on the area, briefly enduring some advice from the friendly lady at the counter. The area was indeed rich in birdlife, and no, he didn't know that one of the few peacefully co-existing grey and red squirrel communities in Britain was just on their doorstep. How fascinating. Then he drove back out of the village, the way he had just come. He parked in a lay-by on a straight and quiet stretch of road, and began to make his way up the wooded bank, at first with difficulty because it was steep, but then with greater ease as the fir trees gave way to hillside peppered with rabbit warrens.

After a stiff climb Hallam stopped and turned to enjoy the breeze – he opened his mouth and made it a shell to the wind, softly howling – then took out the binoculars and gave the countryside an ostentatious sweep for the benefit of any locals who might be watching, following for some time the birds that darted low along the banks. He made his way towards the summit, a further fifteen minutes walk up. At the top the wind buffeted him quite heavily. Eyes watering, he scanned the view below: various prosperous-looking farms covered the valley, which was flanked on either side by steeper hillsides with their crowns covered in rock and heather. Further to the north, the mountains rose, partly obscured by distant weather systems. Straight down the hill Hallam saw a thick covering of pines, not lined up in geometric patterns like the commercial forests but growing freely to act as a windbreak for what must be the house beyond. Checking its position with the road, Hallam concluded that this would be Alasdair's property.

Scattering a few sheep, Hallam made his way down, curving away to the right so as to reach cover quickly, away from the valley road. He circled the property from the safety of the abundant hedges and shrubbery. It was built in the local grey stone, patched with lichen, and the front was adorned with two self-important Scottish baronial turrets. The short drive down to the road had a small cottage at the electric gate which was operated by punching a code into a console on the gatepost. Alasdair, or whoever owned the property, had taken more than the usual amount of care with security for a comfortable rural area like this.

Alasdair was home, judging by the Toyota truck parked at the back, although Hallam did not see any movements through the large kitchen windows or in any of the other windows. He sat and waited. A phone gave out three rings at one point and then stopped, either picked up or taken by an answering machine.

It was not until after 7 p.m. that another car drew up at the gate off the road. A young blonde woman jumped out and tapped in a code on the button console and the gate whirred open. She got back in the car and made her way slowly up the rutted drive. This is it he thought with bitter triumph: proof that he's cheating on Kate. The light was still good enough for him to take five clear shots of the girl from behind a set of ferns as she got out of the car. Her hair was, a mess of curls, she was probably in her mid or late twenties, big-busted with a large crocodile handbag over her shoulder. Her face had the kind of perfect proportions that he found difficult to like, but he warmed to her walk, long and relaxed. She wore bright thick-soled trainers, black jeans and a tight tracksuit top. He surprised himself by feeling attracted to her, and then jealous of Alasdair. Hallam scolded himself for such unworthy thoughts, and then, in an effort to purge them, sought out his reserves of contempt.

He imagined that this girl was thick but convinced of her own intelligence. Perhaps she possessed an unfinished degree in fabric design from one of the new universities. Hallam was snobbish about higher education, even though he had never had any himself. Perhaps in his next CV he would choose Oxford or Cambridge. The girl headed straight to the back door, rang the bell to indicate her arrival, and let herself in. She did not go through the kitchen, and Hallam was left helplessly guessing what might be going on. He circled the back of the house, climbed the bank, keeping well back in the trees.

From here he had a good, almost horizontal view of the upper windows as the house's foundations were sunk into the hem of the hill. The walls were surrounded by a wide moat of gravel, which Hallam noted with annoyance: it made a silent approach almost impossible. A light suddenly came on in the near window, illuminating a green bedroom. The girl came in and dropped her bag on the bed, thankfully not thinking to draw the curtains in the emptiness of the countryside. Hallam drew the Leica binoculars to his eyes and brought her into focus. She pulled her shirt over her head without undoing the buttons, revealing a lightly tanned and possibly even goose-pimpled upper body, then she sat down and took off her trainers and jeans. Was this Alasdair's bedroom? It looked more like a spare room, there were no indications of male occupation. Where was he?

When she stood up again she had her back to the window. She pulled on a thin black negligee – a bit early for bed, wasn't it? – then went across to the mirror and began to apply make-up. This took seventeen minutes. She picked up a thin jumper and, throwing it over her shoulders, went out of the room again, turning the light off behind her. Darkness had fallen rapidly in this time but Hallam only noticed now. He scratched irritably at the midge bites on his neck. They must be occupying an interior room. He would have to risk crossing the loose gravel to access the roof. It was the only way.

seven

He kicked off his walking boots and pulled out his soft black plimsolls from the poachers' pocket of his windcheater. He slipped them on then skirted the fence until he was level with the far corner of the house, which faced out onto the fields. He picked out a sturdy-looking drainpipe leading up to the roof. Without hesitation he descended the few feet of sloping lawn in several short light steps, crossed the gravel with three delicate munches, and placed his right toe on the drainpipe's second bracket. Up went his other foot to the third. Keeping his elbows in, away from the windows on either side, he climbed the drainpipe, his strong, slow movements spiderish in the gloom, then he reached the top and flipped over onto the roof almost soundlessly. He found two skylights, the nearest one looking in on what appeared to be a converted loft, the furthest one to his left over a corridor. It was through this skylight's scuffed glass that he glimpsed a shaft of bright, oddly angled light emanating from one of the rooms. Hallam saw two shadows dart into view, unusually long, from what seemed to be the same figure. Two spotlights then, cast at different angles. They had to be in there.

But from where Hallam was he could neither see nor hear anything properly; the walls and roof were too solid by far, and the skylight was firmly secured. He looked desperately around him, and saw a tall chimney stack not far from where the room must be. He eased the grate off the top of the first pot and put his ear to it. Silence at first, or something near to it; just a regular ticking sound that might as easily have been an insect. Then what sounded like a sigh and a moan. Sex! he thought, with righteous indignation. The dirty sleazebag! Then the first whisper of a voice: Alasdair's, it had to be, hot with admiration.

'Yeah, lovely, that's it.'

'Is this OK?'

'Oh yeay! Higher. Good. GOOD!' A barrage of clicks.

Hallam was disappointed: just a photo-shoot?

'Hold it! Can you keep it there? Yeah, right against it. Fucking YES!' Clickety clickety click.

Hallam's ears pricked up. What kind of photo-shoot exactly? The sort that he didn't want his girlfriend to know about? Or his Perthshire neighbours, for that matter? Hallam felt a ripple of shallow amusement; nothing an anonymous community mailshot couldn't fix.

If only he could see what was going on. Inner rooms were the curse of his calling. At this point Hallam heard the sound of drum and bass echo up through the chimney. The stereo put paid to any further eavesdropping, but at least he need not worry so much about being heard himself. The window facing onto the corridor might allow him a glimpse into the room through the open door; even perhaps an entry. The thought made his heart beat faster, and he registered a familiar burst of excitement in his belly.

He pulled out the thin coil of mountaineer's rope from the haversack, strapped on his belt and tested the metal clips. Then he attached one end to the nearest secure chimney stack at the edge of the roof and threw a leg over the side of the low wall, in preparation for lowering himself down.

He was ready to go. But in this strange rural environment he was nervous. He glanced over at the rope and wondered whether there might be some risk the lasso could ride up onto the pot. He decided to play it safe. He stepped along the wall to tug it down, his head level with the pot.

Something exploded out of the chimney into his face. There was a sharp blow to his cheek and a clatter of grey wings. With instinctive disgust he lifted his hands to cover his eyes, but the movement unbalanced him. One foot slipped off the edge of the roof, and he toppled over into the darkness, arms flapping vainly in an attempt to stay upright. The drop was short and the safety harness did its job, but he was unlucky. As the rope caught, he was twisted violently and his head smacked against the stone wall. He bounced left then right, the impact resounding on shoulder then knee.

He hung there, back arched, arms limp, for several seconds. His vision was blurred, the tears making crystal visions out of the waving starlit sky.

The blood thumped in his temples, accompanying the music drumming against the window to his left.

He was still rotating gently left then right, nauseously. He lifted an arm, his hand seemed a long way away, and gripped the taut rope. Then the other arm responded. He pulled himself round with a huge effort, and brought himself back into position, his feet against the wall, legs bent. But still he couldn't see straight.

He thought about climbing back up again, but he felt too groggy and weak. He looked at the window emitting faint light. Perhaps if he got his foot on the ledge he could lift himself. A stabbing pain seemed to skewer his left eye. Concentrate, Hallam thought. He flexed his knees and prepared to hop over to the left.

He did hop, but the swing of the rope took him further than he anticipated. His left foot went straight through the near windowpane with a loud smash, up to the knee. As he drunkenly struggled to retrieve it without slitting his knee on the shards of glass, the music stopped and two figures casting four shadows filled up the rectangle of light on the corridor carpet. I'm done for, thought Hallam and grinned hopelessly. He began to laugh at the two figures who were staring in disbelief at his leg which had plunged into their private world. His head dropped back, he was unconcerned now. Nothing very much seemed to matter any more. The wind ruffled his hair and the rope creaked. God, I hate pigeons, he muttered or perhaps only thought, before closing his eyes.

Hallam lay on the sofa, a pillow under his head and a cold flannel on his brow. The model – her name was Carrie – turned out to have medical training: she had been designated first-aid expert in the office where she worked part-time, she said by way of reassurance, and her confusion over the circumstances of Hallam's injury caused her to fuss unnecessarily over the practical tasks.

She leaned over him with a frown of concern. His vision still seemed a bit fuzzy, but he noticed that she was wearing one of Alasdair's jumpers. 'How does that feel? OK?'

Her voice sounded weird, unnaturally loud but distant, distorted like an amplified echo, but Hallam smiled weakly. 'Yes, thank you. Much better.'

'Feel sick at all?'

'No, really, I just need to get my bearings.'

She glanced over behind Hallam and stood straight. 'If you do feel sick there's a bucket by the side here. I'll just cool that down for you,' she said, lifting the flannel off his forehead. 'I don't think he's concussed,' she whispered to Alasdair, and walked out. She was replaced in Hallam's field of vision by the man himself. He was wearing a loose-fitting white shirt and jeans. He didn't look very friendly.

'So, what the fuck were you doing on my roof?'

Hallam closed his eyes, then opened them again. 'Just looking in.'

Alasdair didn't smile. 'I want an explanation, Hallam. Either that or I call the police. Although I might anyway.'

'Why?'

'Why shouldn't I? Breaking and entry. Well, partial entry anyway.'

'She's nice,' said Hallam.

Alasdair scowled. 'Is this about Kate? Are you a private eye or something?'

Hallam looked at Alasdair with dwindling curiosity and smiled. Nothing seemed complicated any more.

'Did she put you up to this?'

The man was obviously a moron. Hallam observed that Alasdair, maybe in response to his beatific expression, now seemed slightly ashamed of his paranoid last comment. Hallam turned his face into the pillow. 'No, of course she didn't,' Alasdair answered himself, assessing Hallam with mild disgust.

He leaned in. 'This is off your own back, isn't it? A little freelance pervert, aren't you?'

Hallam kept his eyes closed but muttered into the pillow's duck feathers, 'Just your market, I would have thought.'

A silence, then a tight, restrained voice. 'You've got this very wrong, Hallam. This isn't anything . . . smutty. It's a proper assignment. Proper calendars. I've got this stuff published, you know, reputable men's magazines, mate, not *Fiesta* or *Readers' Wives*. Not the sort of stuff you probably jack off to.'

Hallam looked at Alasdair, suddenly interested. 'Alasdair, the pictures you take, do you get her to look into the camera?'

'What?' As if it was a trick question.

'When you're doing your assignments, do you feel the models are looking at you when they look into the camera? Doing it for you?'

Alasdair's mind went blank for a moment. He struggled to think. 'Well, I suppose, not for me exactly, no. I'm not looking at them either, I'm looking for the image. It's like we're both serving the image. Aye, that's it.'

Hallam smiled and nodded. His suspicions were confirmed: Alasdair was indeed an arsehole. All of Hallam's actions, past and future, had now been justified.

'I've confiscated your film, by the way. What was the idea? Collecting evidence? Trying to turn her against me? Want her for yourself, is that it?' Alasdair looked at Hallam's face and got his own confirmation. 'This camera, the binoculars, all that gear. You've done this sort of thing before, haven't you? You're a stalker. Jesus, man, I thought your mob were jailbirds and schemies, not English public schoolboys working out of an office. Do you really think she'll love you for this?'

Hallam levered himself up on his elbows. 'You won't tell her about this.'

Alasdair began to smile, but it only got halfway, the look on Hallam's face too worrying to enjoy properly.

'Why shouldn't I? If you're going to slander me to her, make out I'm some kind of pornographer.'

'Maybe I won't. If you won't.'

Alasdair assessed him. 'Why the hell should I strike a bargain with you when I've just dragged you in through my own window, with your dick probably just back in your pants?'

'Al?' It was Carrie.

Alasdair looked up and seemed embarrassed. 'Oh, hi, Carrie.'

'I'm off now. We'll talk later, OK?'

'Wait, you don't need to . . .' Alasdair stopped himself. 'OK, we'll speak soon.'

She went. Alasdair considered Hallam again, who now sat up and dizzily felt the back of his head, where a large bump had formed. He tried to stand up and had to steady himself on the arm of the sofa.

'Where's your car?'

Hallam paused to think. He couldn't remember.

'OK, come with me,' said Alasdair with resignation. Clearly Hallam looked pathetic. 'You'll stay here tonight, you're in no state to drive.'

Alasdair took him to the green room where he had seen Carrie undress earlier that evening. Alasdair pulled back the sheets on the bed and pointed out the bathroom next door. He looked critically at Hallam as he tottered to the bed and sat down.

'I'm not taking you to hospital.'

'That's quite all right.'

'Buzz the intercom if you need anything. I mean an emergency.'

'Thanks.' Hallam sat on the bed and looked up at Alasdair who was uncertain despite himself: he seemed to be trying to judge the extent of his visitor's derangement.

'Right then, we'll talk tomorrow.' Alasdair went out and paused for a moment before shutting the door behind him. Hallam strained his ears for the sound of a key turning in the lock, but it did not come and after a second he heard Alasdair's footsteps pad back down the corridor. Either Alasdair was too proud to admit feeling threatened by a sad creep like him, or he grasped the passive psychology of a voyeur better than Hallam expected.

Hallam fell back on the bed and pressed his cheek against the cool linen. He leant over and turned off the lamp, then lay back and winced as his bruise sank into the pillow.

It was 4:06 a.m. when Hallam's door brushed softly against the carpet. The solidity of the building seemed to enhance the profound quiet of the night, and Hallam did little to disturb it as he floated down the corridor, not needing to feel his way thanks to his observations of the building's layout from the roof and his brief but sharp assessment of the positions of the windows and doors on his way to the bedroom; such note-taking was almost second nature to him now, even with a splitting headache.

He tried the second door on his left, the photographic studio, but found it locked. So he continued, on to the main stairwell, around which were two more bedrooms, he presumed, and below them the main hall. He paused there and listened and smelled the air, trying to disregard the suggestion of distant conversation or movement that hovered at the edge of every dead silence. It was a creation of the mind, abhorring aural vacuums. Hallam's instinct told him that the bedrooms on this floor would not be occupied by the main resident. Where would he stay if he was living here? He was drawn to the left. The door he saw was unusually proportioned, smaller than the other two, with a different handle, most likely a later addition. Hallam carefully opened it, and saw a narrow, steep set of wooden steps. Towards the loft, of course. Hallam already sensed that Alasdair was up there; perhaps a whiff of stale sleepy air that carried a tang of sweat. So Alasdair, too, was drawn to the eaves of the house. Hallam smiled: a man after his own heart.

This sense of empathy filled him with quiet confidence. Once he had that feeling, that he was beginning to understand a subject, to get a feel for them, he knew that they were much less likely to detect his presence. It was as if he knew how not to disturb their patterns, and even when they did lurch out of sleep, having half heard or sensed him move through the house, it had the power to lull them back into unconsciousness.

Up the stairs he went, remembering what he had glimpsed through the skylight, already filling in the likely position of the furniture, all his senses alert to the signs that would surely present themselves from underneath the veil of pitch darkness. He turned right at the top of the stairs, the wall behind him.

To his right was the bed: he could hear the quiet breathing. Ahead a window, beside it a desk or table, and a chair. He went towards the chair first, to sit and enjoy this musty aura of privacy, to gauge its atmosphere. His fingers found the back of the chair and as he sat it made a light creaking noise. He heard a rustle from the bed, a shift. Hallam overpowered that noise with his confidence; he leant back and relaxed, allowing it to creak a little more as it received his weight. He sat that way for several minutes, until he knew that Alasdair was down again, out for the count. He reached out a hand and touched what felt like a mirror, in front of it a comb, further along a can of deodorant perhaps, then a book and a pack of cigarettes with a lighter on top of it. He lifted the mirror and brought it up to his own face. It was so dark he could barely detect it there. He opened his eyes wide but there was no reflection. Nothing. He looked over towards the bed. How could Alasdair, or anyone else for that matter, know how this felt?

Alasdair rolled again and snored. Even asleep he was comfortable and confident in a way that Hallam could never hope to achieve; so self-assured that he could abuse Kate's love, and break the trust she had invested in him. In this darkness, though, Hallam knew that his moral indignation was simply a way of handling what he hated in Alasdair, and envied: those traditional male virtues that women still in their hearts seemed to worship. Strength, self-assurance, callousness; in short, all the equivocal attractions that came with sexual experience. Only in circumstances like this could Hallam feel in a position of relative strength. He wanted to teach Alasdair something about the private life of a voyeur: how strange it was, with its proximity to intimacy that would only explode if you reached out to touch it; the addictive solace it provided in moments of acute loneliness but which ultimately only made the yearnings worse; the world of unfulfillment.

He took the mirror and reached out for the lighter, then he stood up. He would show Alasdair what it felt like to be frightened by what you have become and what you yet might be; what it was like to find yourself in the dark, as a stranger, unbearably close.

He went to the side of the bed. Alasdair was lying on his back, mouth open, snoring softly. Hallam smiled with what might have passed for pity and knelt down beside him. He raised the mirror to Alasdair's face, until it was close enough for his breath to cloud the mirror's surface. And then he placed the lighter below it. A flame jumped up in the dark, and another, its reflection in the mirror, equally bright. The yellow light played on Alasdair's closed eyelids, which seemed to flutter. He murmured but did not move, he was far away but floating towards consciousness, rising up to meet the flame that hissed in front of him.

'Alasdair,' whispered Hallam in his ear.

Minutely, Alasdair's eyelashes lifted. They did not open fully and all they could have seen was his own dimly lit face, mouth slack and jaw hanging in sleep, corpse-like.

The flame continued to hiss. Alasdair did not shift, but a sonorous groan emerged from far back in his throat. Hallam stayed that way for a few more seconds, until his thumb began to burn from the heat of the lighter's flame, and he took the mirror away, letting the nightmare that he had hopefully initiated follow its own path into Alasdair's dreams. The door shut softly behind him.

eight

Hallam entered work in precariously high spirits. The elation he felt at having something to pin on Alasdair was tempered by trepidation; partly of course because Alasdair now possessed at least as much damaging information as he did. But there was also a vaguer and more superstitious worry. It concerned the approach of the eleventh of August, a date which had significance pasted all over it, but which, like most portents, remained unhelpfully enigmatic.

Kate was, as usual, already at her desk. Hallam smiled on his way past and spoke his customary good morning, trying to disguise his sudden fear that Alasdair may already have told her about their abseiling encounter. Kate's face did not betray any obvious marks of shock or disgust, however. She grunted a reply, not looking up from her screen. She seemed withdrawn, a trifle glum, though no more than most office workers on a Monday morning. He was halfway to his desk when she tetchily called out his name.

'Yes, Mistress,' he answered in a failed attempt at jocularity. Her face did not shift.

'Have you written that new legacy document yet?'

'Yeah, I've got a draft done. Just a bit of polishing to do and I'll email it across.'

'Hurry it up, would you? The printers have already been on the phone this morning.'

'Sure; it's just you didn't mention a deadline last time.'

'Is midday, OK? Do you think you can you manage it?'

'Certainly, Kate.' Hallam sat at his desk and logged on. Would she be acting stroppily like this if Alasdair had mentioned anything?

He had already thought up a title for the leaflet, *A Legacy For Life*, with a strapline which ran, at the moment: Help Us Continue Cancer Action's Lifesaving Research By Making a Will. This, he envisaged, would be accompanied by a granny-charming picture of a well-preserved old lady with her arms held protectively round two children. The children would be smiling adoringly up at her.

The leaflet was to replace the drab form which had been knocked up years ago and was judged to put off potential donors with its legal phraseology and bureaucratic cover. The aim of this new document was to bring the reader smoothly round to the idea of depriving their relatives of an inheritance and leaving it all to the far more deserving cause of paying Hallam's salary, and others like him who had made a career out of charity. There was also the money needed to research treatments for cancer, of course.

He imagined a different leaflet, freed from the bonds of taste: a picture of some scruffy grandchildren treading dirt into the carpet of a smart retirement home, with avaricious parents looming behind. Do They Deserve It More Than a Decent Charity? Cancer Action: Make That Call.

But back to the real world. If the cover picture did its work, then granny would grope for her spectacles and flip open the pamphlet to glance inside. The next step was to draw her in with some sugary copy on the facing inside page. How to start? Of course, something sensitive and reassuring.

'Please accept our sincere apologies if this leaflet has been delivered at a time of sorrow or illness. It is only intended to provide information on the legacy programme of Cancer Action, which is a registered charity.

'Cancer Action's work has been saving young lives for the last thirty years, thanks to the dedication of our many staff and volunteers up and down the country. We intend to continue with this work, concentrating on out research programme into leukaemia. But it will take more than dedication.'

Dedication, in this office? If anything shakes this organisation out of its lethargy, thought Hallam, it's ambition. Still, what did the public know? He recalled Kate's advice on the legacy market, which was mostly made up of over-sixties: if in doubt, lay on the slush with a trowel.

'Poorly children need and receive our love. You can give them something more: a future. Cancer Action. What better way of putting something back?'

Hallam flexed his fingers and began to fill the document with some mildly mendacious history of the charity's achievements.

Forty-eight minutes passed on Hallam's digital watch before Kate sloped over with a cappuccino from across the road and plonked it down next to him. She hardly ever bothered to go to the coffee shop. It was a peace offering.

'Thanks,' said Hallam, letting a note of surprise enter his voice.

'That's OK,' muttered Kate. She stepped back, then rocked on her heels and looked at her feet. 'Look, I just want to say I'm sorry about that episode on Thursday. I put you in a difficult position. And also for being grumpy just now. I'm a bit ashamed.'

'What's there to be ashamed of?' asked Hallam, preparing to be tortured by the answer. The chances were that Alasdair had gone home with her after the pub. He now regretted his decision not to follow them back and observe them. At the time he thought it would spare him pain. But his imagination had risen to the challenge; photographic equipment, a litre of tequila and a four-speed power hoist had featured prominently. Hallam now admitted to himself that he was beginning to suffer the symptoms of obsession. Or was it love? No, love meant helplessness and exposure. Obsession was better, more controllable. But how was he going to control it? Observation of his subjects usually calmed him by taking him out of himself. Now, with relation to Kate, it was having the opposite effect. He could see that the rules were coming down, along with all their protections, and it scared him.

'I don't think you want to know the answer to that,' she said ruefully, 'but the good thing to take from this is that I am now certain, for sure, that it's never going to happen again. No way.'

'If that's what you want, then congratulations,' said Hallam, attempting to pitch his tone of voice so that it came out concerned rather than bitter. The result, however, was strangely unctuous. Hallam blushed.

'Anyway, I want to make it up to you in some way,' said Kate cheerfully.

'Really, that isn't necessary.'

'Yes it is. I've criminally underspent on expenses this month. I want to take you out for supper, just you and me this time, a few crafty drinks, no dodgy exes. What do you say?'

'Umm,' hesitated Hallam, glancing up at her. 'I'm not sure really.' He scratched the back of his head thoughtfully, playing it out, then winced as his fingernail caught the bruise from the night before.

She laughed. 'Come on, it'll be fun. I need to go through some work schedules with you anyway.' Still he hesitated. She suddenly looked genuinely worried. 'Was I really that bad? Christ, I must have looked pathetic.'

At that moment Hallam's mobile telephone rang. They were despicable contraptions, in his view, but it was office issue and he was obliged on pain of death to carry it with him, particularly on collecting missions. In payment for the suffering she had visited on him, he answered it before replying to her.

'Hello, Hallam Foe here.'

'Hallam?' said a female voice, its tone slightly foreign, as if uneasy with the pronunciation, or nervous perhaps.

'Speaking.'

A pause, an intake of breath. 'Hallam, hi, it's your long lost sister Lucy, didn't you recognise me?'

The forcibly cheerful tone met with silence. 'Are you there? Are you in the middle of something? Shall I call back later?'

'Yes. No.' Hallam turned off the mobile and looked back at Kate. 'Sorry?'

'I think you were about to accept a kind invitation to dinner from your boss who is currently paranoid that she made a fool of herself.'

He blinked, remembered the plot. 'Of course you didn't. Supper would be great, so long as I get to choose the venue.'

'It's a deal,' she said, smiling with a quite flattering degree of relief and pleasure, then went back to her desk. A few minutes later the mobile went again. He answered it reflexively. Lucy belonged to the past; she did not have access to his new life.

'Hello?'

'It's me again. How are you?'

A pause. 'I'm . . . busy.'

'I've had a battle tracking you down.'

'What can I do for you?'

A nervous laugh down the line. 'What can you do for me? I want to know how you're doing. It's been years. I'm back in the UK, I was hoping to meet up. How are you doing?'

'Keep out.'

'What? Hallam, what's the matter?'

Hallam put the phone down and felt his heart beating hard in his chest. He waited for her to call back. What would he say to her if she did? Everything he considered sounded drama queenish and it might only encourage her. He would need to express indifference, a couple of cool insults, then shut down.

He felt hysteria welling up inside. What had she been expecting? Whimpering gratitude for having got back in contact after five years' absence? He wiped his terminal, trying to calm himself down. He peeled the plastic top off his coffee and took a sip. Too much sugar. She didn't call back. After fifteen minutes he got up to go to the toilet, but then realised that he didn't need to and so carried on outside into the street. He had to walk off his agitation.

The Cuban restaurant was not far from the office but distant enough for it to be an escape, and a place where neither Kate nor Hallam were likely to run into anyone they knew. Both of them were aware that it was a suggestive setting, and it seemed to amuse Kate to see Hallam nervous and awkward. Her own confidence rose, she took him by the hand in her big-sisterish way and when he procrastinated over which table they should take, led him firmly to an alcove.

'This was a great idea,' she enthused, looking around her.

'It only opened a week ago,' said Hallam. 'There's dancing down-stairs.'

'Really?' She smiled at him and he veered away from her bright eyes, fearing that she might have guessed his preposterous idea of salsa-ing into her affections. What had he been thinking? Suddenly his plan to bring her out of herself, to play it sophisticated and masterful, seemed horribly over-ambitious. His armpits were damp. He was already longing for the evening to end.

Perversely, she appeared to be enjoying herself. The conspiratorial way she leant forward close enough for him to smell the white rum and cola on her breath was not entirely justified by the conversation about tatty office intrigue. He didn't take a word of it in. The first jug of Cuba Libra arrived and from then on Hallam was committed to the loathsome parlour game of flirtation. He began drinking to dampen his self-consciousness, otherwise he would not be able to function. Her playfulness tormented him, his replies in kind filled him with self-disgust. The charade made him want to cry and all he could do was smile and summon another jest. He became reckless, half wanting to put her off, half wanting something else. But what?

It was too much in the end. Hallam divided into two. The real Hallam rose out of his prattling exterior and began to observe another conversation in another alcove. It was between a skittish young man and a woman somewhat older who was taking a languid, slightly playful, interest in her companion. He recorded the pertinent moments with pity and amusement. Clearly it was all going horribly right.

10:46 'So what chat-up lines work for you?' he asks.

'Someone once told me that I was so beautiful he wanted to suck the dick of the last man who fucked me.'

The young man looks horrified. 'That worked?'

She shrugs. 'It shows commitment, it's respectful. Have you got anything better?'

He thinks. 'Not at the moment.'

10:53 'Do you have a girlfriend?' she asks.

'She's dead. Would you like to meet her?'

She smiles. 'I like creepy guys.'

11:23 'If it wasn't for your dress sense I might have taken you for gay.' He looks hurt. She apologises. 'Don't be offended, I always insult people when I'm trying to compliment them.'

'That's because you can't take compliments.'

'You are gay.'

'No I'm not.'

'Stop trying to be sensitive then.'

'It was an observation.'

11:43 She purses her lips and gives him a dry look. 'Go on then. Try one out. A compliment.'

The young man frowns. 'I think I could learn from you.'

She pauses to think. 'That's not a compliment, that's worrying.' She thinks some more then leans forward. 'What you need is a good male role model.'

'Alasdair?' the young man asks with bitter sarcasm.

The name abruptly brought Hallam back into his stubbornly uninebriated body. Kate grimaced. 'All that stuff you said about fidelity the other night.'

'I was trying to be polite. I couldn't say what I meant.'

'Why not?'

He didn't answer. He couldn't explain.

'What did you mean?' she persisted.

'Cheating on you wouldn't be wrong, it would be weird.'

Kate began to cry, drunkenly. Hallam tried to divide in two again but found that he was unable to do so.

'Kate, I'm sorry.'

The waitress scooted by and Hallam immediately sensed that she was monitoring them. Another observer. He hated her for it.

'I said give me one compliment. Not two. One.' She wiped her nose with the napkin. 'Now give me a refill.' She laughed and sniffed when she saw the look of concern on his face. He quickly covered up with a grin.

'You should consider a career in the Church,' she said.

'Look, for the last time, I'm not gay.'

'You're a good listener, that's all I meant.'

He shrugged. This at least was true. He could listen, he could watch.

Kate peered at Hallam with mock disgust. 'You just gulped that compliment down in one. Like a frog.'

Hallam noted her eyes. My God, he thought, she's totally pissed.

'I don't kiss frogs,' she said.

He started to feel scared. Those eyes were assessing him now with a boozy wariness that could easily be mistaken for erotic intent. It was as if a part of him had ceased to be invisible. He felt exposed. He thought of Verity. This scared him even more. How he hated Freud. But wasn't this what he wanted? Why did he have to want what he most feared? He knew what was coming. Why had he started this? Where were the rules when he needed them?

'Shall I get some coffee?' suggested Hallam, desperate to sober her up.

'No,' she said with loud finality. 'Come back and have one. Bill please!'

His shoulder muscles were aching from the tension. He was genuinely exhausted. The waitress approached with the tab and he wished he could tell her how much he resented her feeding off their conversation, but she carefully avoided his accusatory eye. Kate burrowed in her bag for money.

'It's a bit late,' attempted Hallam. 'I might head back.' But Kate stood up, strangely fortified by her earlier display of vulnerability; so unlike a man. Hallam was required to take note of her body, her breasts. She gave him an incontrovertible stare.

'You're coming with me.'

Hallam was a dead man. Worse than dead: condemned. He stood behind Kate as she cursed and drunkenly rattled the key in the flat door. Dizziness swept over him as the door swung open and he followed her in, one Hallam experiencing this in nauseous Technicolor, the other Hallam like a security camera, looking down at these two fuzzy people, recording their movements in black and white. The crime in progress.

12:19 The young man wipes his clammy palms on his trousers as the woman somewhat older bustles around the kitchen, putting on the kettle, humming tipsily to herself. Classic seductive behaviour. But what is the young man up to? Is he as drunk as she is, leaning like that on the kitchen table top, rubbing the cheek of his sickly grey face? Is he about to throw up?

'Do you like it milky?' she asks, holding up a carton of semi-skimmed.

Hallam's two halves combined again. His vision temporarily went sepia yellow and he wondered whether he was going to faint. How would he explain himself?

He coughed a whimper – not something he had thought possible before. But he was inspired this evening by pure, cornered terror. 'Yes please.'

She smiled and put down the milk carton on the side with heavy deliberation. She looked at him, up and down, and cocked her head. She came up and pressed herself against him. Her fingers pulled his shirt tails out from the back of his trousers and she ran her nails along his lower spine. She leant forward and gently bit his lower lip. His eyelids fluttered and closed.

He stayed on his feet. She pressed herself more firmly against him.

He could feel her pelvic bone against his crotch. She began to move. A second pulse of nausea rose from his stomach into his throat. Her hand moved slyly round from his back to his side, rested there for a moment, then pinched the skin hard enough for him to yelp.

'Hallam, I'm afraid I don't find you very attractive.' Her voice seemed hard-edged despite the slurring. 'You're too young, far too skinny and frankly rather odd.' She stepped back causing a short high-pitched cough of released tension from Hallam. 'However,' she continued, 'I do like to toy with my subordinates. I presume you've had the usual female boss fantasies.'

Hallam had difficulty articulating himself at first. 'W-well, yes, of course. But they've always been very deferential.' She seemed to be waiting for details. 'I'm your willing slave, that sort of thing.'

'Good. Well, this is your lucky night. I'm feeling very empowered. Wait here for a bit then follow me in and sit down.'

Dumbly Hallam stood there as instructed while she slipped off next door in her stockinged feet. He took a deep breath and ran a hand through his hair. He considered running for the door, but then the music came on.

Deja que me quede en tus brazos
dame tu boca dulce de amor

It reassured him. It reminded him of when he was still invisible, watching Kate's sweet narcissistic dances in the mirror. The rhythm lulled his panic and the thought of her body drew him into the sitting room.

She was waiting for him, looking up at the ceiling and softly swaying, hands clasped in front of her. He sat down stiffly on the sofa and watched with a preposterous sense of formality as she began to dance more freely. She wasn't self-conscious at all, she wasn't even looking at him. It was blissful, she had her back to him and was swaying. Almost as if he wasn't there.

Hallam was transported. For the first time in his life, he was experiencing unambiguous sexual arousal in the mutually aware company of a woman. She tossed her hair to the side as the rhythm picked up and looked down at her moving feet; she ran her hands down her hips and slowly reversed towards him. Hallam was beginning to imagine. But then, with a smooth twist of her heels, she got him in her sights, and those terrible brown eyes began to explore his face. He twitched as she came towards him. Her eyes, he wanted them off him. She leant down for a kiss but he thrashed his head to the side, away from her. He could sense the warmth of her breasts close to his face, her lower body moving left and right. He wanted her away from him. She went down on her knees to corral his face, to try and kiss him again. He willed himself not to scream and push her violently away. Instead he shrunk from her, hiding his face, pretending to rub his eye.

'Don't,' he whispered. 'Not yet. Dance. Please. Over there.' He indicated the far side of the room, and tried to give her a smile of encouragement. She paused, piqued, but the drink was coursing through her along with the rhythm and she didn't seem to mind. She straightened up and slow-boogied back across the room, watching him all the time.

'Don't look at me. Turn.'

'But I want to see what you're thinking.'

He looked so frustrated that she shrugged, raised her chin, twirled round and continued to dance with even less inhibition than before, looking out of the window at the midsummer night sky, still pale at the margins.

> *estréchame en tu manos y*
> *hazme una caricia*
> *no me dejes y avédate mi lado*

Yes, that was better. He felt that he had found the shadows again. But what was she doing now? Her hands had gone up in front of her, she was unbuttoning her shirt. He pushed himself up on the sofa, transfixed. She was touching her own breasts, taking off the belt of her trousers, tugging them down a few inches, turning round again . . . The shirt fell to the floor, but he hardly saw it. She was a blur now through the bars of his shaking fingers as she came for him again. 'Don't touch me,' he pleaded. 'I'm gay, I'm gay.'

They lay together on the large sofa, shoulder to shoulder. Her shirt was back on, one button refastened.

'Explain the erection to me then.'

'I was thinking of my career.'

She did not seem convinced. 'Venereal disease, is that it?'

He rolled his eyes. 'No.'

She frowned.

He continued, seeing the need. 'And, look, you are very attractive. But I am,' he paused and closed his eyes, praying for guidance, 'I am politically very committed to the gay cause and I would regard any dabbling in heterosexuality as, as . . .'

'You've got a boyfriend?' His refusal had sobered her up, but only enough to turn her into a physical rather than a sexual threat.

Hallam took a deep breath. Something deep inside him would not allow him to claim that he had a boyfriend.

'No.'

'Now for some reason I believe that. The rest, I'm afraid, is suspect.' Hallam despaired and looked out of the window. Her voice dropped. 'I am about to get very, very offended, Hallam. Unless you give me a reason very soon, a convincing reason.'

Hallam gritted his teeth. He turned to her. 'I am a virgin.'

She paused, she carefully did not laugh, then she frowned again. 'That's a bit arrogant, isn't it, at your age?'

'Is it?'

'Pretentious. No one's good enough for you, I suppose.'

'It's not that unusual.'

'Alasdair lost his when he was eleven.'

Oh, perfect, thought Hallam.

'Still,' she continued, 'you do have other things in common.'

'What?' Hallam began to shout, dragging himself up to look her straight in the eye. 'We don't even share a gene pool. He's . . . a simian. Although,' he calmed himself, 'I don't know him very well, of course.'

'On the outside, granted, you're different, plus he's quite a bit older. But you've both got that introspective observant side, only you've not seen it.'

And you've not seen the side I've seen, thought Hallam.

'He's arrogant, I know,' she continued. 'The macho rig worker turned artistic genius. He gives me a hard time about my parents having money. The fact is, he's from a perfectly respectable Aberdeen family himself, they'd probably be horrified to hear the way he goes on about how hard he had it. Don't you think it's odd the way people re-write their past to suit what they've become or what they think they want to be?'

This confused Hallam. He had rarely paused to consider matters of class; as a pervert he was above such vulgar forms of definition. But he thought about that last sentence of hers and it seemed to reverberate through him, in unexpected directions. Its immediate effect was for him temporarily to lose his crippling self-awareness; as if this notional facility everybody had, not only for re-writing their past, as she said, but for re-inventing themselves, had the power to liberate him from what that past had caused him to become. Or at least to give him leave from it. Kate leant over to pick up her cup of coffee from the floor, which caused her to brush against him. She sipped the cooling drink, and fell back against the cushions with a little sigh.

Hallam, afire with all this shared intimacy, was struck by a thought as unexpected as it was unwelcome. Was it possible that he, Hallam, had moulded the past to suit himself? That he had fictionalised it somehow for his own ends? It was true that sometimes he wondered about his memory; not its vagueness but its unfeasible intensity. There were memory sites that he revisited with almost religious fervour every night – Centre Point, the footsteps passing by his door, the white driveway lights, the waters of the lake. Were they real any more? Or had they metamorphosised into fantasy?

And what of his ardent hatred for Verity?

Hallam wanted to expel the thought of that woman from his mind. He twisted round to face Kate. He leant forwards and kissed her hard on the mouth. Her lips were still warm and wet from the coffee. He could tell she was slightly startled, unsure even, but after a moment her lips parted and she curved her back as his arm encircled her and drew her tight.

But then she stopped him. She took his forelock in her fingers and slowly pulled his head back.

'I'm not sure I want the responsibility,' she said.

'We don't have to penetrate. I just want to go to bed with you.'

She laughed. 'Was that very naive or very experienced?'

'Please.' He tried to keep the desperate longing out of his voice. 'I'd hate you to think I was arrogant.'

She paused. Hallam's thumb slid across her breast. She breathed deeply and closed her eyes.

'Nothing serious?' she asked.

'Deadly flippant.'

'Right then. Upstairs.'

Hallam took off his clothes and lay back naked on her bed. He heard the taps running in the bathroom. He gazed up at the skylight and saw his body reflected there, suspended above him, the returned gaze oddly detached, the body pale against the dark coverlet. The bathroom door opened and Kate slipped in a few seconds later. She turned out the light and instantly Hallam's suspended body gave way to stars. He saw the steadily blinking lights of an aircraft as it passed overhead on the long descent. Eyes on the city below. Then it was gone.

'Psst,' said Kate. She lay down beside him. They both smiled shyly at each other, eyes shining in the dark. Then he rolled towards her, into her arms, and out of sight.

4:17 in the morning and everything was possible: a good life, a shared life, a happy one even. Perhaps happiness was important after all. Kate lay still next to him, breathing steadily. He was completely sanctioned to reach over and touch her if he so wished. The barriers had come down.

Hallam lay there in the dark and exulted at the possibilities. The odds were long, but right now it felt as if they were all fixed irresistibly in his favour. The rules were no longer necessary.

The piercing tone of the mobile phone reached right up the stairs and Hallam, dozing pleasantly, was tempted to ignore it. Then he realised that it was getting closer, along with the clink of a tea tray.

Kate entered in her dressing gown and laid the tray down on the bottom of the bed. She handed him the mobile. 'Go on, it might be important.'

Reluctantly he lifted himself up on one elbow and pressed the green button. 'Yeah, hello?'

'Hallam, good morning.' It took him half a second to realise who it was; that peculiar accent again. 'It's Lucy here. Sorry, did I wake you up? I was trying to catch you before work. Are you OK?'

'Look, can't you just leave it?'

Kate was pouring tea, and listening.

'This is absurd. I'm in England, I want to see you, and anyway I've never been to Scotland which is ridiculous. But not as ridiculous as us not having been in contact for five years. Come on, we've got so much to talk over, it's important.'

'Like what?'

'You've not been in contact with Julius or Verity, have you.' It didn't sound like a question.

'No. Have you?' He instantly cursed himself for asking her a question, and prolonging this conversation.

'I spoke to him yesterday, to arrange a visit. It must be time we all got back together. A reunion. What do you think?'

'Get back together?' Hallam went pale, and Kate gave him a short glance over her mug of tea. 'You must be fucking joking. Now get lost.'

'Please, we need to talk this over calmly. Will you be around this weekend?'

'No, you can't come up. I'm not having it.' Kate got up and went out of the room, Hallam raising an arm to her, wanting her to wait. He heard the bathroom door shut.

'Are you alone?'

'Yes.'

'Are you at home?'

'None of your business.'

'OK, fine, I'm not checking up on you.'

'I've got to go to work now. Don't call me on this number again, OK?'

'I'm staying in London with my friend Sarah tonight, but I'll be on the move. I've left my mobile number on your answering ma—' Hallam pressed the off button and chucked the mobile on the duvet. He breathed deeply, then heard the bathroom door open again. Kate came back in to pick up a fresh bottle of moisturiser, but she didn't meet his eye.

'Sorry about that. Hey, hold on, where are you going?'

'I'm getting ready for work. Shouldn't you be?'

'What's the matter?'

'Oh, nothing.'

'That was my sister on the phone, she's completely nuts, phoning me out of the blue.'

'You've not mentioned her before.'

'Lucy. She's been away for years, South Africa, and now—'

'Hallam, I'm not a complete idiot. You spun an impressive line of bullshit last night, and congratulations, you do a seamless imitation of a virgin, right down to being a crap shag.'

'Kate . . .'

'This was a hideous mistake, but it's at least partly my fault. Let's forget it. Now go home, and I'll see you at the office.'

'You've got it completely wrong. I can prove it to you.'

'Don't bother. Look, even if she is your sister, it doesn't matter. Let's just forget this. I was smashed, I'm your boss, this is not good policy. And if you tell anyone else about it I'll kill you.'

Hallam was speechless. Kate disappeared again into the bathroom. She turned the lock.

He lay there, suddenly unwelcome in the bed. He got up and began to get dressed, cursing his sister under his breath. The thought of reconciliation repelled him.

Hallam entered the office, glanced at Kate and from her closed, hostile face concluded that she was not bothering to maintain an appearance of cheerful professionalism. In a way it was a relief because he was not sure he could have handled it. He found that he could bear the injustice so long as there was still hope. She's angry, he told himself, she cares, although he recognised that this was hardly grounds for optimism about a future relationship.

He had surprised himself with the sudden shift in his aspirations. He had never even considered the possibility of a relationship. This was why, he now realised, his life had been so simple. He sat down heavily at his desk and logged on, which simultaneously seemed to activate a profound depression.

He gazed about the office, at the posters and photographs for various charities and international aid organisations clogging the walls; rows of images of human suffering and need. For the first time he was forcibly struck by the personal and moral vacuum that this job had become for him. He walked into this office and worthwhile existence was suspended. This was the giving business after all; an industry called charity. He reflected upon the ingenious ways in which life could turn you into what you hated most.

This job had once suited him. Its rules had seemed familiar and easy to master. He had instinctively understood the way manipulation could be disguised as benign concern. Verity, he supposed, must have taught him that. He had even learnt to relish the task, with the requisite veneer of irony, of course. Now he merely disgusted himself. He took a brief look over the text of the new legacy document that had been sent back by Kate with suggestions for revisions – mostly sensible, he had to admit – and after an hour or so he emailed the corrected copy back through. It was good work, he knew, and now a source of profound personal shame.

He looked over to Kate's desk. She was on the phone, crouched behind the terminal, hugging the receiver in a way that usually denoted an intimate personal call. He did not need to guess who was on the other end: Alasdair. He caught a flash of a smile round the side of her terminal. It was not for him. She was falling straight back into Alasdair's arms, despite his best efforts. Perhaps even because of his efforts. And because of Lucy of course.

Eventually Kate came over to Hallam's desk with a look that made it clear she was on a purely professional mission. 'That was Alasdair on the phone. He wants you to call him, he said it's about the gallery down south that you mentioned to him. Here's the number.' She dropped a Post-it note down on his desk.

'Thanks,' he said.

He expected her to walk straight off but she waited, as if she had something more to say. His hopes leapt.

'I've just been told that Mrs Carter died yesterday.' Hallam did not know how she expected him to react. He did not know how he expected himself to react. 'She went rather quickly, didn't she? I wonder about some of these heart failures with cancer. They're pretty generous with the painkillers at the end, it must be tempting to swallow a few too many.'

'How did you get so fucking cold-hearted?'

Kate was shocked by his vehemence but she rose to the occasion. 'How do you know it's cold? You got nowhere near.'

He was furious that she thought his accusation was motivated by her spurning him. Although of course it was, partly. 'Someone died,' he said.

'And remarkably promptly too. Do you have this effect on a lot of people?'

He went a vivid red. 'What do you mean by that?' His voice was almost a gargle.

Kate looked disconcerted, then laughed nervously. 'I hope you didn't put anything in her tea because you've netted us one million pounds. Her solicitors were on the phone this morning. That's most of the inheritance.'

One million pounds. It registered, even through his newly acquired bitterness and disillusion.

'Congratulations. You'll probably get a call from one of the bosses in the London office. I told them it was mainly your work. I wouldn't be surprised if they offered you a job down there at some point soon. You should consider taking it.'

Hallam took a moment to process the implications of what she had said. He could feel her watching his response, and as the pain of rejection began to expand, he looked up and saw her eyes glisten with what looked like malicious pleasure. How typical of Kate, he thought, that such a blow should be delivered as a form of congratulation. But then Kate's air of mean triumph wavered and immediately Hallam felt a rushing sense of regret and tenderness. She was meant for him, and the force of this conviction surprised even himself. But he did not say anything. Kate turned and returned to her desk, then went off in the direction of the toilets.

Hallam slumped back in his chair. This was all so unnecessary, he thought. If only he could show her that she had misunderstood everything. If he could keep Alasdair clear of her somehow, just for a while, then he could work on her, bring her round. The beginnings of a plan began to shape itself in his mind. Only then did he recall the substance of that other information Kate had given him. That Mrs Carter had died.

Hallam was still not sure what he felt about this. Guilt? He picked up the phone and resolved to rediscover his humanity when he had the time. But even as he began to dial, seeking escape from his conscience through activity, a part of him was trying to justify his indifference, justify his actions, justify his job. What was more important, he asked himself, the living or the dead? But he had been answering that same question day in day out for the last nine years, and every time his answer had been the same. The dead, the dead, the dead.

'Lucy?'

'Yes? Is that Hallam?' It sounded as if she was in a car. 'Can you hear that? It's my old motor, still going strong after all these years! Sarah's loaned it back to me.'

A brief silence. 'I want you to come up to Scotland.'

'You do?' She was obviously surprised. 'Really?' There was pleasure in her voice now, and it acted like a provocation.

'But it's not because I want to see you,' Hallam shouted, 'it's because you've fucked up my life again and this time you're going to put it right. You've got a talent, Lucy, and it's for fucking me up.'

'What have I done?'

'I want you to show yourself to someone and explain to them who you are and confirm that it was you who phoned up this morning and that you're not some girlfriend of mine.' A gasp, and then a squawk of suppressed laughter. 'Don't you dare laugh, you bitch.' Hallam realised that he had yelped and turned round to see if Kate had heard him. Fortunately she was not back at her desk yet.

'When would suit you?' Seriousness was reinstated in her voice.

'As soon as you can.'

'Great. Is Saturday evening OK then? I've got a dinner party on the Friday and I've got another long drive after that. I can't wait to see what you look like now. Any surprises I need to prepare for?'

'Just because you're coming up, don't think this is going to be some happy reunion. I hate your guts. Give me a ring when you know what time you're coming.' Hallam put down the phone. He scratched his head violently with both hands and rubbed his face, then dialled Alasdair's number, not allowing himself to pause. He got the answering machine. He cleared his throat and waited for the beep.

'Alasdair, it's Hallam here. I got your message although I presume you weren't really calling about the gallery. I'll pay the bill for the breakage and if there is anything more you want to discuss, then why don't we do it in person at my place. Saturday evening if you can make it.'

nine

Hallam opened the door to his flat and came face to face with his mother. Or at least a younger version of her. He stepped back woodenly as Lucy, lightly tanned and sporting short bobbed hair with streaks of blonde, laughed, dropped her arms round his shoulders and kissed him on both cheeks.

The oval face, the small dimples and slightly raised chin, even the thick hair tucked impatiently behind the ear; it was the ghost of genetics come back to haunt him.

Lucy gave him a frank, smiling assessment, faint wrinkles around her eyes bringing a maternal aspect to her face that he had never imagined could reside there. Through his daze he already sensed himself surrendering to her, as if out of reverence for the other person he saw etched on her features.

'Gosh, Hallam, you've grown up. Look at this flat.'

That accent again, but at least her voice firmly established Lucy's personality behind this sacrilegious resemblance. With the ease that Hallam had always envied in her, Lucy wandered through the long thin flat and glanced airily through each door, raising an eyebrow in mild surprise at the cleanliness of the place. Perhaps she thought he had tidied it for her benefit. This irritated him because the truth was, his real home was in the rafters and the absence of clutter was the result of non-occupation. She did not think to look up at the trap door and the loft above; he had taken the precaution of putting away the ladder.

'Do you mind if I make myself a cup of tea? I'm parched.' She filled the kettle and shook her head ruefully. 'I was in Cambridge last night. My old uni friends are still a bunch of boozers. Geting up this morning and hacking through the traffic was hell.'

Hallam felt like a stranger in his own flat. He tried to resent rather than admire the way she managed to conjure up a welcome for herself everywhere she went. But as he stood in silence and watched her bustle about the kitchen, searching out the mugs, he found he was unable to.

It took all of his stubbornness and sense of grievance to prevent himself from abandoning the plans he had in mind. He reminded himself that he didn't need Lucy and she most certainly didn't need him. He must be strong, look after himself – after all, wasn't that what she had told him all those years ago before driving away and out of his life? If he stuck to the plan, it would all be for the best. For him, anyway.

'No . . . flatmate?' she asked. She was stepping carefully around the Kate issue.

'I'm no good at sharing.'

'It's lovely,' she said admiringly.

'It's a funny-shaped space, but it suits me fine.'

'You sounded just like Julius when you said that.'

'What? No I didn't. Did I?' She had plucked a hidden neurosis as only a sister could.

Lucy laughed, as if it wasn't important. 'You even look like him.'

'I do not. We look completely different.' There was panic in his voice.

'OK, OK, easy does it. It's just that with the short hair . . .' She poured water from the kettle into a mug. 'I popped in on the Hall on my way up from London. Do you have any herbal tea?' She took a teabag from the box in the cupboard.

Hallam stood there, stunned. 'You met him at the Hall?'

She grinned. 'Yeah, for lunch. It was outlandish.'

Hallam felt the blood rush to his face; jealousy first, then anger. 'But we swore we'd never return. No, you swore!'

Lucy went blank. 'When did I swear?'

'The day of the last supper. When we were walking up the road to the Barkham. You swore you'd never go back unless . . .' he faltered, 'she died.'

'Did I?' Lucy shrugged and dunked the teabag a couple of times, before tossing it into the sink. 'Well, I must have been pretty fucked off.'

'You were,' said Hallam. 'Is she . . . she's not . . . ?'

'Dead, you mean? Oh no, firing on all cylinders. In the prime of spite. Have you really not been in contact at all?'

Hallam stared at her. He had always believed, without thinking about it directly, that there had been some tacit agreement between them to abandon the family as a failed project. That was the only way he could make sense of Lucy moving out of contact for so long. The idea of returning to the Hall had acquired the status of a forbidden fantasy in his mind. Now this long exile from his grounds had been rendered meaningless at a stroke. He couldn't make sense of the past five years. What had he been thinking?

'Not even a phone call?'

'No.'

'That's strange. Julius gave the impression he knew where you were and everything. He even told me where you worked. That's how I got your number. What about money?'

'There was the will, I got that when I was twenty-one. I bought the flat with it.' Hallam spoke in a weak voice. He remembered wondering how the lawyers had tracked him down at the time, but then he had moved and put it out of his mind. Just as he had put out of mind the letter, unread, that had accompanied the money.

'Did you get anything else with it?' she asked casually. She was referring to the letter, of course. It had presumably been entrusted with lawyers those eight years between the death of its writer and his coming of age. Had Lucy received anything similar. Did she know for sure of his?

'No.' He did not want to talk about this. Instead his mind circled back to the belittling notion that his father had kept track of him. Of course, he should have known that there was no hiding in the modern world. Julius had probably known where he was every step of the way. Hallam's cherished ideas of heroic isolation continued to shrivel, and in their place new and childlike questions reasserted themselves. Why hadn't Julius tried to contact him if he knew where he was? But then, why should he? Why hadn't he made the effort himself? Because, Hallam answered himself, he had been banished.

The door buzzer sounded.

'Expecting someone?' asked Lucy, and took a sip of her tea.

Chanby Hall. Still there. 'Has it changed?' he asked.

'Not much,' she said. 'Apart from the back. Aren't you going to get the door?'

He blinked once, then walked out of the kitchen to the front door, and lifted the intercom receiver. 'Hello?'

'It's Alasdair.' The voice tinny, monotone. Hallam buzzed him in, then stood for a moment, trying to remember through his confusion what Alasdair was doing here. Of course he had invited him. Hallam undid the latch on the door and turned back to see Lucy, still in the kitchen, who was fishing in her bag for a packet of cigarettes. She plucked one out by its white filter and lit it. She seemed so composed as she sent a stream of smoke from her lips to the ceiling. Alasdair's footsteps were ascending the cramped circular staircase. Then they stopped by the door.

There was a wary pause. Then a hand came out and tapped three times on the doorframe. Hallam didn't say anything. Alasdair cautiously prodded his head through and registered Hallam. Then, over Hallam's shoulder he saw Lucy in the kitchen. Hallam turned to look too. She did look beautiful, standing there by the sink, drawing on the cigarette in that self-contained manner of hers. She tapped the cigarette in the ashtray and smiled hazily through the smoke. 'Hi,' said Hallam to Alasdair.

Alasdair looked slowly back to Hallam, with an expression both sly and knowing. The thought evidently running through his mind was: coward, bringing a woman along to keep things civilised.

'Good evening,' he replied in a droll tone.

'Come in.'

'Thank you, I will.' He stepped in and let Hallam shut the door behind him. Hallam noticed a feral quality in Alasdair's manner; a sharpness around the nose and mouth, a sense of self-control in his movements. Alasdair shot swift glances into the other rooms on his way through to the kitchen, as if checking for possible ambush. But there was also curiosity in his assessment of the flat. It suggested they were rivals. A flattering thought. Promising, too.

'Hi,' said Lucy, holding out her hand briskly, 'I'm Lucy, Hallam's sister.'

'Alasdair Cruickshank,' he drawled, with ironic formality. 'How do you do?'

They shook hands. Alasdair smiled and held her gaze slightly longer than necessary. Then with a theatrical flourish he swung round to face

Hallam, causing him to flinch. 'I'm very sorry, I'd have brought some wine if I'd known.'

'I can nip down for some later,' said Hallam. 'Lucy, Alasdair here's a photographer.'

She raised her eyebrows, politely impressed. 'Really? What kind?'

Alasdair gave Hallam a quick glance, trying to gauge whether this whole situation was some sort of game, but Hallam's serious expression seemed to reassure him.

'Anything really, except weddings. And dog portraits.'

'For artistic reasons?' There was light mockery in her voice.

He thought for a moment. 'I suppose they must scare me.'

Lucy looked at Alasdair coolly and took another drag. No polite laughter: evidence that she found him attractive.

'I imagine children must be a problem.'

'I tell myself they're dwarfs.'

The two of them smiled at each other faintly. Hallam felt irritated, although he knew he ought to be pleased that everything was going so well.

'Drink anyone?' he asked, dutifully.

'A glass of wine would be nice,' said Lucy, tossing away her barely touched tea.

'Back in a minute then,' said Hallam, and picked up his jacket. As he was walking out he heard Lucy ask Alasdair how he knew Hallam.

'Let us say, a shared friend,' Alasdair replied.

The wine had been drunk, and the topics of conversation had included the pleasures of South African safari, the manly perils of deep-sea diving and the deeper challenges of artistic endeavour in the medium of photography. Lucy got up to go to the toilet. As the door shut, the sociable smile faded from Alasdair's face. He uncrossed his legs and sat forward. His voice became clipped and businesslike. 'What's going on with Kate?'

'I've stuck to our agreement. I've not told her anything.'

'I don't mean that. I mean what's going on between the two of you?'

'Nothing.'

Alasdair paused then sighed at the lack of co-operation. His gaze hardened. 'You're not the only one who watches.'

Hallam digested the comment slowly. 'You surprise me, Alasdair. I never took you for insecure.'

'Drinks at the Cuban place. Back to her flat some time after twelve.'

'So?'

'I followed you.' Alasdair leant forward. 'How does it feel, being watched?'

Hallam shrugged and smiled. Underneath, however, he was furious with himself for not noticing or being prepared.

'Did you fuck her, Hallam?' Alasdair tried to be mocking but it did not disguise the torment beneath.

Hallam continued to smile. So Alasdair didn't know. Even better. Hallam enjoyed the novel sensation of having the upper hand.

'Do you know the sad truth? She's using you to try and make me jealous.'

'Is it working?'

Alasdair's eyes dilated and he clenched his fists. 'You're a pervert, and I'd happily rip your dick off because I think it'd be a service to society. But I'm going to give you a chance. I don't know what you're capable of but I don't want you anywhere near her outside of work. No watching, no following. Do you understand? If you keep it up, I'll kill you.'

Hallam leant forward, made reckless by the wine and the knowledge that he was on home territory. 'Well, since you've joined the brotherhood, Al, let's share a little knowledge. What else did you see then? Did you see us make love? Did you see the way she looked at me, the things she did for me? Or have you just been imagining it? And what does that make you?'

He half-expected to be attacked but Alasdair did not move. Even his mouth maintained its droll grimace. So Hallam continued. 'Because, guess what, I don't have to imagine anything. Do you miss the way she presses her hand down on the side of your face when she's pumping away on top? And how rough you were with her sometimes, those slaps and squeezes which hurt her and which you weren't exactly sure she enjoyed as much as you. And the guilt around your eyes when she went quiet afterwards.'

'She told you that?' he asked quietly.

'Remember that skylight above her bed, and how you like to keep the light on? Even with the blind down it was a grandstand view. That's right, mate, I was there, every rancid grunt and thrust of the way. And when you lay there afterwards like a great punctured balloon and she padded off to the toilet and locked the door, I followed her round, just by the window, and I saw the disgust on her face as she washed your slime out of her.'

Alasdair's shoulders had bunched, a muscle worked reflexively in his jaw. But he waited, as if Hallam might have more to say. Then with a great effort he sat back and smiled. 'It was nice of you to join us,' he said, reverting to his ironic drawl.

This response genuinely surprised Hallam. He had succeeded in shocking Alasdair, but he detected something else in those pinprick eyes, an expression beyond anger. Excitement, possibly. Was Alasdair feeling unexpected pleasure from the idea of being watched? They stared at each other in silence. The hostility had transformed into a new tension, an unspoken dialogue of opposites, dare and counter-dare. Had he found the chance of a perfect consummation for his obsession after all these years, and was that tentative affirmation he saw in Alasdair's expression? Hallam encountered disgust and enlightenment simultaneously, but it only lasted a second. Lucy came back in and she must have heard Alasdair's last comment because she sat down next to her brother on the sofa and smiled in mild embarrassment, misunderstanding. 'I wasn't that long, was I?'

Alasdair picked up his jacket and got ready to leave.

'Are you off?' asked Lucy, surprised.

'It was a pleasure to meet you, Lucy. Maybe see you later.'

Hallam addressed Alasdair in a light voice and put a hand on Lucy's knee. 'Well, what a good idea, why don't we all meet again? Like I did with you and Kate, eh, Alasdair?'

If Alasdair understood the significance of the invitation he did not show it. Instead he turned towards the door.

''Bye.' Lucy sounded a little disappointed that the party was breaking up so abruptly.

Hallam got up and opened the door for Alasdair, who slung a heavy arm round his shoulder and put his lips uncomfortably close to his host's ear. 'I feel sorry for you. But you're an interesting case.'

'I hope you learnt something.'

Alasdair's eyes unfocused for a moment. 'Perhaps I did.' He stepped outside and started to descend the stairs. But then he turned and looked up at Hallam, thoughtful, one hand resting on the stairwell's central stone pillar. 'Tell me, which is worse: seeing or imagining?'

Hallam leant against the doorjamb, and looked out through the narrow window above Alasdair's head, at the grey tenements dimly lit by white lamps, at the shadows of other people's lives sliding across the windowpanes. 'Imagining.'

'And what's worst? Watching or . . .' Alasdair paused, 'being watched?'

Hallam answered with the sympathy of someone who had asked himself similar questions. 'You don't have a choice about what's in you. Don't worry about it.'

Alasdair appeared perplexed. Hallam smiled with the knowledge of his one certainty. 'It's all there is.'

Alasdair seemed to be satisfied with this. He nodded, then raised a hand in farewell and slowly made his way down.

Hallam shut the door and returned to the sitting room where Lucy had lit another cigarette. He sat down, self-absorbed.

'Funny chap, your friend,' Lucy commented as she picked up a magazine from the table.

Hallam looked up. 'Did you like him?'

She shrugged and flipped a few pages of the magazine. She seemed unconcerned, another positive sign, in her case. 'So am I going to meet this girlfriend of yours then? That's what I'm here for, isn't it?'

'Meet me at work tomorrow. She's my boss.'

Lucy put down the magazine and adopted her frank tone of voice. 'Why are you so angry with me?'

'I'm not like you. I don't do indifference.'

'Don't be so fucking arrogant.'

He assessed the hostility in her face. Was her response calculated to prove that she did care after all? He sneered his bitter amusement: she was a phoney, and there was nothing he held in more contempt.

'I had problems too. You're not the only one. But I can understand if you don't want to see me again.' She stood up and made for the door. He followed her.

'That's right, walk away again.'

Lucy stopped, realising that she had forgotten her bag. She had to turn round and head back to the kitchen to pick it up, enduring his gaze. 'Meaning?' she said briskly, hooking the strap over her shoulder.

'Five years ago you walked away, and dropped me in the shit. Your call to the newspaper about the development of the lakes, Lucy, don't you remember?'

'It wasn't me.' She had managed to put an almost convincing level of indignation into her voice. Hallam slowly shook his head in disgust. She headed for the door again, only to halt once more. What was it now? He followed her gaze down to the left. There, in the corner, was a spare coil of nylon rope. It had been there for so long that Hallam had grown blind to it. She picked it up and held up the noose end which now suddenly appeared invidious. When she turned round he saw that she had gone pale.

'What is this for?'

He blushed, knowing what she feared it might be for (loop it round the neck and kick away the chair), and knowing himself what its real purpose was. What could he say?

'I do abseiling. As a hobby.'

'So you've still got your head for heights then?' She moved slowly towards him.

He became nervous. 'Yes, so what?'

She reached out quickly and grabbed his wrists, turning his palms upwards to inspect them. She ran her thumbs over their rough surfaces. It seemed to convince her that he was telling the truth, because her relief came in the form of a smile. She lightly squeezed his fingers.

'They used to be so soft when you were a baby.'

He pulled his hands quickly away and wiped them on his trousers, as if it might remove the gesture of affection.

'Who else would have called the paper,' he asked, 'if not you?'

Lucy shrugged. 'Verity?' She went into the sitting room and sat down on the sofa. Hallam followed.

'Why would she sabotage Julius's project?'

'To pin it on you. To get you thrown out.'

He hesitated. Verity was capable of it, he knew that. He resorted to accusation. 'You were on her side.'

'It was never friendship. She trapped me with her confidences. She knew I was the only one who could come between her and Julius.' She paused. 'Look, OK, we were friends for a while. My friends at Cambridge loved her. My friend Alex loved her. Did I mention Alex? We almost had a relationship until I told Verity about him. She was really sweet at first, took us out to lunch, and the next thing I knew, she was having an affair with him. Once she realised I knew, she was completely brazen about it. She threw herself on my mercy, knowing that then I couldn't say anything to Julius. And it drew me in, made me responsible for it too somehow. I can see that now.' She glanced up at him. 'I expect you're wondering why I didn't just tell Julius.' It was the one thing that he was not wondering, as it happened. But she continued. 'He seemed happy. It seemed wrong. Then she began to ask me to provide alibis when she was seeing Alex. And I said yes. I suppose I didn't want to let on that I was jealous or that she'd hurt me. She is a genius at transferring guilt, believe me.'

Is. Verity in the present tense. Hallam had difficulty entertaining the thought; his stepmother had been locked up in his past for so long.

'That's why I left, Hallam, and why I stayed out of contact. It wasn't about Alex, he wasn't anything special in the end, but I couldn't take any more of the manipulation. She poisoned everything, my whole idea of the family, and I hated myself and I thought you'd be better off not seeing me again, and that you'd have an easier time of it without me. South Africa was the way out. Along with all the rest.'

Hallam assessed what she had said. He had a nose for people who had been through analysis and her confession had the smell of the couch all over it.

Since he did not say anything she smiled weakly. 'Well, I'm chucking in that diamonds job. I've had enough of squinting with a hangover at little bits of rock. I was thinking of doing something worthwhile like you. Aid work maybe.'

'Stick with diamonds,' said Hallam. His comment seemed to come from a distance.

'So how did you cope?' she asked, a note of curiosity creeping into her voice. 'All things considered, you've come through it incredibly well.'

He took a deep breath and looked at her again. 'I put it beneath me.'

Lucy sat back, and nodded thoughtfully. 'I think I know what you mean.'

'I think you don't.'

She absorbed the hostility that had flared up again.

'Why did you do it, Hallam?'

'What?'

'I heard what happened after I left. The nails in the tree.'

She actually thought that he was capable of doing it. His own sister. He clenched and unclenched his fists. Maybe they were right. Maybe he was capable of it. In fact, maybe he was capable of a great deal more.

'The tree surgeon was all right in the end, sort of,' said Lucy eventually. 'He got some use back in his arm. They sewed it back on him at the infirmary. Compensation too.'

'Did Julius tell you all this?' he asked.

'Yes, he did.'

'And what did you think?'

Lucy laughed nervously. Hallam's eyes skittered over her. She rubbed her hands between her thighs, as if warming them up. 'I . . . found it hard to believe.'

'At first?'

'So you didn't do it?'

'You didn't think to check with me.'

'Dad said that afterwards you told him—'

'It doesn't matter about Julius,' Hallam said, jumping suddenly to his feet. 'What . . . about . . . ME?' And with that last word, he looked wildly about him, to the windows, into the other rooms, peering up at the trap door for some chink in the wood through which someone could, conceivably, spy on him. Were they there, listening in, noting down this impotent squeak of self-assertion?

Lucy watched him, scared, from the sofa. 'Did you?'

Hallam scratched his head; he laughed, he rubbed his neck; and then he looked down at her with dry eyes, decided to lie. 'Sure.'

Lucy held his gaze, but he saw the fear and it made him pitifully proud. Until he realised that maybe she was not scared of him, but for him.

'Well?' he asked. 'Aren't we supposed to cry and hug now, isn't that what they do in therapy? Now that it's all out.'

Lucy seemed to deflate. She leant her elbows on her knees, ran her fingers through her hair and shook her head. 'All out? You call that all out? Jesus.'

'What do you care?'

She looked at him then, and Hallam regretted asking. She was about to open her emotions wide, in the manner of someone who is capable of being loved. He resented and envied her capacity to do this.

'You're right, I didn't care,' she said. 'Back then I thought I could drive away and leave it all behind and that meant you too. I hated her and I wanted you to hate her too. I made things worse for you. I encouraged you. And I am so sorry for manipulating you like that.'

He waited in case she was going to go on, then nodded sagely and raised his eyebrows sarcastically. 'My, thanks for the apology.'

She wiped her eyes, embarrassed by the tears that had sprung up. Hallam wanted to dismiss her then; to send her back behind the protective glass, to his past. But she had destroyed that barrier and humiliatingly, he had to know.

'What was Verity like when you visited?' he asked, cheeks scorching.

Lucy suddenly lightened and leant forward, as if she was imparting gossip. 'Christ, it was awful. She'd put on this really formal lunch, I felt totally underdressed. And it was all such a false celebration, because I knew she didn't want me there. She cooed over me like we were long lost girlfriends, kept going on about the redecorations, the redesigns, the new interiors, everything knee-deep in silk and brocade.'

'And Julius?'

'Clinging. When I first turned up he looked sort of scared. But after that he was all over me, staring at me when he thought I wasn't looking. He'd not seen me for ages, I know, but it was like he was searching my face for something.'

'Or someone,' muttered Hallam. The dead are in all our faces, he thought.

'I wanted to see Dad. I wanted to see if there was a chance, however small, of some kind of reconciliation.'

'They killed her.'

Lucy frowned. 'It was suicide.'

'They were screwing together right under her nose. What did they expect?'

'There was illness. Infidelity happens.'

'You weren't there, you were at university. What do you know?'

'He told me what happened.'

'Did he now. So tell me what happened.'

'You know this. She was just out of hospital after an episode. She seemed to have stabilised, and then . . . Julius has tortured himself about this. Maybe you have too.'

He shook his head. 'He's lying.'

Lucy got up to come over and comfort him, but he shook her off violently.

'Get off, sit down. Hasn't it occurred to you that the two of them might have planned it to happen? To push her into it.'

'Think about what you're saying, Hallam. Dad's not a murderer.'

'It was obvious that Julius was cheating. He made it obvious. It was a matter of time.'

'You don't know this.'

'What would you do in . . . *her* situation? What is the first thing you would demand? That Verity goes. But does Verity get sacked? No. Julius says no. So what can she do? Leave? Where to? Not to her family, there aren't any left. To her friends? Where are they? Back to the hospital she loathed?'

'Stop.' Tears were running down Lucy's face now.

'That's why she killed herself. Because he left her no alternative. They may as well have held her under with their own four hands.'

Lucy wept. Then she grabbed her jacket and rushed out of the door and down the staircase.

Hallam felt enervated by his cruelty. He strode over to the window and looked down, waiting to see her emerge at the bottom of the building. She couldn't win him over, no chance. It was all justified, even if his pleasantly glowing sense of righteousness was not quite matched by a calmer belief in being entirely right. It did not seem to matter right now, in the afterglow of the confrontation. This must be what they call moral conviction, he thought. He savoured his new sense of power.

Lucy came into sight, clattering over the cobbles. He wondered whether Alasdair was watching the mouth of the close, waiting to bump into her, or whether perhaps they had exchanged numbers or she had mentioned her hotel when he had gone out for wine. Whichever way, Hallam had a hunch that Alasdair wouldn't let him down.

Hallam lay on his mattress in the loft. The smell of wood and quietness no longer lulled him. Instead it felt stifling. He turned over and squeezed his eyes shut, but the letter would not let him sleep.

At last, with an almost petulant whimper of frustration, he sat up, rolled off the mattress and sought it out. He had tossed it away all those months ago, acting indifferent, trying to fool himself, but sadly he knew exactly where it was: in the corner, under the rumpled computer print-outs and legacy literature, in its thick envelope. He took it out and returned to the mattress. He opened it without pausing, his fingers operating as if by remote control, by a need so long denied that it seemed hardly his own.

'My Darling Hal,' it began. This was as far as Hallam had got on the morning that he had received it those few days after his twenty-first birthday. His mother's intimate use of his abbreviated name was enough to make him recoil and thrust the letter away. Now, like then, he was seized by an instinct, strengthened by strictly observed habit, to retreat from this source of turbulence and pain. This time he did not obey it.

'If you ever come to read this it will mean that the lawyers have done what they promised and that I have left you, probably a long time ago. It may be that you wanted to forget me and who knows you may have succeeded, and if so I apologise. I appreciate that by running away from pain and suffering I only pass it on, but I do not apologise for that, even to you, Hal, because nothing needs less apology than the desire not to live.'

Hallam threw back his head. He was laughing, with genuine pleasure. He had never known his mother as an adult, he had never had the chance to talk to her about her thoughts and feelings; how could he have done when he was barely thirteen? He was enjoying the attention, this mother to son chat, so long delayed, even if it was a suicide note. So nice to catch up: so how WERE you? Hallam laughed wildly again. Why hadn't he done this before? he asked himself. What had he been so scared of?

'I love you as I write, I want you to know that, but as you're reading this when I am dead, and the dead don't love, there's no point pretending. Even as I write I can feel I am dying, the decision is being made, it's done. And that takes everything with it, except, oddly, for the time being, the desire to tell the truth. Anyway, you're old enough now to hear the truth, although I can hardly guess what kind of man you are. It feels ridiculous addressing one's son nearly ten years into the future, you might even think that it's in slightly bad taste, considering what I have to tell you.

'She has driven me to it. Oh, I know, the decision is mine, and it doesn't help not having a mind you can trust, but she has made living insufferable for me. They are childish things she does, but childish things are often the most savage.

'For instance, she switches my pills. My prescriptions, the lithiums and all the others. Actually, it is no joke, my most recent sojourns in the secure ward – you know the joys of that from your visits – have been its direct result. Blowing my top when I need calming, crushing descent when I need stabilising, it really is most distressing. I have no proof of course, and I'm hardly reliable, am I?

'And the rest. The taunting obviousness of the way she flaunts her affair with Julius – you MUST have noticed, even at your age (the age you were). It's humiliating, I suppose, but above all incredibly annoying.'

Annoying? Now he remembered the way her mind would switch back bizarrely on itself, probably through a prescription haze, but then, now and then, become lucid and pressing. Through the utterly inappropriate moments of levity, there was a growing sense of weary matter-of-factness.

'I do appreciate Julius needs escape from me. In fact, I know for certain that he will be happier when I am gone. Although this is not a reason for what I am going to do, end my life, I mean, just a pleasant consequence. I can't say I think much of his taste in women, although she is extraordinary in her own way.

'It IS childish what she has done, you see. As childish as the other stuff, leaving the gas on and suggesting it was me, questioning whether you are safe in my charge – which, really, is ridiculous because you were always safe with me.

'I wonder more whether you will be safe without me. I can hear her moving around downstairs as I write, the sound of her steps.

'I am going now, Hal. Let this upset you, it will help you to live better eventually, if that is what you want. Enjoy the money, it's not much, is it?

'Do you know, I'm not at all sure that this is very interesting. I had better go and get organised.'

She had not bothered to sign off. Hallam let the letter rest on his knees. He lay back on the bed. His mind was curiously blank. A great and leaden calm settled on him and he slept.

ten

Hallam was at work the next morning, when reception phoned. Lucy was downstairs, doubtless feeling guilty for storming out the night before. He asked for her to be shown up, then glanced over at Kate who was at her computer. She had been studiously avoiding Hallam's glances since he came in. When Lucy appeared, Hallam rose to meet her, noticing with some satisfaction that Kate was very alert to the entrance. He grabbed the opportunity; he rushed forward, gave Lucy a (by his standards) warmly fraternal kiss and pulled her over to be introduced before Kate could bolt for the toilets.

'Kate, this is my sister Lucy, the one I told you about.' Both women were slightly flustered, even Lucy, but she quickly laughed and held out a hand. 'I'm not as bad as he makes out.'

Kate hesitated, then smiled.

'Have you noted the family resemblance?' inquired Hallam, with a hint of told-you-so.

'Yeah,' said Kate, 'you're the ugly version. Anyway, nice to meet you, Lucy. I'd better answer that phone, I'm waiting on a call.'

''Bye,' said Lucy.

Hallam took her to his desk. 'Thank you.'

'That's OK. Look, I'm sorry for walking out like that last night. Me turning up out of the blue and everything.'

'Forget it.'

'Are you sure?'

'Sure.'

She smiled and seemed to accept his move towards reconciliation in good faith. 'Do you know, your friend Alasdair gave me a call at the hotel, and asked me out.'

'Really? That's nice of him.'

'Did you put him up to it? To get me off your hands?'

'No. We might have to consider the possibility that he liked you on your own merits. He's an eccentric soul.'

'In what way eccentric?'

'Well, let me see. He's considerate, interesting, solvent, non-alcoholic, self-assured and – now this bit's strange – he doesn't shag about.'

'Are you being nice to me because we're in public?'

Hallam frowned and inspected his fingernails. 'I didn't mean to be.'

'So do you think I should say yes?'

Knowing her, she already had, but he thought that he ought to encourage her anyway. 'Nah, you've hardly got anything in common. Anyway, what's the venue?'

'A place called Black Bo's. Not that I've agreed yet,' she added quickly. 'Why don't you come along? I'm heading north the day after. I thought I might take a gander at the Highlands.'

'I've got a date tonight.'

In response to her silent query about who his date was with, Hallam surreptitiously nodded in Kate's direction. This was of course untrue, but then Lucy hadn't been totally honest either.

'I'll see you before you go, though.'

'Speak to you later then.' Lucy kissed him – Hallam even proffered his cheek – and he walked her out past Kate with elaborate attentiveness.

As he returned to his desk, Hallam realised that these small charades of affection were dangerous: they slipped past your defences and too easily became real. It was funny how he could so easily handle the big things, the letter for instance, which had given him an almost unnatural inner peace by merely confirming his suspicions, and thereby settling his most deeply held and feverishly avoided anxieties. No, it was the little things that he found the worst. Tenderness, for instance. He breathed deeply and sat down.

The phone rang. Hallam sighed.

'Hello, Cancer Action, Hallam Foe speaking.'

Silence.

Hallam put a professional smile in his voice to disguise his impatience. 'Hello, Cancer Action? How can I help?'

'It's Gordon Carter here.'

Hallam had been waiting for this. 'Gordon, we were informed of your loss. Can I just say how sorry we are—'

'Sorry? I'm surprised you're still bothering to be insincere now that you've landed your million.'

'I work for a charity, Gordon, I haven't gained anything personally from this.'

'No, your motivation isn't anything as simple as money, is it? I might have been less repelled if it was.'

Hallam sighed audibly. This was achieving nothing. 'What can I do for you?'

'I'd love you to return my inheritance.'

'Your mother made a decision of her own free will to leave—'

'The courts will decide that. That's not really why I called.'

'The courts?'

'Your employer will be receiving notification from my lawyers about the terms of my late mother's will, and whether she was of sound mind when she made her amendments just before her death, and indeed whether she made her decision of her own free will at all. Your methods are pretty unorthodox, Hallam. I don't know what they taught you at Newcastle University, but it certainly wasn't ethics. What was it you studied at university, by the way?'

The index finger of Hallam's left hand tapped nervously on the desk. He didn't answer.

'Foe?'

'Yes?'

'Did you really go to university? Because that was what you told your employers, wasn't it, when you were given your job?'

'Yes.'

'Goodbye, Hallam.' The line went dead.

Kate came over. 'Good work on the legacy leaflet. Your sister seemed very nice, but it wasn't necessary to show her to me. What happened wasn't planned, Hallam.'

'I realise that,' he said. But it was planned, he thought. I planned it.

'What I mean is, I feel as if I might have been a bit irresponsible with your feelings.'

Hallam's right eyebrow expressed mild surprise. 'Thanks.'

She rushed on. 'Look, you already know that I'm on the rebound with Alasdair, and the fact is I still don't know how I feel about him.'

'That's OK. Really.'

'But you should know that I don't regret . . . well, I do wish I hadn't, but . . .'

'Forget it.'

'No, I won't forget it, because I feel privileged that you opened up in the way you did. But I'm just wondering if I was really the right person, what with work and everything.'

'Honestly, that's OK. It was a one-off.' She still didn't look entirely convinced, so he put a twist of resentment in his voice. 'Look, if you remember, I did have my own slight misgivings.'

She blinked hard, as if to force back the embarrassment. 'Of course. Sorry.'

'I'm more worried about you,' he continued, softer now. 'What's the matter?'

She chewed her lip anxiously. 'Do you mind me talking like this? About him?'

'Not at all. So long as you don't mind me keeping out of it, if you know what I mean.'

She groaned with pent-up frustration. 'It's just, he's been calling me constantly, and I've been putting him off, but now the bastard has suddenly gone cold on me, and I'm angry for caring but I'm just wondering if he's seeing someone else.'

'And if he was, what then? You'd want him back even more?'

'No! Believe me, I don't want him back. Maybe I want back what I thought he was. Not who he is, or at least who I think he is. If he's seeing someone now, then I think in the end it's going to help me move on. D'you see?'

'Mmm.' He nodded in what he imagined was the concerned but detached manner of a sensible friend.

'Oh shit, I'm so sorry to pile all this on you.' She dropped a hand on his shoulder, where it lay for a moment. 'Come on, let's forget it and sink a couple after work.'

Hallam's face brightened, but then he made a little tut, as if remembering. 'I can't do that, I'm afraid. I'm seeing Lucy this evening.'

'Oh, of course. Sorry.' Kate suddenly looked embarrassed. 'Oh please, don't think . . . No, I'll shut up.' She turned and went back to her desk in disarray.

He phoned the restaurant. 'Hi, I'm just phoning to check what time dinner's been booked for this evening. The name's Cruickshank. Eight thirty? Of course, thanks, my mind's a sieve. For two, that's right.'

The car park was opposite the restaurant and set back from the road. On the second storey Hallam watched through his Leicas as Alasdair arrived on time. He paused at the glass door then went inside, turning briefly to shut it behind him. He seemed to have a little trouble with the handle because he stood there for a moment and Hallam could not be sure whether he was also taking the opportunity to look out. Either way, he was met by a waiter who showed him to the table, which was, as chance or design would have it, reserved right by the window. Hallam was afforded a perfect view, even if the place filled up. Alasdair sat and fiddled absent-mindedly with a napkin as he waited for the fifteen minutes that it took Lucy to arrive. She had dressed casually for the occasion, trousers as usual, a close-fitting cotton top, hair messy but attended to. They smiled and kissed and Alasdair ordered some wine. It was eight forty-nine. Hallam recorded it in his pocket notebook. He took a couple of photos with the aid of a zoom lens, then he returned to observing the chatting couple through the Leicas. The minutes passed and his terse recordings filled up one page, then two. He noted such details as a hand touching another on the table, the ordering of a second bottle of wine, Lucy going to the ladies.

Yet Hallam realised that he was losing his touch. He had watched the process of seduction many times, usually with disdain for the coyness and clowning, the faux earnestness of the men and the slow cow-like blinks that denoted female encouragement. But now, he could see, his detachment was corrupted by having been through this nightmarish game himself.

He kept having to remind himself that he was watching Alasdair and his sister, not himself and Kate. He felt surges of protectiveness and hatred, envy and a sort of engaged fascination in the outcome of the evening. In comparison to this, the previous encounters he had observed in various corners and apartments of the Old Town were cheap soap opera. There was no entertainment or escapism in this. He both feared and desired a successful outcome.

The couple's conversation beyond the glass window was unimportant. It was in their bodies: Alasdair's bunched back as he stirred his coffee; Lucy's playful toes dangling a shoe under the table; their languid glances towards one another. All of it drew Hallam to one irrefutable conclusion. The plan was working.

Alasdair ordered the bill. Hallam went on ahead and positioned himself on the roof of a tenement across the road from the four-star Ramparts Hotel, a Scottish baronial building halfway down the Royal Mile. Lucy's room was on the third floor. She never skimped with travelling expenses. It was a peculiar expression of pride, Hallam thought, for someone whose job, despite the association with gems, only paid a modest wage. Perhaps Julius had managed to slip her some more cash on her visit – another compelling incentive for reconciliation that, naturally, she had not lowered herself to mention.

As Hallam expected, the couple went directly up to her room, not even pausing to take in a drink at the hotel bar. He reflected sourly that Cambridge had taught Lucy something more sophisticated than playing hard to get. He was trying to fire his resentment of his sister but all he could muster were petty grudges and bitchy observations that in another context might have been almost affectionate. As soon as the light went on she stood at the window for a moment, unwittingly allowing him to frame her with three or four good shots. Then she crouched down to inspect the contents of the mini bar. Alasdair stood near the window too, smiling at something she said. The room couldn't be very big, however swanky the hotel. She sat down out of sight on what must be the bed. Hallam caught him, too, with the zoom, fairly clearly. If only he could get the pair of them together, for a truly incontrovertible image.

Lucy stood up again and sloped over across the window with a couple of small spirit bottles, chatting away nervously, it seemed. She turned to sit down but his hands reached out round her waist and pulled her down on him. She jackknifed and fell backwards out of sight. Hallam saw nothing for a while, just the flash of a bare elbow, then the flick of a blonde bob. He waited.

Six minutes later he saw Alasdair stand up, naked. He held out both hands and pulled Lucy off the bed and into his arms. She was down to her underwear. This was Hallam's opportunity. He took one exposure, then another as they kissed. But then Alasdair suddenly twisted her round. It must have surprised her because he could see a look of vague alarm in her face as he pushed her up against the window, bending her down with one forearm round her waist, and the fingers of his other hand thrust up the nape of her neck.

Either she was in pain or experiencing visceral pleasure. Pleasure, Hallam told himself, shaking, as he took one more shot. But then he stopped as her neck seemed to bend painfully against the windowpane. He let the camera fall from his hands and swing from his neck as he groped for the binoculars and trained them on target. Pain.

Soon afterwards, Lucy was pulled from the window. She flopped out of sight, discarded. Alasdair was left there, panting. After gathering himself together he came right up to the hotel window, his genitals flush but spent, and stood for a moment with a hand on each hairy hip, as if admiring the city observatory against the dark blue sky. He looked invigorated, pleased with himself.

Hallam counted the seconds. One minute fifteen and the naked figure of Lucy flitted behind him on her way to the bathroom, clutching a towel to her front, causing Alasdair to glance round and smile. But then presumably she shut the door behind her, because Alasdair dropped his look of casual satisfaction and became serious. He returned his gaze to the window. He seemed to be staring out intently but no longer at the sky, more in the direction of Hallam, although there was no way that he could be seen from his vantage point. Slowly and deliberately Alasdair nodded.

Alasdair had moved away from the window and was getting dressed, when two small tears fell from behind the Leicas and skimmed Hallam's cheeks. His unblinking gaze was still fixed to the shaking eyepieces even as the yellow-lit window started swimming in his vision. He had found his opposite. They had connected. His obsession had been sated to the point of self-disgust. With Alasdair's assistance, and the letter, everything had changed.

He could leave it all behind now, couldn't he?

He had horrified himself, but there was pride too. He told himself that his business was almost done here, and that a new and even more challenging path was unfurling before him, with an objective that it was his absolute duty to carry through. Hallam had observed all his life. Now, he decided, it was time to act.

Hallam walked into the office at 9:28 a.m. with a satchel under his arm. Kate was looking worried; she had been watching the entrance, waiting for him to come in. He went straight over to her desk.

'Hallam, we've just received some bad news.'

His grin was sickly. 'I bet mine is worse.'

'It's not a joke, Hallam. We've received a writ. About the Carter bequest.'

'That's not news. This is.' He pulled a large brown envelope out of his satchel and dropped it on her desk. 'Go on,' he said.

Kate opened the envelope. She pulled out a sheaf of enlarged photos and began to flip through them. Her frown slowly fell away; her whole face lost animation. Hallam placed the notebook down next, and opened it for her at the relevant pages.

'My observations,' he said, drily. He then delved into his satchel, looking for his letter of resignation.

'Is that . . . ?'

'Alasdair and Lucy. My sister. Indeed.'

Kate put down the photos and hardly bothered to look through the notes. Instead she twisted her chair round to face him. 'This may sound predictable, but why?'

Hallam still couldn't find his letter. 'Don't worry, I don't want anything from you. I wasn't expecting you to forget Alasdair or to fall for me. In that case I'd have sent you those anonymously, although I expect you might have guessed anyway. Whatever. I just wanted you to see that he's wrong for you, that you can leave him behind now. And also . . .' Hallam's voice started to shake, despite his best efforts. 'And also that I'm wrong for you as well; that I'm a pervert. That you should stay away from me.'

'What are you talking about?'

'It doesn't matter. Oh, sod it.' Hallam gave up looking for the letter, which he had carefully worded the night before, and grabbed a pen from Kate's desk. The sudden movement caused her to push herself back in her chair. He noted her repulsion, and felt self-pity blossom as he scrawled

'I RESIGN' across the back of a newsletter. He signed it with a dramatic flourish, then made for the door.

'Where are you going?'

He paused, but did not turn round. 'I'm going home.'

eleven

On his way back to the flat Hallam stopped in at a chemist to buy a bottle of bikini line depilatory cream, the strongest they had. After that he went to a corner shop where he bought a packet of the very cheapest sausages he could find. He was disappointed that none were past their sell-by date, and had to settle instead for an eight-pack of only vaguely suspect economy chipolatas.

At the flat he put his purchases into a black rucksack, along with some dark clothes and his usual abseiling equipment. To these he added a sleeping bag, a groundmat and a water bottle. What else? A screwdriver, some tight leather gloves, a small can of oil. He opened a large drawer and took out his old camo jacket, which lay rolled up in the back. It had stiffened and become moth-eaten after years of neglect, and on reflection Hallam decided to dump it in the rubbish bag; he would buy a new one before catching the train. However, he remembered to take from the jacket's inside pocket the big ring of keys for the Hall. Utility was foremost in his mind on this trip. There was no room for sentiment.

And immediately he was tempted by it. Hallam peered further into the recesses of the drawer and dug out a plastic bag. Carefully he emptied it, and out flopped the old badger pelt. He stroked the slightly balding snout thoughtfully and put it in the rucksack also. It would be his one indulgence.

The phone started to ring. Hallam waited for the answering machine to pick it up. After his scratchy recorded message, Lucy came on the line.

'Hi, Hallam, it's Lucy here. Just tried you at work but someone said you had gone home. Hope you're OK. I thought you might want to know all about my hot date last night. You're right, he is a bit eccentric. Give me a call at the hotel or I'll try you later. 'Byee.'

She sounded sunny, entirely normal; completely divorced, it seemed, from the wrinkled-up face which he had seen pressed against the windowpane of the Ramparts; a face made stupid and brutish by the sexual act. How it degraded people, including himself. Once again Hallam cursed himself for the string of compromises that had arisen out of his obsession with Kate, and he reflected briefly on the repercussions it had had on those around him: his sister's unwitting prostitution for his own ends; Alasdair's discovery of his inner exhibitionist; and Gordon's disinheritance to the tune of one million. His conscience undulated beneath these thoughts but was soon stilled as he threw himself back into the tasks of organising his departure. He washed the dirty dishes and threw his bed linen in the washing machine. He wiped surfaces and scoured scurf. He performed detailed cleaning tasks with cotton-wool buds. Finally he stacked his now voluminous collection of logbooks in the drawer, which he locked then vigorously buffed.

At the front door he looked behind him at the flat he was leaving. He wondered at the mildly pathological behaviour that caused people to tidy and purge their homes before a period of absence: the fear that things left unattended might decay and attract vermin. This was the problem with his life. He had left his past behind without having it scoured and purged. Things had gone bad. His task was to return and put these matters right.

Silently admonishing his gloomy thoughtfulness, a trait which he was increasingly growing to despise in himself as a form of dithering, Hallam drew himself back to business, and action. He did not forget to pick up his binoculars before locking the flat.

He arrived at Leicester train station, the point of his departure half a decade before, in the late afternoon. He stepped onto the platform and walked through the grand Victorian building, past the Barkham Hotel which had not changed, and towards the centre, which had. Developments had sprung up everywhere. He saw a new shopping centre here, fresh roads and flyover there, more prosperity in every direction. He was in his home town; a modestly resurgent provincial city, content with itself, alien.

At the bus station Hallam took the extra precaution of using the main bus route to Melton rather than the rural service which could have taken him through Chanby itself. The single-decker lurched through the traffic until, twenty minutes later, the congestion eased. Hallam jumped off at the large and sprawling village of Cold Satchville, already paranoid that a passing driver might recognise him, although his face would have been unfamiliar to most locals even five years ago, so seldom had he ventured outside the grounds.

He sat in a pub that was just opening its doors to the early-evening punters. He had chosen it specifically for its longstanding local reputation for being both busy and unfriendly. The road it sat on was heavily used by lorries and the passing trade meant that the staff were indifferent to strange faces. He sat in the corner and waited for dusk. He consumed a brick of lasagne and sipped carefully at two pints of anonymous keg lager. His rucksack was stashed unostentatiously behind him, under a table, and was ignored by the few regulars who congregated mainly around the fruit machine and in the poolroom next door.

The banality of the surroundings soothed away Hallam's nerves about re-entering the forbidden territory just a few miles to the west. He briefly considered the situation back in Edinburgh: the prospects of a legal challenge to the bequest, the chances of damaging press coverage, and the exposure of his fictitious CV, which would surely scupper his career in the charity sector. None of it seemed terribly important; indeed he already felt marvellously unfettered sitting in this grotty Leicestershire boozer, and raw freedom conferred beauty even on the manic trill of the fruit machine, on the chipped green ashtray, on the sweep of the fireproof burgundy curtains. These commonplaces were a blessing to him now, a brief respite from this exotic mission whose objective he still doubted he could achieve for reasons both operational and personal. Retribution was still an unfamiliar concept to him, and he shrank from the responsibility, but it was clear. Why else would his mother have written him that letter? It was his right to know the truth, and she had taken the step. She had made no mention of revenge, that was true, but what need was there to give him instructions, unless she thought him a coward? He felt ashamed that he had delayed reading the letter for so long, and for entertaining these doubts.

Noticing that it had grown dark, Hallam slung the rucksack over his shoulder and left the pub.

He took the right turn away from the lights of the main road and up the hill, heading west. Just beyond the last redbrick farmhouse, he jumped over the roadside ditch and shoved his way through a gap in the hedge, and then over a loose barbed-wire fence. A dog barked, and he glanced towards the lights shining from the farmhouse. The barking stopped, he quickly crossed the fallow field, jogging his way in the direction of Chanby. When a car motored by in the opposite direction he lay flat on the grass as an extra precaution; the beams of its headlamps were dispersed by the hedge and only dimly illuminated the undulating field beyond.

He stood up, brushed himself down and was on his way again. He found that he was beginning to enjoy himself; the warmth of exercise coursing through him, the mild southerly climate and the smell of trees on the wind all induced an ambivalent nostalgia for his early youth. He was glad to be back as an adult.

An hour and a half later he paused to rest in a spinney just beyond the outskirts of Rigby, a small hamlet made up of four bunched cottages and a straggling outhouse. It was ten seventeen. He approached Chanby by curving round and coming in from the south, thereby keeping a distance both from the road and the line of houses that marked the beginning of the village. This way he could cross the main street in a patch of relative darkness, and quickly find cover in the meadow at the bottom of the grounds.

Hallam liked being diverted by these practical considerations. However, his excitement was slowly being replaced by a nagging sense of disbelief that he was actually intending to go ahead with his plans. He suppressed it and pushed on, reminding himself to be wary of the closing-time traffic, not that there would be much of it in this sleepy corner of the county. If he was cautious, he reminded himself, he need not commit himself any further than he felt ready to go.

The only serious risk of being seen was from the Pankerton Arms, which popped into view through a stand of dead elms. A crack of light was barely visible, due to the landlord's habit of keeping the curtains tightly drawn to avoid the attention of any police car that might object to lock-ins.

From behind the elms Hallam saw that the pub car park was empty. He knew that he ought to wait another hour to be safe, but now he was so close. Was he imagining it or could he see the dark smudge of the grounds' trees beyond the meadow? He stared into the darkness until his eyes hurt, but the geography of the grounds was indelible in his mind.

Gatewatch to the left, Lower Point away to the right. Their pull was irresistible.

It was then, crouching in a field opposite the old local, that Hallam experienced a second and more profound sense of homecoming. It was not an invigorating rush like the first, but more a sense of context, of remembering that he was the product of a family and a place. He cast his eyes around him. Very little had changed, but there was no reassurance in these familiar surroundings. Hallam preferred the anonymity of the city. The village's sedative atmosphere was to be fought, at all costs.

With cool professionalism he hopped over the barbed-wire fence, crossed the road in ten or eleven steps and vaulted over the wall that marked the Hall's traditional boundary. He lay flat behind it for a few seconds, in what appeared to be dry horseshit. He listened for movement or any sign of having been spotted. Nothing. He was in.

He lifted himself up on one elbow and checked the road both ways. Empty; only the faint hum of traffic accelerating up a far hill. Then, just as he was getting to his feet, he heard footsteps on the pavement, emerging from round the corner.

Quickly Hallam dropped down against the wall. It had been built over a hundred years ago without mortar, according to the local custom, and the bricks bulged out precariously over the pavement. To his horror it seemed to totter from the impact of his rucksack and shoulder. Hallam put his hands over his head. The wall steadied. He breathed again.

The footsteps came closer, heavy, plodding, as if snow-clad. They were drunks returning home on automatic, Hallam concluded, a theory backed up by the lugubrious silence that had at first unnerved him slightly. The patter of a small dog's paws could also be heard. A loud belch resonated only feet away.

'That would be a sigh in Pig City,' observed one of them. The county's elastic vowels pulled Hallam straight back to seventeen.

'You what?' The voice sloppy, content.

'A saying of my uncle's. Get your nose out of it, Reg.'

Hallam prayed that Reg had not detected the economy chipolatas, but the dog owner's impatience saved him. Reg was dragged away with a hoarse gasp and the scrape of claws on asphalt.

Hallam waited for their footsteps to fade and then allowed himself to peer over the wall at the two departing pedestrians, who were heading for the small housing estate further along. When they had disappeared out of sight, he at last made his way up the meadow, passing close by the spot that Jenny had once frequented, but which now lay empty. Hallam smiled faintly at the memory of all the logbook entries that these few square feet of cover had spawned, then he looked up. There: he could see the trees clearly now, he could even hear the breeze in the upper branches of Lower Point.

He climbed over a second barbed-wire fence and swiftly strode up the public footpath, confident that he would not meet anyone coming the other way at this time. On his left he noticed how the hedge that bordered the Hall's bottom lawns had grown still higher and thicker, and that a wooden fence had been installed to prevent anyone on the path from seeing in. There was graffiti on the slats.

At the top of the path he emerged beside the war memorial, facing the cemetery. In the centre of it, Chanby parish church continued to prod its stump at the sky. The question was how to get up there. He quickly scouted the cemetery. It was empty, quiet and clean; not even a beer can in sight. He went straight to the church entrance and tried the thick oak door. The heavy circular iron handle would not budge: it was locked, as he had expected. He would have to scale the wall, despite the backpack, which was a heavier load than he usually contended with.

Returning to the tower end of the church, he looked up, hands on hips. The copper lightning rod ran up to the weather vane, passing a gargoyle through whose gaping mouth he could see a smudge of the night sky. That was no help. He could either try and lasso one of the crenellations on the first tier of the roof or attempt the lead drainpipe on the near side. He opted for the former; the pipe looked too spindly for comfort.

He aimed for a crenellation near the buttress, so that the rope would be hanging in deep shadow if anyone walked past. He tied his end of the rope to the rucksack and climbed up. Once he was on the roof he pulled the rucksack up behind him, keeping a close eye all the time on the cemetery gate that led onto the estate's main road.

He then climbed to the ridge of the church roof and used the same method to scale the square tower. He pulled the rucksack up over the low wall and placed it against the base of the steeple. There was about a foot of space: just enough to lie on out of sight. He thought about organising his things in preparation for a night's sleep, but he could not resist the temptation to take a preliminary look at the grounds. Slithering back down the rope he loped off along the Hall's private path and disappeared into the shadows of the trees.

He opened the gate cautiously to ensure that it did not creak, for despite being surrounded by shrubbery, Hallam was aware how far the noise could carry – conceivably up to the master bedroom where Verity and Julius night already be sleeping. He padded past the towering wellingtonia with its shabby thatch of drooping branches, towards the stables. All this was the same too. He backed into the narrow passageway between the stables and cottage; carefully checking the windows at the back of the Hall for light. There was none. The moment was approaching: his first view of the lakeland.

Hallam stepped softly, yet he could hear the echoes of his feet and heart as he came to the passageway's arched mouth. Then he stood, forgot all good intentions of stealth, and gaped.

What lay in front of him was a large building site. This he had been prepared for. But in the middle of the mud, cement-mixers and concrete foundations stood an outlandish edifice: a huge metal mast shaped like a V, with two satellite dishes adorning each finger. As the clouds slid by above, dim moonshine fell upon the obscenely defiant instalment, causing its dishes to glint like knuckle-dusters.

The contraption took Hallam's breath away. It was beyond offensive. He stepped forward as if on stilts and began to take in the devastation surrounding it: the shimmer of windows in a long wide pit, some kind of environmentally friendly burrow he supposed – what the papers had called Hobbitland all those years ago. Around the edges of the site were a few freshly planted conifers. And to the right, where the long grass and lakes had once spread to the horizon under the shadow of Centre Point, was an expanse of nothing. Flat, uninterrupted turf on a gentle, sterile incline.

Hallam's stunned gaze returned inevitably to the twenty-foot V. He moved his feet slightly, making a soft sucking noise in the mud, and simultaneously a large piece of board covering a ditch some few feet in front of him suddenly rose up and disgorged a black-clad figure who pelted across the mud and leapt at him.

The figure's shoulder rammed Hallam straight in the solar plexus and sent him flying backwards. He hit the ground with jarring force. His assailant gripped him tightly round the waist.

Hallam struggled to breathe as a rough-palmed hand grabbed him by the throat and a heavy pair of knees pinned down his arms. Looking up through his watering eyes he could see a fist raised up to strike and he tried in vain to twist away. Violent assault was so intimate, Hallam reflected in that long, slow moment as he prepared for impact. And not even an introduction.

Half a second passed and his nasal septum was still intact. Another half-second.

'Who are you then?'

Hallam writhed again but he was well and truly pinned. He looked up at the face of the man, who was wearing a woolly hat and an almost comical look of surprise.

'Hallam?' the man said.

'Carl.' Hallam coughed and gasped. 'Good evening to you.'

'Nobody told me you were coming back.'

'Get off me.'

Carl rolled off him and stood up, confused and embarrassed.

'Nobody told you,' said Hallam with difficulty, clutching his guts and trying to sit up, 'because nobody knows.'

The two of them sat and drank in turn from Carl's thermos of sweet tea, regarding the satellite mast.

'Your father calls it the Salute,' explained Carl, 'but for the record it's meant to provide the underground village with a satellite signal when the residents eventually move in. If there ever are any.'

'Why did he have to make it so big?'

'A practical work of art is what he calls it. In fact it's to wind up the locals who opposed the development. There's no planning permission for it. He'll have to pull it down, I expect.'

'Since when has he been into art?'

Carl shrugged. 'Modernism and progress defying conservative backward thinking,' he said, the neutral monotone suggesting that it was a quotation from his employer.

Hallam sucked in his breath. 'You must love it.'

'The clever bit supposedly is that apparently the two-fingered gesture originated with English archers who taunted the French knights at Agincourt and Crécy with it. Because if the archers were ever caught, the French would cut off those two fingers so they wouldn't be able to pull back a bowstring again.' Carl took a slurp of tea. 'Funny stance for a landowner to take, isn't it, but there you go.'

'Has there been a lot of trouble about this development, then?'

'It hasn't stopped. Ever since . . .' Carl hesitated. 'Ever since you went away, there have been kids coming in here, vandalising the site, nicking stuff; they even took to smashing up the plants and spraying graffiti. It was the townies to begin with, the ones that demonstrated, anyway, but there's locals too. They've changed the locks up at the Hall. A bit paranoid, if you ask me. It's only teenagers.'

'Have you been sitting in that ditch all night waiting to ambush someone?'

Carl shrugged. 'There's one little bugger in particular I'm after. I've got my suspicions who it is. Anyway, I've made it quite comfy down there. Nice to have a bit of peace and quiet.'

'Have you got a girlfriend?' asked Hallam.

'No, mate. Married.'

Hallam threw his head back and cackled. 'Don't tell me — Jenny!'

Carl's face shut down. 'That's right, and you'd better watch your mouth.'

Hallam's grin faded into incredulity and then something more respectful. 'Sorry, Carl, I didn't mean—'

'That's all right,' Carl quickly interrupted. 'Just . . . leave it.'

'Right. So she forgave you then?'

Carl raised his voice. 'I said, leave it.'

'Kids?'

Carl scowled. 'Not yet, she doesn't want them. What are you doing back here then? Visiting the folks?'

'Not exactly. Like I said, Carl, they don't know I dropped by, and I don't want you to mention it.'

'I'm sure they won't ask. Where are you staying?'

'Nearby.'

'For how long?'

Hallam shrugged and scratched his ear. 'I take it Verity and Julius are in at the moment.'

'They hardly leave, in case the neighbours get up to something. I'm on full alert when they're out, like tomorrow morning. She's off to the hairdresser's and he's got an appointment with the council. Julius said if there's any surveyors or other officials turn up then I'm to phone him on his mobile right away. He's paranoid they're going to send people in to tear the mast down.'

'Does he still have the same secretary?'

'No, Nicola left years ago now. They've had a few since.'

'That'll be Verity.'

'I wouldn't know,' muttered Carl, discreet as ever. He tossed away his tea and got up. 'Well, I'm off. It seems pretty quiet tonight. What are you up to?'

Hallam glanced up the hill. 'I might take a wander around.'

'You'll not find much up there. Yet.'

Hallam didn't want to think about it any more tonight. 'Night, Carl.'

Carl tightened his thermos then stopped and faced up to Hallam. 'You probably know what they were saying about the spiking of that tree. It wasn't you, was it?'

'Thanks for not assuming, Carl.' Hallam wasn't answering any more questions.

'You're up to something. I can feel it off you.'

'Nothing that will affect you.'

'It's the grounds I care about. Your dad's big ideas, they're all right, but me, I believe in stewardship. Looking after what's there. Your grandad, for instance, he only bought this place after the war for the lead piping. Knocked down two wings and a whole floor for it. But he did it responsibly, for a scrap merchant. It was all ugly Victorian additions he got rid of, and now it's back to its original Queen Anne shape. That's all right, that's got style. In fact, that's what I'm interested in doing with these grounds. I know you might hate me for this, but I reckon they were right to get rid of those lakes. They were too far gone. And that oak, it was coming down sooner or later anyway. Sometimes you have to let go.'

'Thanks for the bracing folk wisdom, Carl.' Hallam's voice was cold. 'Send my regards to the wife.'

Carl scowled. 'Don't do anything stupid, Hallam.' With that he turned and trudged away down the back drive.

Hallam sneered briefly, then turned and looked up the desolate incline. Carl wouldn't volunteer anything to Julius about him being here. Far too loyal, that man.

* * *

Hallam woke up with the dawn and his first sight on opening his eyes was the church's ancient sandstone masonry just a few inches from his nose. He closed his eyes again and shifted his weight off his shoulder, which must have been bruised last night by Carl. Still, not too uncomfortable. The low wall had sheltered him from the chilly breeze, and he'd only woken up once in the night, during a very light shower. He stretched out and smiled.

He felt privileged to be lying here at the base of the stump, almost certainly the first person to have slept here in all the building's five or six hundred years. He rolled round in his sleeping bag under the tarpaulin and hitched up the groundmat. He patted down the rucksack to make it a more comfortable pillow, then lay on his back to face the light blue sky which was being traversed by plump, unthreatening clouds. He breathed in the moist clean air of early morning and listened to the birds. Their calls soothed him, reminding him of summer days in Centre Point, and he dozed again until the first audible coo of one of Verity's doves, which immediately caused him to tense, as if woken by an alarm clock.

Hallam checked his watch; it was seven fifteen. He reached into the rucksack and fished out his Leicas. Moving over to the wall, he swept the larger part of the front lawns, the east side of the Hall and the visible stretch of the drive as well.

He pulled out his logbook and pen. Although he was aware that a documentary record of the next few days might conceivably present legal hazards in months to come, he decided that posterity demanded some kind of testimony. Slipping the notebook in a pocket, he pulled on his new camo jacket, gathered up the equipment he would be needing today (let's see now, rancid-smelling chipolatas, depilatory cream, balaclava, gloves, oil can, mobile phone, Hall keys) and dropped down onto the roof, and from there to the ground below.

7:46 Builders arrive in lorry.
7:55 Carl arrives in same old Astra.
8:23 Builders start work (the drill).
8:36 Verity (first sighting, hair still long, for now) + Carl at top lawn; discussion of herbaceous border.
8:49 Small car arrives. Secretary? Old, frumpish. V's choice?

Two pages later:

3:15 Dark blue Jaguar (Julius) leaves.
3:48 Carl mowing bottom lawn (foul mood).
4:06 Verity leaves. Hair appointment? (silver BMW, new model).

Hallam was positioned in the shrubbery below Gatewatch as the BMW disappeared, with Verity's trademark solo blink of the indicator. Hallam noticed that Gatewatch, along with all the other lookout posts had been liberated of the platforms and treehouses. Still, at least the trees had survived. Hallam wondered if Verity would have simply car-parked the whole grounds by now were it not for Carl. With that bitter and quite possibly unreasonable thought, he took out his mobile phone and waited for Carl to make his pass in the tractor mower before he dialled the number of the florist in Cold Satchville.

'Good morning,' said Hallam. 'I wonder if you could make a delivery within the next hour, to Chanby Hall in Chanby? You could? Excellent. How much can I get for two hundred pounds? Is a credit card OK? And the sender's name is absolutely confidential? Excellent. Lilies. Can you also include a message. It goes as follows: from a secret admirer, with love.'

His next problem was access to the Hall itself. Carl's news that the locks had been changed was a major worry, but there was one access point Hallam guessed they might have overlooked. The first thing was to reach the Hall without being spotted by Carl, who had probably chosen to mow the front lawns this afternoon specifically so he could keep an eye on the drive. Hallam was pinned down until he took a break.

It took Carl a further forty-three minutes to fill the trailer with grass cuttings, by which time Hallam was beginning to worry that Verity or Julius might return and ruin all his plans. He could dodge the secretary, who was unlikely to stray far from the office orangery, but the risks rose exponentially if anyone else was inside.

At last Carl hefted the grass bucket to the trailer and emptied it onto the conical mound of grass cuttings, then flattened it down with large circular motions of his hands. There was love in those movements.

He hopped onto the mini tractor and towed away the trailer towards the compost heap at the back, leaving a fine cloud of green and brown fragments that tumbled through the grey diesel fumes. Hallam sniffed long and haltingly. It was the smell of the early days.

But this was his chance. He put on his black balaclava and thin leather gloves to avoid fingerprints or detection if security cameras were about – although in truth he rather liked the SAS chic of it. Once Carl was away round the curve of the drive, Hallam made his dash, sprinting past the driveside lamps, three, four, five, going from rhododendron bush to detested rhododendron bush – how they'd flourished. He trotted round the front, reassured by the fading sound of the tractor but still feeling exposed as he went by the Hall's main door. He hung back at the corner, checking in case the secretary was about. Her car was parked there at the back, alongside Carl's. Hallam was shaking. He was so close; the power of the place was bearing down on him.

There was the metal lid to the old coal chute, with the same padlock still attached. Glancing all around him, Hallam ran up to it and made a quick inspection; it was spotted with rust, but he was counting on the internal mechanism still working.

He pulled out the can of oil that he kept with him for stubborn locks in Edinburgh tenements, and squirted some inside. Then he pulled out the keys, quickly selected a Chubb and with shaking hands tried it. It wouldn't fit. Try another. Not that one either. He glanced behind him, trying to suppress the first intimations of real fear. How many minutes before Carl came back? Four, five? He tried another, it got halfway in and then seemed to jam. He thrust it further inside. Hallam thought he could hear the tractor engine coming. Hadn't Carl even taken a cigarette break? What kind of fool enjoyed his job like that?

Hallam wiggled the key furiously and at last it slid home. He turned it and the lock opened. Flushing with relief, he tore off the padlock and shoved it in his pocket. The tractor was coming closer. He stuck his fingers underneath the lid and pulled. And pulled again. It creaked. The back door of the Hall opened. Disaster: the secretary.

With the full force of panic, Hallam dragged up the lid and squeezed himself feet first into the blackness, pulling the rucksack with him. His jacket snagged on the lid. He heard the Hall's telephone ring, a woman's soft curse and the door shut again. He scrambled on the chute, his plimsolls briefly gaining purchase, long enough for him to free his jacket and lower the lid above his head. Hallam glimpsed the red smear of the tractor on its return journey just as his rubber-soled toes slipped on the dusty chute and he went rolling down with an ominous rumble into the bowels of the Hall.

He dropped out of the chute feet first but landed jarringly on his backside on a low mound of coal. He lay still for a moment and allowed himself a groan of pain, then shifted, causing the coal to crunch, and rubbed his coccyx. He paused again, listening for any sound from above that might suggest the secretary or someone else had heard anything. Nothing, or so it seemed.

It was almost entirely dark in the cellar, and cold, but he remembered its layout well enough. He groped for the rucksack and found the torch. The thin strong beam revealed the cellar pretty much as he had seen it five years before. Brickwork blackened by dust, with the far section of the cellar separated by iron bars, behind which loomed Julius's collection of wines and ports, some of which had allegedly been laid down for Hallam's twenty-first birthday. Hallam got up and tried the gate. It creaked open. Careless, thought Hallam, very careless. He could liberate some of his inheritance later.

He began stealthily to climb the narrow stone steps that led, he remembered, to a small room adjoining the main hallway. But then he stopped and flicked the torch beam over himself. He was coated in coal dust. He would leave a ridiculously obvious trail.

There was only one thing for it. He mounted the top step and tried the door, which was locked. He selected a key from the ring. It fitted, but inserting it prodded out another key which fell and tinkled to the floor on the other side. He waited. He opened the door and rotated a glance, slow, measured. At that moment a loud bell went off – a long jangling note from the other side of the wall, so close that he could hear the judder of the electric motor beneath the ring. He snapped the door shut only to realise: of course, the doorbell. It had to be loud to be heard from all corners of the sound-absorbing Hall. The flowers must have arrived.

Re-opening the door a crack, Hallam listened to the secretary as she went to the door and opened it. A brief conversation, a gasp of admiration, a laugh and then the approach of two sets of footsteps.

'Why don't you put those there, on the table. And those? Over there for now.'

'There's more to come,' said the man.

Hallam began to undress, keeping an ear trained on their progress. By the time he was down to his underpants, socks and balaclava, the delivery was completed. He heard the florist's van reverse and drive away. While he waited for the secretary to return to work in the office, Hallam took out the necessary equipment from his rucksack. He placed the screwdriver on the tiled floor alongside the depilatory cream and rancid chipolatas, which were now discoloured and slippery in their transparent plastic packaging.

One sock off, then the other, and he stepped carefully into the Hall proper. The chilly tiles sent goose pimples up his thighs. Last of all, he pulled off the balaclava and gloves. These he placed on the dusty pile of clothes just within the cellar door, which he then softly shut. He picked up his equipment and tiptoed in his pants to the hallway.

He glanced left and right, but the secretary was talking away on the phone. Praying that the alarm system was not active in the rest of the house, he sashayed with elegant haste through pots and buckets of white lilies, red roses too, some thorns just lightly grazing him as he hopped off the floorboards and up the broad carpeted stairs. He couldn't stop himself from sniggering at the thought of what havoc those pollen-spewing flowers would play with Verity's allergy.

At the top he looked around in surprise at the entirely new decor: the striped French upholstery; the patterned turquoise wallpaper; what looked like eighteenth-century cupboards – all of it incredibly expensive and, in Hallam's eyes hideous. Thank God he had taken off his clothes; every footstep would have indelibly marked the plush pale carpets. It was as if Verity had mummified the Hall of his memory in silks and ribbons and plump settees. On he went, heading directly for the master bedroom and, more specifically, the en suite bathroom.

Verity had surpassed herself in the bedroom. It was an orgy of cushions and flouncy pillow covers, dominated – naturally – by a large mahogany four-poster bed. Hallam had always been surprised that a woman of her reserved character (and he knew what reserves) should be so lush and velvety with her interiors. Perhaps this was because his imagination stopped short of her interior life, although it did seem logical that she had one. There was calculation, of course, and sex. But the rest? Conscience? A past? Hallam realised that he knew virtually nothing about her past.

He saw a large ceramic tray on the dresser, which contained spare sets of keys. Hallam looked quickly through them – keys were always useful – and dug out one on a Jaguar keyring. On to the bathroom, where a large cast-iron bath stood in a corner of the whitewashed wooden floor, flanked on all sides by full-length mirrors.

In these mirrors Hallam saw his own reflection from top to bony bottom. His eyes and wrists were encircled by black coal dust which had found its way in through the balaclava's eyeholes and between his cuffs and gloves. Together with his scrawny body, clad only in discoloured white pants, he resembled something pitiful and half-starved; a skunk perhaps.

Hallam suppressed his doubts by concentrating on the job in hand. He found two shampoo bottles, one with a matching conditioner. The first was a standard brand – Julius's, he presumed – and the other a dermatologically tested, studio-developed, probably super-expensive hair cleanser which could only be Verity's. Everybody has a physical focus for their vanity and hers were those thick, soft locks.

The bottle of conditioner was nearly full. Hallam unscrewed the top and poured about one-third of the transparent, lightly-fragranced contents away down the basin. Then, with scientific delicacy, he flipped open the depilatory cream and transferred the same amount to the conditioner bottle. The consistency of the liquids did not exactly match, but it would do. Hallam rescrewed the bottle and shook it, before placing it back in its position beside the bath.

Next for the shower rail. This was the more difficult and time-consuming job but Hallam considered it worth the trouble. For it was, in his opinion, the most ingenious and subtle of the plagues he was arranging. First he opened the sausage packet, which gave off the rich sweet odour of rotting offal. Taking up the screwdriver, he climbed up on the sides of the bath and began to unscrew one end of the shower rail from the wall.

This did not take long. In fact one screw came loose more quickly than he expected and it dropped down into the bathtub, rattling down towards the plughole. He got his foot in the way just in time. Letting out a jittery sigh he retrieved the screw and then took up the chipolatas. One by one, grimacing, he fed the slimy suppositories into the end of the shower rail, poking them along with the aid of the screwdriver. A bit of steam from the bath or shower would really get them honking. Hallam had picked up this idea from an irresponsible internet site during an idle hour at work. The author had suggested prawns but Hallam, unable to resist a personal touch, had slightly amended the recipe. He grinned with satisfaction as he began to screw the rail back into position.

A car's wheels scraped to a halt on the gravel outside. He tensed. Surely that couldn't be Verity; not yet. He ran to the window. It was. He could see the high-slung silver rear of the BMW down below.

Once again, panic coursed through his limbs, but he had to finish the job. There was still time. She would be occupied with the flowers for a start, he hoped. He jumped back up onto the side of the bath and tightened the last screw, just as the first scream of outrage echoed up from downstairs. Goose pimples rose all over Hallam's exposed skin as he scooped up his equipment and made for the door, pausing only to look back and check that he had not forgotten anything. He tiptoed to the bedroom door to hear what was going on downstairs and assess his options for escape.

He heard the fury in Verity's stamping footsteps downstairs as she raged at the secretary. 'You stupid woman, how could you let someone bring these flowers into the house?'

'But I don't see the problem.'

'My allergy! Didn't Julius tell you?'

'Verity, believe me, I had no idea—'

'Get them out! Right now! Get Carl, why didn't he say anything? Christ,' she groaned, 'it's coming on already.' Hallam heard her panting experimentally, followed by the hiss of an asthma inhaler, then the back door opened and Verity fled outside.

More footsteps clip-clopped rapidly down the hallway accompanied by the rustle of flowers being carried out by the armful towards the back door. The process was repeated for over three minutes while Hallam looked round desperately for somewhere he could hide, in case Verity took refuge upstairs. He heard Carl's voice by the back door now, trying to calm her down.

'Who would have sent them?' she cried. 'Who would do this?'

'Is there a card or something?' asked Carl.

'I don't know. Go and look.'

Hallam heard Carl's footsteps circle the hallway. Then they stopped, before heading hastily back outside. Hallam crept to the top of the stairs. Perhaps if he made a dash through the front door . . .

'Are they all out?' he heard Verity ask at the door.

'Yes,' said the secretary.

'Have you opened all the windows downstairs?'

'I'll do that now.'

'I'm going upstairs. You didn't put any upstairs, did you?'

'No.'

A moan and three puffs of the inhaler. 'I've got to lie down.'

Hallam retreated to the bedroom. Where should he go? Where could he hide? All the doors to the other rooms were shut, apart from her bedroom, and he had barely ten seconds to make a decision. What if the other doors were locked, or if they creaked? What if she checked for more flowers? She was coming up the stairs. There was only one thing for it. The bathroom cupboards.

Hallam skidded back into the master bedroom, dropped the depilatory cream, picked it up again and ran through to the bathroom, the equipment crushed to his bare chest. With his free hand he opened the first full-length cupboard. It was filled with drawers. No good.

He heard Verity reach the top of the stairs.

He tried the second. It was filled with shelves laden with unguents, bath crystals and soaps. No good. He tried the third. He heard Verity enter the bedroom. A clothes rail containing a couple of light dressing gowns and a Japanese kimono. Hallam stepped in and reached out for the cupboard door. The cream slipped from his grasp again. He managed to catch it between his knees and in this comic pose sank into a crouch and softly shut himself in. A moment later he heard Verity bustle into the bathroom.

A silence. Had she noticed something? The smell, perhaps, or some smudges of coal dust on the cupboard mirror? Had he forgotten the sausage wrapping? No, it was here in his hands, greasy, the sweet stench filling the stuffy confines of his hiding place.

He heard a sigh, then a vigorous scraping sound which he realised was Verity brushing her hair. Vanity even in the midst of crisis. Perhaps she sought to calm herself, perhaps it helped her think. Then there was the clunk of the toilet seat going down. The hiss of tights and knickers on a brisk descent. Oh no, Hallam thought, I don't want to hear this.

A second later he heard the quiet piddle of urine in the pan. It sounded so vulnerable; how completely at odds this private human function was with the iconic status that he had given her – his inverted mother figure, his nemesis. Right now she was nothing more than a woman sitting on a toilet, her guard utterly down.

He then realised why he was here. His desire to kill Verity had always been present, among the crowd of hopeless desires that had filled his hours in Edinburgh, but he had never thought to single it out until now. Since he no longer sanctioned denial, what was stopping him? Civilisation? He thought back five years to the teenagers gathered around the display cabinet of combat knives in Leicester's army surplus store, and began to understand the nature of their fascination.

In the gloom of the cupboard Hallam's knuckles whitened experimentally round the screwdriver. What if he burst out of the cupboard right now and punctured that little taut stretch of skin between her eyes with the point of the tool? Wasn't that what he was here to do? To act, to kill?

It had all the deadly symmetry that he could desire. His years had been spent outside real life, and he had been exiled from it by this woman. It was she who had condemned him to be an observer. This would be his triumphant return to the world of participation; breaking back into life again, at the expense of hers. Wasn't that what he wanted?

No. It was not just about personal grievance, it was on behalf of the dead. He must do it for the right reasons, without undue emotion, in the rational manner of a legal execution, and at the appointed time. Retribution. Yes, that was the word he had chosen.

Verity blew her nose with a painful sob. The toilet flushed. A rush of water in the basin and then she went out. Her footsteps passed along the landing towards the stairwell, and then down. Hallam's body relaxed by a degree, and then another. It was too late to kill her now. But also, he reflected, too soon.

'You're fired!' he heard Verity scream downstairs, followed by a sneeze. 'Now get out!'

His immediate concern was to escape without detection. The roof? He could wait until nightfall, and come down a drainpipe. But then he remembered that he would have to retrieve his clothing on the cellar steps or run the risk of Julius discovering them on his way to get some wine. He couldn't leave evidence like that lying around.

Amid the salvoes of calculation, Hallam's fretting suddenly fell silent. He realised that his escape could be perfectly simple. He waited until he heard Verity go outside, then he calmly stepped out of the cupboard, paraded the length of the landing, and strolled down the stairs with perfect self-assurance. Like a duchess, he thought triumphantly. It was a precious moment, that leisurely descent in his underpants while just down the hall he could hear the secretary packing up her belongings, and the sound of Verity outside, berating Carl in a totally unjustified manner for not having intercepted the flower delivery van.

Hallam felt exhausted but placid. He had the same sensation of utter confidence that he had experienced that night he visited Alasdair's bedroom. He was now intimately re-acquainted with his subject, and with that his talent for being invisible had returned. He had regained the Hall.

He did not hurry to reach the cellar steps although he was only seconds away from being discovered by Verity, who came stamping through on her way back upstairs, snuffling and gasping with the onset of her allergy. He softly shut the cellar door behind him and put his clothes back on, warmed by the thought that there was so much more fun to come.

He settled down in the cellar to wait until nightfall. His self-confidence did not extend as far as risking detection from Carl in broad daylight, now that he had been put on full alert. He was in no hurry and, besides, he quite liked it down here, despite the cold. It made a change to be underneath his subjects for once.

He decided to select a bottle from his father's rack. But which one? As usual he fell back on the dictates of his superstitious lexicon. With the aid of his torch he counted eleven rows along, eight up and pulled out what looked like a rather smart bottle of Cabernet Sauvignon. It seemed a little too chilled in his hands, but if his father's taste in wine was as pernickity as he remembered it, the vintage was likely to be superb. He pushed the cork through with the screwdriver, taking pleasure from the thought of how much this would annoy his father were he here to see it. Then he raised the bottle and silently toasted himself and the success of the first phase of the operation.

twelve

Hallam had scooped out a primitive recliner in the pile of coal and was approaching the bottom of the bottle by the time he heard Julius return. His father must have had other business in town, being back this late. He went straight upstairs to see his wife who had, Hallam guessed, already gone to bed.

Now was the perfect opportunity. Hallam took one last pull on the bottle and got a mouthful of dregs. Gagging, he tossed the bottle away in disgust, and it skittered across the coals before hitting the wall with a tinkle of breaking glass.

'Arse,' said Hallam, and spat. Still, they wouldn't have heard that upstairs. He got up with difficulty and grabbed his rucksack, then fixed his unsteady gaze – now accustomed to the dark however – on the chute. Than he had a thought. He returned to the wine rack and picked at random another bottle, which he put in the rucksack for later.

Now he was ready. Scrambling over the coal, he put one foot on the lip of the chute and searched for a handhold. Not so easy getting back up.

'Shite.'

He took a couple of steps back on the coal pile and attempted a run-up. As a mounting procedure it should have been a dismal failure, but somehow his drunken lunge enabled his tough fingertips to find purchase on a welded joint. With his nose painfully pressed against the dusty metal, arms at full stretch and knees painfully lodged against the sides, he managed to inch a leg up and wedge himself in. Slowly he pulled himself up, the rucksack causing much inconvenience, until eventually he was able to open the chute's metal lid and taste fresh air.

He flopped onto the concrete, panting from the exertion, and let the lid down softly. He remembered to replace the padlock before deciding to return indirectly to the church via the front lawns, for fear of passing the back door, where he knew a security light would be activated by any movement. He went by the dustbins and caught a whiff of fresh flowers. The stem of one red rose hung out forlornly from one of the bins.

Passing through the trees on the drive, he looked up at the front of the Hall and saw the shadow of his father in the master bedroom, through a gap in the shutters. Hallam groggily pondered the great myth of privacy, threw up one arm in a grandiose manner and then let out a thunderous belch that might have passed for a sigh in Pig City but was louder than he had anticipated. This was immediately followed by a short but distinct shuffle from the shrubbery not far away.

Had he imagined that? Hallam sank back into the shadows of the nearest tree as swiftly as he could manage, and waited. Nothing. Very slowly, he backed himself against the tree trunk, looking all around him. More nothing. He could reach the path to the church now without any difficulty but the risk of being spotted was too high, and he might lead Carl – or whoever it was in that bush – to discover the centre of operations.

But surely it couldn't be Carl. He would never be so stupid as to let himself be heard when he was staked out under cover. It had to be someone else. Hold on, thought Hallam, perhaps it was one of the local vandals. Of course! Filled with supreme confidence, Hallam strode across the lawn and stood right by the large shrub. He thought he could see a pair of feet inside it.

'Hello?' whispered Hallam in as unthreatening a manner as he could. There was no answer. He tugged one of the bigger branches like a bell pull. 'Anybody in? It's only me.'

A tiny rustle, then an adolescent's curse and the sounds of a scuffle.

'Who's me?' came a tight little whisper from the shrub.

'Hallam Foe.'

'Fuck!' The crash of branches being fought through and a small figure burst out, heading for the drive.

'No, you've got it wrong,' shouted Hallam as quietly as he could. 'I'm on your side.'

A second figure broke out of the shrubbery, but hesitated. It turned out to be a boy of about fourteen. Hallam tried to smile reassuringly.

'Are you the lad from the lake?' the boy asked.

Hallam thought about this. 'I suppose so, yes.'

The boy nodded in the direction of his companion, currently hovering by the gate. 'It was his older brother that saw you in there. He was on a dare. Nobody had the guts to go back for ages, until us.'

Hallam remembered, all those years ago, the figure fleeing across the fields as he had pulled himself out of the lake.

'Is it true you eat road-kills?'

'No.'

There was an uncomfortable pause. The boy's companion waved to him urgently.

'Right, I'm off.'

Hallam thought about asking him to keep this quiet, but there did not seem to be much point. The boy jogged away. Hallam looked back at the windows of the Hall, then slipped away himself, mindful that Carl or Julius could have been drawn by the noise. He would have to get a move on.

Hallam opened his eyes and fought his way out of his sleeping bag, reaching just short of the low wall. He emptied the meagre contents of his stomach into the rain gutter in three wine-reddened heaves. As he slumped onto his side, gasping, he heard his vomit begin to drip onto the path from the gaping mouth of the gargoyle.

He pulled the second empty wine bottle from under his back, where he had let it roll late last night. Maybe the extended nightcap hadn't been such a good idea. He opened his weeping eyes and looked up at the sky, which was grey with a solid and seemingly immobile block of cloud. He groaned, shifted his foul tongue around his mouth, and wished that he had remembered to fill up the water bottle. His bladder was uncomfortably heavy with urine, so he got on his knees and began to piss away the streaks of sick from the rain gutter, causing the gargoyle to emit a further stream of even more disgusting waste.

He crawled back to his sleeping bag and had just wearily wriggled back inside when he heard the creak of a gate from the estate side of the cemetery, followed by approaching footsteps. Peering carefully down, Hallam saw the vicar on her way to unlock the church. He prayed that she would not notice the puddle of vomit and piss on the path and then look up to see the slaver dripping from the gargoyle's lower lip.

As it happened she did not. She stopped to pick up a few stray pieces of litter from the grass and then passed out of his sight into the main entrance. Hallam heard the heavy lock being turned and the oak door swing open, at which point he noticed movement on the Hall's drive. A red van on its way up – the emergency plumber! Presumably he had been called to check the drains. The chipolatas were doing their job already.

If all went to plan and the smell in the bathroom continued to worsen, Julius would perhaps call someone in to check under the floorboards for the source of the stench. Pest control would be summoned, on the lookout for rats or similar rotting vermin. And ultimately, as the stench crept into their bedroom where Verity might still be laid up with her allergy, they could conceivably be forced to call in the vicar and attempt an exorcism. Tee hee.

Until the sausages were discovered, however, there would be no firm evidence that she was being persecuted. The mystery of these serial misfortunes would provide a valuable psychological dimension. Hallam wondered whether Verity had washed her hair yet.

Once the vicar had gone on her way again, Hallam started to feel better. It occurred to him that he might check his telephone answering service. Making himself more comfortable against the rucksack, he turned on his mobile phone and tapped in the number. The first one was from Lucy, sounding impatient.

'Hallam, where are you? Give me a ring as soon as you get this. 'Bye.'

The second was from Kate.

'Hallam, what the fuck did you think you were doing? I sincerely hope you weren't trying to impress me. You need to call me, Hallam, we've got to deal with this, not least the work situation. You can't just walk away. And besides, what about me, you son of a bitch? Call me. Now.'

This call provided shallow amusement for Hallam now: all of this chaos was happening in another world. The next call, from Lucy, sounded more panicked.

'What's going on here, Hallam? Where are you? I've just tried to talk to Kate, but she was being very weird. She doesn't seem to have a clue where you are. Look, I'm sorry about some of the stuff that was said that night, don't take it too hard. And for God's sake, don't go and do something stupid. I'm going to try work again. I love you. Please call me.'

He snorted at the cutesy declaration of attachment. Next. Surprise,

surprise, it was Kate again. He could tell this immediately from the short sigh of self-restraint that began the message.

'Hallam, I really need your help on this Carter matter. I really believe we can sort it out, so long as you call me soon. Also, I want you to know that . . . that I want to hear your voice telling me that you're OK. Please. Call me anytime. Lots of love.'

Hmm. More rational-sounding, this one, even an attempt to appear as if she cared about him. She must be getting desperate. Hallam wondered what sort of conference Lucy and Kate had had together; what had been revealed, what temporary grievance-bedevilled alliance they may have hammered out. Lucy must have greater powers of charm than he had given her credit for if Kate had managed to forgive her the many disturbing implications of those photographs. Either that or Kate was under serious pressure from lawyers and superiors at work; she always became more polite when matters turned urgent.

Hallam grinned; in a perverse way he was beginning to enjoy all this attention from the women in his life. Then he realised that this was not a perverse response at all, in the eyes of normal people, or according to the therapy-influenced analyses that Lucy doubtless subscribed to. It was an utterly explicable, low-grade human desire for attention. Since when had he started to enjoy attention from women? He used to shrivel at the idea of them even looking at him. Since when had he started to act or respond like other people?

It was a genuinely worrying development. He knew all too well what his 'normal' subjects got up to behind their closed doors and open windows; he had compiled simply too much evidence for them to be considered anything like suitable role models. He would have to consider these and other pressing issues in more detail, later. Once he'd got this job out of the way.

One more message. Hallam was expecting Lucy again, but instead he was startled by the foppish tones of Alasdair.

'Good day there, Hallam. How are you? Me, I'm still a wee bit sore after that extravagant sexual pummelling, but wonderfully satisfied nevertheless. I must say your sister confirmed the old adage that the mad ones are better in bed. Not that much of it was in the bed though, eh, old chap? Anyway, I must get on, but I just wanted to check that you enjoyed the performance. We aim to please. *Arrivederci*, dear boy, and if you have any other fucked-up relatives needing to be fucked, then you know who to call.'

Two beeps followed. Hallam turned off the mobile and frowned. He picked up his trusty Leicas and weighed them in his hand, then leant back and trained them on the old weather vane above him, which had rusted solid while indicating a north-easterly wind now decades past. He never failed to enjoy the crisp clarity of the German optics.

The sound of building work up at the back lakes rumbled on during the morning, but Hallam was prevented from going up to observe because of the lack of cover in the full light of day. He had to keep his distance even at night. There was a high risk that Carl would be skulking nearby, and he did not want to test his old friend's loyalty once again, especially since the plagues in the Hall must surely have raised suspicions in his mind.

The siege mentality of the Hall, already well-established before Hallam's return, and the crisis within, made him more wary about venturing into the grounds at all. However, the arrival of a car containing what Hallam thought to be a doctor, and the fact that Verity had not shown herself out of doors all day, when her habit was to oversee Carl's work (much to his irritation), indicated that his depilatory gambit could well have paid off. He shuddered deliciously at the nastiness of his actions, and savoured his powers of malevolent ingenuity. Where did he get it from?

His hangover made Hallam realise that he had not eaten for a very long time. Food was a problem, because he did not want to show his face in the village, nor did he want to walk the few miles or so to the next one and risk running into someone he knew, or missing some development back at base. He could easily last another day or so, and that was all he needed.

That afternoon Hallam idly played his Leicas over the estate, and noticed a net curtain being peeled back in the pensioner's maisonette at the top of the road. He could see the old lady peer myopically out from her chair by the window, as she had done ever since her stroke six years before. Brisk entries in Hallam's logbook all that time ago, written down during dull periods of observation, testified to this. He had given it little thought at the time but now he considered how interminably long the retirement years dragged on in the modern world. For all the changes at the Hall and in his own life, this old woman's patterns had remained exactly the same.

Perhaps that was everyone's fate in the end if they lingered into old age; to become a crippled voyeur, positioned by the double-glazing, driven by incapacity and boredom to feed off the carrion of other people's comings and goings when the misery of TV's daytime schedules drove you away from the screen. At least he would be more prepared for it than most, if he made it that far.

It was a rental car that had attracted the old lady's attention. It pulled up by the pavement at the top of the road, but the reflection on the windscreen prevented Hallam from seeing in. Then the door opened on the driver's side.

Lucy put on her sunglasses and stretched her back. The passenger door opened, and out came Kate. She squinted up at the church and then looked over towards the grounds of the Hall. Hallam remained absolutely still.

The two of them made their way through the church gate. Kate was aiming straight for the church itself, obviously curious, but Lucy tapped her elbow and the two of them headed down the path that led directly into the grounds. What was going on? Had Lucy phoned Julius? That question was answered almost immediately when first Lucy and then Kate ducked out of sight, presumably having seen someone come round the side of the Hall. It was not the reaction of lunch guests. Lucy rose up on tiptoe and peered over the hedge, towards the lawns, then the pair of them crept past the war memorial and down the public path.

Once they were out of sight, Hallam trotted down the steeple's thin metal ladder and slipped out of the church, temporarily abandoning caution. He ran down to the Hall's private gate and vaulted over it, then slipped down the covered path through the shrubbery which opened out onto South-West Traverse. From here he could see Carl right on the far side of the lawns, patiently making his way along the lawn edges with a strimmer. The whine of the motor over that distance acquired a strangely disembodied sound.

Then it stopped. Carl had turned off the strimmer and was standing straight. He cocked his head in a way that suggested he was listening, and then went over to the fence. It had to be Lucy. Perhaps she was checking with Carl to see whether he had seen Hallam anywhere, and the chances were that Carl would tell the truth, particularly if she gave him her own version of events.

There was no way Hallam could get close enough to hear what was being said, and he felt impotent rage at the thought of Lucy turning Carl against him. Hallam's fuming was interrupted by approaching footsteps on the path and he had to slip round the other side of the shrub and sink into it to avoid being seen.

He immediately recognised the ambling footsteps. The shlip of the lighter confirmed that it was Julius on one of his smoking expeditions; he would most likely be heading down towards the pond, quite possibly looking to chat with Carl. This would be the first time that Hallam had seen his father up close in five years.

It was something of an anticlimax. As Julius passed, just feet away, Hallam could only see the back of his father's head, which was marginally greyer than before. Other than that, his figure and gait had barely changed. The waft of panatella smoke drifted back with the light breeze – even the brand of tobacco was the same. Hallam made his break and quickly ducked back down the path Julius had emerged from, keeping to the verge for the sake of silence. Then he saw Carl pop back into sight and spot Julius. Carl guiltily looked at his feet, wiped his hands on his trousers and picked up the strimmer again.

Hallam sprinted back to the church. He climbed up the ladder to the bell chamber and pulled himself up onto the roof just in time to see Lucy and Kate making their way back up the path towards the car.

They came to the fork that led either to the church or the small car park. Kate stopped. 'Can we have a quick look around? I love these old village cemeteries.'

Lucy looked at her watch, then shrugged. 'Why not? There's not much else we can do, for the time being.'

'If that was your dad, why didn't you say hello?' asked Kate.

'I don't want to explain why we're here.'

'Doesn't he have a right to know?'

'I don't see why.'

They started to walk again. 'I can't believe that Hallam's capable of violence,' said Kate.

'Of course he is,' snapped Lucy. 'He's unstable, isn't he?'

Why thank you, dear sister, thought Hallam. Although she was right of course.

The two women stepped round the dried remains of Hallam's sick on the path.

'You don't know that,' said Kate.

'I'm his sister.'

'And I'm his boss.'

'He resigned.'

'He absconded.'

The two women stopped, stared hard at each other. Lucy poked her finger at Kate. 'I want to help Hallam. You just want to track him down so you can use him as a scapegoat for this writ.'

Kate scowled. 'That is . . .' she paused, 'partially untrue. My prime motive is to find him safe then give him a good bollocking.'

They continued to tour the cemetery, performing a full circle round the church. Hallam followed them from above, passing silently from griffin to gargoyle to griffin.

'I get first go,' said Lucy. 'I can't believe he had to show you the photo with my nose pressed against the windowpane. It was completely unnecessary.'

'I thought he caught your likeness rather well,' said Kate sweetly. 'Was it your first date?'

Lucy shrugged. 'It was the only thing Alasdair seemed good for.'

'Hallam wasn't even good for that.'

Hallam flinched. Kate seemed to regret her presumably unpremeditated reaction. She looked away as Lucy processed the information.

'So that's what this is about,' said Lucy at last. Kate kept quiet. Lucy batted Kate's shoulder with the heel of a hand. Kate didn't react. 'You're worse than I am,' said Lucy. 'Twenty-two years old. Your direct subordinate at work.'

'At least we didn't do it in a hotel window,' Kate muttered.

Lucy's eyes narrowed. 'Is he in love with you?'

'It didn't mean anything. He said it was fine. He said he didn't want . . .' Kate faded out.

Up on the roof, a single tear of shame ran down Hallam's cheek.

'If you're suggesting that I'm responsible for his actions,' Kate blustered, but she lacked impetus and capitulated instead. 'OK, so it was a mistake. We're even.'

There was a pause then Lucy held up her hands. 'Let's just try to make sense of it. It might help us find where he is.'

Kate sighed and ran a finger along the inscription of a plaque mounted on a tomb. 'He may have just dropped by on a quick visit. When was it that Carl said he saw him? A couple of nights ago?'

So Carl had informed on him. Hallam found himself betrayed from every direction.

'Yeah. But I've just got this feeling . . .' Lucy paused, as if sniffing the air, and Kate stopped too, in front of another plaque. Kate frowned and stooped to read it.

'Anne Foe.' She straightened up and turned to Lucy. 'Anne Foe?'

'Mother,' said Lucy matter-of-factly. 'Suicide. Or misadventure, if you prefer.'

Kate looked closely at Lucy. Lucy, it seemed, just stood there, but she had her back to Hallam and he could not see his sister's expression.

Kate put her hand up to Lucy's face. Lucy inclined her head slightly. They stood like that for a while.

Hallam was moved and also very jealous. He wasn't ready when Lucy suddenly twisted round and looked up at the church. He dropped out of sight and waited, breathless.

'What is it?' asked Kate.

A silence. 'Nothing,' answered Lucy. 'Let's get something to eat. We'd better think about arranging some kind of surveillance.'

Hallam heard their footsteps return to the car. He did not move until he heard the engine start up and disappear down the road, and then he shook his head.

Amateurs.

As early evening came on, Hallam saw Carl through the trees, loading shovels and other garden equipment into the tractor trailer, tidying up in preparation for going home. The builders had already packed up for the day and a great peacefulness descended on the grounds; even the fantails, floating back in towards the dovecote from their trees and perches, did not inspire the usual disgust in Hallam. He had always loved this time of day. But now, of course, it was poisoned, like everything else.

Carl climbed onto the tractor and started the engine up, but then, strangely, turned it off again. He stepped down and wandered over to the far side of the grounds near the main gate. With his back to Hallam he put his fingers in his mouth. Hallam strained to hear his call but the whine of a car passing through the village prevented him. Carl then walked up towards where Hallam was hiding, behind a collection of large rhododendron bushes, and again put his fingers in his mouth. What came out was their call of old, a long piercing bird cry that started as a low throb and ended as a staccato series of chirrups.

He paused, waiting for a reply. Instinctively, Hallam's hands went to his mouth, the fingers forming their old pattern; his desire to respond was almost overwhelming. Then he smiled ruefully and let his hands drop.

Carl waited, for longer than seemed necessary, then returned to the tractor.

After nightfall Hallam made his way down from the church, safe in the knowledge that he was not being observed by Kate or Lucy. He had watched with amusement when their stake-out was cut short by the arrival of a police squad car, which had been called by the granny in the maisonette, who must have thought they were girl burglars casing properties in the area. After questioning, their names had been taken down, and they were told to clear off. This they did, cheeks burning in shame as one or two other neighbours peered out with hostile curiosity from their gardens and front doors. Lucy must have lied about her identity, not wanting Julius to know she was there.

Hallam found his way in the dark down to the front of the grounds and took up position, surveying the windows of the Hall through the pillars of the stone palisade that divided the two lawns. He was hoping for a glimpse of Verity, but the windows of the master bedroom were firmly shuttered and she did not appear in any room which had its lights on.

What was his next step? What was holding him back? And, duty aside, what was stopping him from thoroughly inspecting his own desires? His new and overriding principle had been to act, which he believed could offer a radical solution to all his problems. And yet, was he even sure what these problems were? Hallam found himself swinging between moments of pure operational clarity and profound personal confusion.

One more test of his conviction, he thought. One more dress rehearsal. He resolved to be ruthless with himself. Which tree was best placed to send the clearest possible message to the Foe master bedroom? Hallam stood up and moved over to the base of South-West Traverse. The wind rushed through the upper canopy and he heard the gentle creak of one of its boughs. He reached out a hand and touched the trunk.

*   *   *

It was 3:08 a.m. when Hallam slipped the key in the padlock that secured the stable doors – late enough, he supposed, for Carl to have gone home. The key turned smoothly and Hallam was careful to lift the floor bolt fully, so that it did not drag along the wide semicircular groove in the cobbles.

He stepped inside and savoured that smell again, of oil and grass cuttings and settled dust. His torch beam flickered across the work table littered with screws and small engine parts, over the mini tractor and trailer, down to the line of six plastic petrol cans beside the wall.

He went over and lifted them each in turn, to check which were full. He lifted two, a gallon of fuel each, and took them to the door. Then he paused. He lifted his head and sent the torch beam wobbling over the roof and the holes in the planking through which he had once observed the lovers below. How clearly he remembered that time, lying flat on his stomach, his breath clearing a little fan shape in the dust.

Hallam started from the higher branches and let the petrol course its way along the boughs and down the trunk. When the first can was empty, he let it drop to the turf below and began the second, which he winched up on the end of his rope.

Six minutes later he was standing by the base of South-West Traverse, bending over to set down the second can. He looked around him. Silence, darkness around him, extending as far as the bottom of the top lawn, where the Hall's lanterns gave the grass an unnatural lustre even in the middle of the night. The shutters were all closed.

Hallam pulled a metal lighter from his pocket, flicked it open, lit it and without any hesitation lobbed it towards the base of the trunk. A gust of wind caused the tongue of flame to shoot off diagonally into the night sky. The foliage crackled and spat. He turned and walked calmly away through the small gate and into the cemetery as the heat and greedy roar scorched his ears. With that noise he felt his life swinging irreversibly towards its fate. Now he knew that courage was unnecessary, because in his heart there was no longer any choice.

A second tongue of flame, this time high and vertical, briefly drew his eye through the net of brambles along the cemetery's edge.

It was a busy morning. The police arrived for a sombre inspection of the blackened stump, which tapered to a charcoal point about fifteen feet up. It made Hallam think of First World War photographs from the Somme battlefield. Two constables made a few inquiries around the estate. The once egg-shaped but now pudding-like journalist did so too, but was denied access to the grounds by Julius and Carl, who remained by the tree after the police had left. From among the shrubbery Hallam caught a few of their words.

Julius sighed. 'I can't help feeling responsible for this somehow. The Salute will probably have to come down anyway if the council get their way. The last meeting was dire.'

This caused Carl's anger to break through his introspective frown. 'It's not your fault, Mr Foe. You've put care and money into these grounds. It's those bloody idiots in the village. When I catch one of the buggers trespassing they'll know about it.'

Julius smiled affectionately and patted Carl on the shoulder.

'Well, we won't back down without a fight.'

Hallam looked away; Carl's brown-nosing of his employer never failed to irritate. At which point he thought he saw the figure of Verity peering down from the bedroom window. But as soon as Hallam fastened his eyes on the movement, it was gone.

Later that day Hallam listened from the church roof as the vicar stood at the entrance and helped a parishioner stick up posters for a charity jumble sale. She mentioned that the police had only one decent lead regarding that shocking explosion – a pair of young women who had been spotted by Mrs Ashford and whom the police had briefly questioned.

The parishioner, a lady in her fifties, said the culprit had to be someone local. The vicar remarked that either way it would keep the *Argos* well-stocked with material for stories about rural crime. They talked about the journalist and how the police weren't at all exercised about the felled tree: too busy, they agreed, with their usual grubby urban obsessions, such as burglary, drugs, care home paedophile rings, etcetera.

Hallam was lying naked beside the church stump and undergoing the long-delayed operation of changing his underwear when he heard the little gate swing open and the shuffle of approaching footsteps. Hallam's feet cycled hurriedly in the air as he pulled his pants up, then he crawled to the wall to look, pushing aside his pen and half-filled logbook.

At first he was baffled by the face of the woman hurrying up the path. She was a middle-aged boozer by the look of the reddened, puffy face, but with a hunched-up posture and timid scuffling gait that had an eccentric pensioner's vulnerability. The latter effect was enhanced by the ridiculously exotic lime-green turban she was wearing. Was Verity consulting some kind of New Age gypsy palm-reader to ward off the evil eye? But as she got closer and he saw, beneath the turban, the baldness at the back of the neck and above the ears, Hallam realised with a shudder just who this bizarre derelict might be.

Verity.

Hallam put a hand over his mouth and wondered if he had uttered the name out loud, because at that precise moment the woman glanced nervously around her. Her profile confirmed it. Seeing no one, Verity turned the corner of the church and went inside. Hallam buttoned up his trousers and slipped through the bell chamber's trap door and down the ladder to the stone floor at the back of the church. He stood there, partly hidden by the thick bell ropes. Yes, there she was: he could see the turban making its way up the steps and into the family pew, where it was partly obscured by the wooden ornamentation that doubled as a discreet partition from the rest of the congregation below.

He had never guessed that Verity might be religious. They had gone to the Easter and Christmas services and tossed some large banknotes into the collecting plate to fulfil the now token obligations of late twentieth-century pseudo-gentry. But here she was, on her own. Hallam was doubly fascinated; enough to take more of a risk than he would otherwise have considered.

He broke cover and slipped across the cold stone floor to crouch behind the grey medieval tomb of the Hall's old residents. To his left were heavy purple wall hangings adorned with crosses of gold thread. He waited and peeked round the corner. Her head was bowed. Was she praying? It hardly seemed possible. But it looked like it. She was completely still, with her eyes tight shut.

Hallam waited and watched. Beyond the altar he could see the arched window, which was not stained with gaudy pictures of religious scenes like most churches but plain. Behind it a weeping willow could be seen growing in the cemetery on the other side of the wall. He had always been touched by its poetic simplicity; it calmed him now, giving him confidence in his own invisibility.

He slipped forward again, this time out of view, and silently climbed up the stone steps to the pulpit on all fours. He was barely five feet away from her now, but if he kept his head down there was no way she could see him. He was sure that she could not have heard him either. So when she spoke, his whole body jerked.

'I don't know if you're listening or not. I know you don't like to reveal yourself.' She paused, as if waiting for some kind of sign or response. Receiving none, she continued.

'Thank you for the flowers. I bullied the shop girl into telling me. You shouldn't have paid by credit card, unless you wanted me to know it was you playing these games. Did you want me to, and *are* they games?'

'I hope you don't think I'm going to break down and repent for the things I've done. I don't regret a thing. But I have some good news for you. A tumour. No one else knows, certainly not Julius. You and I both know he runs from illness, and I would have preferred to enjoy these last few months before the outward signs started to show. But you've put an end to that. So, what next? I know what you want to do, even if you don't. And I want you to know that I want it too. Fast.' She paused then, her voice shaking but courageous. 'Are you a coward?'

Verity and Hallam both waited. Birds chirruped outside, just audible over the sound of a lawnmower down the road.

'The trouble is, you're not going to tell me, are you? Or maybe you're not there and I'm just going mad. Yes, that's probably it.'

Hallam heard her rise up and make her way out of the pew. And then those shuffling footsteps retreated down the aisle and out of the door – so different from the metronomic stride that had measured his sleeping hours. He stayed there for a few minutes, leaning back against the pulpit, and contemplated what she had said.

Was she really asking him to act, or was she, too, playing a game? Hallam frowned as he got up, and continued to think as he unhooked the wall hangings, rolled them under his arm, and made his way back to the roof.

That afternoon Hallam ventured down to watch Carl as he replaced one of the driveway lights that had been kicked in, probably by one of the boys that Hallam had encountered the night of his escape from the Hall. That was when he saw a young man with short brown hair and a thin mouth come cruising down the road on a mountain bike. He stopped just beyond the main gate and watched Carl with a cheeky grin on his face.

'We could see that tree burning all the way from the top of the estate.'

Hallam recognised the voice from the bushes. Carl kept working.

'Who did it then?'

'The police are on to it,' said Carl, not looking up.

'Not much chance of catching them.'

'We'll see.' Carl began to screw a new bulb into the socket.

'Bloody hooligans,' said the boy. 'Just see if they don't break it again the moment you turn your back.'

Carl straightened up with a smile, but didn't turn round. The young man decided that it was probably time to leave and twisted the bike round. Then, with quite dazzling speed, Carl burst through the gate and grabbed the boy round the neck in a half-nelson, dragged him off the bike and onto the grass within the gate. The boy was pinned.

'Right, you're trespassing now, you bastard, and I'm going to smash your face in unless you tell me who's behind that tree-burning.'

'It wasn't me.'

'It was you with that graffiti though, wasn't it? Who was it? Your mate?'

'Fucking get off!'

Carl landed a solid punch on his shoulder.

'For fuck's sake, Carl, it's only a tree.'

'There's a woman in that hall who's being messed with. Who's behind it? Who is it?'

'What? I don't know what you're on about.'

'Names.'

'Hallam Foe!'

Carl's expression changed. 'What?'

'I saw him in the grounds, two nights ago. Ask him.'

Carl rose to his feet. The chances were that he had noticed the disappearance of the petrol cans from the stable, and with no sign of a break-in, the evidence must surely have pointed to someone with keys. Hallam, for instance.

Carl looked out over the lawns thoughtfully. 'Get off this land,' he said quietly. The young man got up and staggered out through the gates. He picked up his fallen bike and pedalled away up the road indignantly. Carl went calmly back to work.

Hallam returned to the church stump. He dialled Kate's number.

'Hello?' she answered.

'Hello, Kate, it's your crap shag calling.'

'Hallam,' she answered smoothly. 'You're not the first. Where are you?'

'I've been practising on my own, it's better for my self-esteem.'

She sighed. 'I hope you don't expect me to apologise. You didn't.'

'Can I speak to my sister, please, if you don't mind?'

'OK. Hold on, how did you know she's here?'

But at this point the receiver sounded as if it was wrenched away and Lucy came on the line.

'Hallam, are you all right? Look, don't worry about the Carter affair, Kate omitted to mention that it is unlikely to reach court, and besides—'

'I'm not the least bit worried.'

'Oh. Good.'

'Where are you?'

'We're staying at this stuffy little B and B in Melton. You should see the wallpaper.' She laughed, but hearing only silence from Hallam, she continued more seriously. 'Where are you Hallam? I know you were in Chanby. Carl said.'

'I know.'

Lucy began to shout. 'How dare you take those pictures of me? What are you, some kind of pervert?'

'Technically, yes, but the point is I'm misunderstood.'

There was a pause here, a hand over the receiver. Hallam guessed that Kate was telling Lucy not to scare him off. Her tone became more conciliatory.

'I mean, why? You don't need to peep.'

'Not any more, maybe.'

'What are you planning to do?'

'Lucy, I honestly don't know.'

'Is this to do with what we talked about? Are you still angry with them? Please don't do anything stupid.'

'I wasn't intending to,' he replied a mite proudly. 'But I want to see you. And Kate. Where did you say you are?'

'We're in Melton. But don't worry, we can pick you up. Where are you, Chanby?'

'No, you can't come here, the locals will pounce on you. The police think you're involved.'

'In what?'

'I'll tell you later. Let's meet tonight, somewhere in Melton. Suggest somewhere.'

'OK, if it's not too far. The Greased Pig. It's a pub in the centre. Nine o'clock?'

'See you then. With Kate, OK?'

'Hallam?'

'Yes?'

'Will you turn up?'

'Why else would I have phoned? I need your help.'

'OK. 'Bye.'

Hallam put down the mobile, lay back, and waited for evening to come.

As the day closed, he registered the sound of crows from the copse of dead elms opposite the pub, the drone of a car from over the hill, and the steady chug of a diesel generator from farm buildings beyond the cemetery. He saw the sun go down over the fields in the west and noted how the grey clouds pinkened around their edges along the sky. Like scabs, he concluded despondently, before turning his attention back to his filthy fingernails.

A chilly wind fluttered over his arms and scalp. It suggested to him that summer was giving way, even though it was only mid-August, the eleventh of August, in fact. He pulled the church wall hangings over him. Now was the time to complete what he had come here to do. And that, he now openly acknowledged to himself, must surely be the execution of his stepmother. After all, what else could he have been building up to over these last few days?

He reassured himself that this was not going to be just another brutal act of murder. He was working as the agent of a greater power; not of religion exactly, but of natural justice. Yes, he liked that. The concept of natural justice was reassuringly vague and brought the right smack of moral authority to his vendetta. He knew that he was not well cast as a tragic hero, but he had to acknowledge that revenge was a more compelling raison d'être than charity fundraising.

But how could he know that he would go ahead with the execution for the right reasons when his head was muddied by myriad personal animosities? Were these reasons, in themselves, enough of a spur to ensure that he actually went through with it? And if he failed in his duty, how could he ever escape the knowledge that he had failed the memory of the dead parent in whose name he was pursuing this mission?

If he did not act, then what would happen to him? Where would he go? He already felt like a ghost. He had begun to take a melancholy pleasure in haunting this landscape of his past, and the longer he stayed here, the worse it would become. This voyeuristic half-life was, after all, his addiction. He had come here to shake it off for good, but if he wasn't careful he would end up falling back into it again, more hopelessly than before.

Hallam attempted to pull himself together. He should go down and scout the grounds in advance. He should clarify his plan, which was to fake an assault on the satellite mast, and thereby create the diversion that would draw Carl up there and hopefully also lure Julius out of the Hall, leaving Verity alone.

He believed he meant to kill her. He felt the potential within himself, sometimes as a bass drum in the chest, sometimes as a tremolo in the throat, and he was amazed. He was moving beyond fear to helplessness, a feeling compounded by his seeming indifference to the consequences of murder. It was not courage; he simply did not believe that arrest and trial and prison would happen to him. His imagination stopped after Verity's killing, because it would be the end of his story as well as of hers. He could only assume that if he managed to go through with her extinction, then he could manage his own too.

Hallam scratched his greasy hair furiously in a physical effort to expel these gloomy ponderings. Sentence had already been passed. The thinking was over. He gnawed at the shank of a fingernail.

But he had to answer his doubts. Wasn't revenge what his mother would have wanted? Wasn't she the victim, after all? And if his mother would not have wanted it (just suppose), and if she wasn't technically the direct victim of Verity (this was true), was that enough to win Verity a reprieve? And what if his mother was making it up?

Mother. This was not a word that he was in the habit of uttering, even to himself, even mentally. It was too strong, too sacred. Now, suddenly, he appeared to be capable of rationally considering her hypothetical feelings, as if she was not dead. He should judge her by her actions, which in her case involved a desperate act of violence. It was a parental example that he was determined to follow.

But how could he kill Verity? It was not in him. It was no good.

At this point of deepest despair, Hallam heard a car pull up beside the church gate, followed by the approaching footsteps of perhaps four people. They were chatting merrily among themselves, about a wedding they were going to, about the music they had in mind.

They unlocked the church door and went inside. They had keys? Hallam was sure that the vicar wasn't there, so it couldn't be an evening service. The church was only used one out of every three Sundays. Hallam's concerns mounted when all four of them gathered in the apse directly below him. And then he realised.

Campanologists.

The cheerful wittering came to a halt and he heard the first creak of ropes being pulled. Just a few feet beneath him, the line of old bells shifted. And then it came, the first appalling strike, and then another, and another, and soon the bells were tumbling left and right, emitting peal after enormous peal. Hallam threw all his kit down to the grass below. He jammed the heels of his palms against his ears, but it made little difference. He couldn't think. It was unacceptable, it was unassailable, it was downright medieval, and the celebratory racket drove Hallam off God's roof and onwards, with an irony that did not escape even his vibrating mind, towards a reckoning he might otherwise have missed.

thirteen

Hallam approached from the back of the lakeland development, skirting a derelict farm cottage. The night sky had clouded over, and it was only the glow of lights from the estate half a mile away that gave the surroundings any definition. He passed a pile of old masonry covered in nettles, and stopped to pick up two brick ends. They were not dissimilar to the ones his mother had put in her pockets to weigh herself down. He hefted them; they were about right. He took them with him.

Coming round the side of the cottage, he saw the Salute with its satellite jewellery, basking in the glare of the security lights which had been newly installed that day: one of the measures that Julius had taken to protect his property after the tree-burning. Hallam heard a guard dog bark hoarsely from behind the Portakabin. It must have been spooked by the shadows, or perhaps the bells that continued to ring out their good cheer over the village. A light showed in the Portakabin where the recently arrived security guard was making himself a snack, judging by the smell of monosodium glutamate and loosening noodles.

Hallam could not prevent himself from pausing to savour the odour which he would normally have found distasteful. His stomach contracted from suppressed hunger, his knees began to shudder, and for a moment he felt the full weight of his nervous and physical exhaustion. But again he willed himself on. This was just the moment when discipline was required, and to prove it to himself he took an extra-cautious roundabout route back through the fields. Minimise the risks you can control, he told himself, until the job is done.

The bells fell silent as he passed along a drainage ditch. An auspicious sign perhaps? He nimbly hopped over a barbed-wire fence that divided a field of barley from a copse, and then he froze. Through the trunks of the trees, silver-sided from the security lights on the right, there seemed at first to be nothing wrong; everything was utterly still, which combined with the angled artificial light to give the impression of a film set. However, Hallam's instincts still warned him against moving. Was it something he had heard? He waited, continuing to scan the trees. He did this for so long that he began to see shapes emerging from previously innocuous shadows. That bolus on the far trunk started to resemble a protruding head; the stump to his right, partly obscured by a second tree, was it in fact the crouching figure of another observer?

Something kept him nailed to the spot, with an insistence that did not seem to him the product of his imagination alone.

Then he heard it: the short crackle of a walkie-talkie, to his left, unfeasibly close. With exquisite care, Hallam turned his head to look. A figure rose up out of nowhere, it seemed, heavily camouflaged, clad in branches and leaves, caked in mud. It raised an arm to its head. Hallam considered whether to run.

'Luke? Wake up, Luke.'

It was Carl. The gardener cursed softly under his breath, waiting for a response. He had obviously lost none of his camouflage skills, learnt during his weekends with the Territorial Army as a teenager. Carl had taught eleven-year-old Hallam some of the tricks after work, and Hallam remembered how even this informal introduction to the art of not being seen had gripped his imagination.

Carl rolled his eyes and Hallam was close enough to see the moist whites of them in the blacked-up face. But Carl had not detected him. Luck, and many years of practice, were on Hallam's side.

Eventually a response came through on the walkie-talkie.

'Yur.'

'Luke?'

'I'm eating.'

Carl adopted the chummy egalitarian tone of a professional trying to raise the game of his amateur colleague.

'It's dead up here in sector three. How's it with you?'

There was a grunt, a scrape and then a crackle as the security guard presumably set aside his meal and tabloid to peer through the Portakabin window.

'It's going cold.'

'I'm coming back now. See you in five minutes, OK?'

Carl waited for a response but didn't get one. He put the radio back in his camo trousers, picked up the baseball bat that was lying handily by, and slipped away, panning left and right as he went, but thankfully not behind. Hallam counted one minute and began cautiously to follow; it was the safest way.

He returned to the bushes in the cemetery where he had stashed his rucksack. He took out the badger pelt and fitted it onto his head. He partially unfolded the purple wall hangings and wrapped the brick ends in them, then put the package under his arm and made his way towards the back of the Hall. He saw his father through the French windows of his office, working at his computer. Hallam reached the wellingtonia and looked out from the shadows towards the pebbled car park where Julius's Jaguar was. He would have to be quick. He took from his pocket the spare keys that he had stolen earlier from Julius's bedroom.

Dropping his package at the base of the tree, Hallam took a deep breath and ran towards the car. The crunching of his strides seemed hugely amplified. He pressed the button on the electronic keyring and the car doors unlocked. He jumped in behind the wheel, clipped on the seatbelt and stuck in the key.

The big engine revved loudly, Hallam rammed the gear lever into reverse, let off the handbrake and lurched backwards. He put the vehicle into drive and powered towards the stables, the car's big back end swinging in the loose pebbles. He glimpsed, from the corner of his eye, the back door open and Julius standing in the light. Julius ran forward a couple of steps, then stopped, turned, and screamed, 'Stay there, lock the door, don't come out!' So Verity was definitely in, and alone, Hallam concluded as the car's sleek right flank clipped a stray wheelbarrow and sent it pirouetting across the concrete.

He splintered a wooden gatepost and barely made the corner round the side of the stables, but then he was on target and pressed his foot down solidly on the accelerator, the shiny bunched bonnet directed at the mast, his hands at ten to two as prescribed by the Highway Code. The Portakabin flashed by on his right, then the car bounced violently over the rough ground and ploughed into the base of the mast.

The impact threw Hallam forwards and then back, face pressed deep into the maternal bosom of the airbag. Even over the scream of the engine, stuck on full throttle, he could hear the creak of bending metal as the mast toppled to the ground at about forty degrees to the car. Dazed but uninjured, Hallam unclipped his seatbelt. The driver's door was stuck so he squeezed past the headrests, fell into the back seat and from there scrambled out onto the dried mud of the site. Some broken quills of bracken still grew here among the brickies' cigarette butts, all that remained of the vast pillows of wild grasses that had once swayed here.

Hallam managed to stagger away into the darkness before Julius came panting up through the stables passageway, under resistance from his panatella lungs. Hallam saw the horror in his father's face as he witnessed the crumpled embrace of the vehicle and toppled edifice. The Jaguar's engine was howling at an unsustainable rev count and Hallam knew it would cut straight to Julius's heart: he would have to turn it off, and this would buy more valuable seconds. Or maybe Julius thought the driver was caught in the wreck, injured, and that he would have a chance to beat him up before the emergency services arrived.

Hallam was right. Julius bent over, seeming to whisper negotiation with his outraged lungs, and then jogged to the aid of the car in distress.

Hallam went in the opposite direction, sprinting with a delirious level of adrenaline that lightened his limbs and seemed to fix his face in a rictus or a grin. He reached the wellingtonia, wrapped himself toga-like in the thick fabric of the wall hangings (they would serve as protection from the shards), and picked up the brick ends. With one weighed in each hand, badger pelt wedged wig-like on his head, Hallam became an improvised figurehead for natural justice. He ran towards the French windows of his father's office, the palatinate toga flapping behind.

This was it. His rational mind was subdued, it was now an issue of fear. Hallam approached the window. One brick for the glass, the other for her skull. It would be like killing a sick old dog, he thought, imagining the downward blow of the brick against her temple, the soft body twitching at his knees. If only he'd actually killed something as big as a dog before. He'd once winged a blackbird with an airgun, aged twelve, and that had taken four point-black shots before its hideous reflex spasms were stilled. The image of that poor bird flapping hoplessly on the lawn hung in his mind even as he prepared to throw the brick. If the glass didn't shatter completely, he would shoulder-charge. Subtlety was no longer a priority.

As Hallam pulled back his arm for the throw, he saw, in the arched window, his victim appear. Again, as in the cemetery when she was wearing the turban, Hallam had trouble identifying her at first. She was now wearing a wig of straight black hair. Her inflammation had reduced, it seemed. She wore the black kimono which he had seen earlier in her bathroom cupboard; he had drawn her from her bed.

There Verity was, ten feet away and staring out, it seemed, directly at him. For a moment Hallam forgot how light works. He took two steps back. Then he remembered: he could see in through the window but she could not see out. He took an extra second to inspect her more closely. Verity possessed a chameleon quality that unnerved him, and he was again obliged to adjust the image of the hate figure that had sustained him for so long. She looked attractive, younger than her years. Then he asked himself what she was doing there at the window. Was she just staring at her reflection?

A reasonable voice in Hallam's head suggested that if he really was hoping to bludgeon his stepmother to death then perhaps now was the time. He raised his arm again to throw, but again he hesitated. Was it worry for her husband that he saw in those staring eyes? No, it wasn't that. Hallam inched forward and steadied himself. She still couldn't see him.

Verity lifted one arm slowly up to her head. She gripped the wig and pulled it away. She let it drop. Bald-headed, she suddenly seemed so naked. And Hallam saw the dry eyes of extremis, and he realised, with the certainty of nightmare, that she was not staring at her own reflection. She was looking through herself, out into the dark, at what she absolutely knew was there: her death. Yes, she knew he was there. Just as she knew during those meetings with his father in the stables all those years ago, when the same dry eyes had stared up at the roof. Just as she knew he was there in the church, when she prayed out loud and coaxed him towards their mutual destruction. How she knew him, and how she controlled him, even now, in her new role as a willing sacrifice.

Hallam chose her left breast for his aim, just at the tip of the embroidered dragon's tongue. He could feel her eyes on him. It was then that his throwing arm ceased to shake, and Hallam was filled with pity for his subject. Only now did he believe that she really was ill. He realised that he did not want to kill this woman, but the reasons only began to articulate themselves after the decision had been made, and he had dropped the brick on the ground. He would not give her what she wanted. Not only for pity, but because she was an irrelevance.

Hallam turned away from her and walked a few steps up towards the stables. He could see a figure growing in the mouth of the passageway, backlit by the security lights. It was his father; the curve of the shoulders and the shambling gait were unmistakable, but the silhouette soon merged with the darkness again. Hallam waited.

Twenty-four seconds later Julius came close enough to see. When he caught sight of Hallam standing there, wrapped in his religious wall hanging and badger-clad, he did not seem surprised.

'I'm going to call the fire brigade,' said Julius in a weary, practical voice. 'Someone joy-rode the car into the mast.'

Hallam realised that Julius, not unreasonably, had taken him for Carl in the dark. His eyes had not adjusted yet, obviously. But when Hallam did not reply, Julius paused on his way to the back door.

'Where were you, Carl? And that bloody security guard, what are we paying him for? Is he down the front?'

'I managed to evade them,' said Hallam quietly.

'Who is that?' Julius began to walk towards Hallam, peering at him in the darkness.

Hallam groped in his trouser pocket, pulled out the torch and lit it under his chin. There was the clatter of a chair from the arched window, but Hallam's attention was fixed elsewhere. He turned off the torch.

Julius stopped, and put his hands in his pockets, as if groping for some change. 'Oh,' he said, 'it's you.'

'Hello, Father.'

Julius did something more difficult than keep calm, considering the circumstances. He showed irritation. 'I can't believe you've trashed my car again.'

Hallam was overcome by untethered hilarity. Tears pricked his eyes. He picked up the brick end and flung it, striking Julius a glancing blow on the shoulder.

'Ow,' said Julius, rubbing his arm.

Hallam's voice was hoarse with accusation. 'You made me ruin my life.'

Julius frowned, and looked up into the night sky. 'Why is it always the parent's fault? I used to think the same thing too, of course, but to be honest, you never paid me much attention anyway, and you were always a little odd.'

Tears were now streaming down Hallam's face, snot blocking his nose. Julius looked at him and smiled. 'You haven't done that badly. Last time I checked, you had a steady job, a flat. I rather admired you skipping university. You can lie convincingly, it's a valuable asset in life.'

The wind was taken out of Hallam by the paternal compliment. He did not know how to handle it.

'You were supposed to be my father,' he said, trying to stick to the pertinent issue. 'You were supposed to be her husband.' Hallam gestured up towards the lakeland development to indicate who he meant by 'her'. 'You're not supposed to be glib.'

Julius rubbed his cheek. 'I think you're being a bit harsh on me there, Hallam. Your mother and I were very happy for years. And as for you, what about those hours I spent putting up those treehouses? You loved them. In fact I seem to remember—'

'Dad, you self-deluding lunatic, she committed suicide. She drowned herself in your lake. What does that tell you?'

'It tells me she was clinically depressed.'

'You were fucking Verity.'

Julius was suddenly very angry. He took a step forwards.

'I saw you in the stables with her,' said Hallam, 'from the loft above. Don't deny it.'

Julius paused and frowned. 'Anne didn't know. We were talking about a divorce anyway. You don't know a fraction of what it was like.'

'She told me in a letter that she knew. She told me what Verity was doing to her, driving her to it.'

'Oh yes, and what else did she tell you? That we were all ganging up on her, switching her pills, turning on the gas? Hallam, she was constantly making up accusations. She said some quite extraordinary things about you, for that matter.'

Hallam looked more closely at his father's face. All he could read was exasperation.

'She was ill, Hallam, and she killed herself. Accept it. The past never makes sense if you look too hard. But if you have to do it, pick an explanation that helps, not one that drives you mad.'

Hallam stalled. How could he know that this was not good advice? Maybe Julius was right, maybe nothing did make sense. He felt desolate and desperate.

The white driveway lights flickered on. Both Hallam and Julius turned; perhaps they had been activated by Verity inside the Hall. They saw a face, faintly skull-like in the underglow of the white shining lamp; a face that seemed to Hallam to combine the features of both Lucy and his mother.

'What are you doing here, Hallam?' asked Lucy's voice.

He was looking for this. He was looking for her, whichever she was. Hallam cried out, 'Why did you leave me?'

'I had to get away from myself.'

'What about me?'

'You came second.'

'But suicide? It was selfish.'

'Have some fucking respect,' she snapped. Then she imitated Hallam's voice: 'What about ME?'

'You promised you'd be there for me. Always.'

'It was truly felt, Hallam, but it never comes true. You have to look after yourself.'

'But she was my mother.' He was despairing, not expecting an answer.

'Yes she was, the best mother she could be, for as long as she was able.'

Lucy then walked towards them, and in Hallam's eyes she looked more herself again, freed from those transfiguring driveway lights. Carl came out of the shadows, close behind her. His unease was evident, even behind his mask of boot polish. The now sweaty security guard arrived at the rear, tugging harshly at the dog's leash. Lucy's voice acquired a cheerful tone as she looked at Hallam close up. She did not seem surprised by his garb.

'Shouldn't you be in Melton? Kate's going to be furious, sitting in that pub on her own. I knew you wouldn't turn up.'

She took the second brick out of Hallam's limp hand and glanced over to the window where Verity was now hunched, wig back on her head but slightly askew, hands cupped against the window in an attempt to see through it. Lucy sighed and let the brick drop.

Verity straightened up and hurried out of sight, adjusting her wig as she went. The Foe family waited in silence until she timidly put her head out.

'What's going on? Julius? Who's there?'

'Get back inside and shut the door,' snapped Carl. Verity was too uncertain to lose her temper with Carl, too proud to obey. Carl softened his tone and shepherded her back inside. 'Really, Mrs Foe, it's OK. Just wait inside and your husband will join you in a minute. And please don't call the police.'

'Who's out there?'

'Just some locals. Nothing to worry about. Your wig's crooked,' he added discreetly, which persuaded her to turn round and hurry back in. The door shut.

Carl turned back to his employer, his employer's daughter, and his former friend. 'Right, Mr Foe,' he said, 'I know you're my employer and I've always taken that to mean you could expect my loyalty in most things. And you still can, only I want to get a couple of things straight. These are my terms. You can call them blackmail if you like, I don't care. There's nothing to be done for the back, but I want a proper budget for the upkeep of the rest of these grounds, with cash flow and financial planning. I want plantings of deciduous trees. Proper ones, oaks, horse chestnuts, beeches, and I don't care how bloody long they take to grow. And I want some new equipment, that tractor's about fucked. And I want co-operation on that plan for the herbaceous border. And another thing, that gazebo plan of hers. Forget it. Otherwise when the cops arrive I'm telling them the lot, and so far that includes vandalism of property, the destruction of protected trees, attempted murder, and I can always leak your latest plans to the paper, Mr Foe, if you force me. Well, what do you say? Have I missed anything?'

There was an incredulous silence, broken only by the distant throb of approaching sirens. Hallam inspected the rip in the knee of his trousers. Lucy shifted her feet on the pebbles. Julius brushed himself down and took a bent cigar out of his pocket, which he straightened and lit.

'What you say sounds reasonable, Carl,' he said.

'You, Hallam, you're just like your father, except he's got his stupid underground village and you went the opposite direction, up into those treehouses. You're both so bloody self-obsessed and . . .' Carl paused, 'peculiar.'

'Right, Carl,' said Julius, whose briskness indicated that he had received sufficient lecturing for the evening, 'you can go home now. Thanks for everything, we'll talk tomorrow.'

'Right,' said Carl, composing himself again. 'Goodnight.' He walked away, straight-backed. The security guard and dog lingered.

'Go on, sod off,' said Julius, and they went too. Julius then went in to check on his wife.

Lucy and Hallam stood silently together for a moment. Then he turned to her. Softened by the shadows her face seemed more like their mother's than ever.

He looked at his sister with gratitude, at those beautiful inherited features and the good things they reminded him of. And whenever he wished to recall his mother's love in the future he knew he would come back to this eternal half-second on the pebbled car park of Chanby Hall, with the sirens curling up the drive, when his mother was absent but so obviously there.

fourteen

Hallam turned off the Royal Mile, roses under his arm, and into Urquhart's Close. It felt strange to be looking up at the tall grey tenement rather than down on it, as had been his perspective on former visits. The outer door was locked so he rang the intercom of Kate's flat. He was uneasy. He had not seen or spoken to her since his return from Leicestershire and she had not answered his telephone messages. What was she doing in there? He was not used to being kept in the dark about his subjects' lives. But she was no longer a subject, he reminded himself sternly; indeed he no longer had any subjects. It was all part of respecting other people's privacy. It made him feel doubly bereft.

Predictably she did not answer, although he knew her routines inside out, and found it difficult to believe that on a Saturday morning she would be out shopping or seeing friends. He had to talk to her. He wanted to tell her about all the steps he had taken towards becoming a normal person. He had burned his logbooks. He had tried to initiate some ordinary friendships, however scorchingly embarrassing. He had even attempted social interaction with his neighbours. He wanted to tell her that he would apply himself fervently to improving his sexual technique.

Why wouldn't she answer? He buzzed again. And again. Eventually Hallam stepped back, stared up longingly at the unco-operative windows, and sighed. He was determined not to revert to his old methods. Determined.

It felt as if he had been off the roofs for months, although the truth was nine days, ten nights. He looked around him at the Edinburgh skyline, the castle, the blackened fang of the Highland tollbooth, the Salisbury Crags, the parliament's scaffolding. Perhaps it was time he found a new city, without quite so much voyeuristic temptation. But he suspected other cities, like villages, like towns, were all the same.

Along the valley gutter he went, between the pitched rooftops, over the trap door, towards her skylight. For so long his porthole into a secular paradise, now it was a forbidden intrusion. He crouched down. The skylight was open a couple of inches. Hallam told himself that he should announce his presence before looking in. He gripped the outside of the window frame with both hands, closed his eyes and told himself he should knock, or cough or call her name. He did not want to startle her. But pehaps she wasn't there after all. He listened, and thought he heard the soft hiss of a personal stereo. Stealthily and with exquisite guilt, Hallam took a look inside.

There she was, on the bed with her eyes shut, in a tracksuit, with headphones on. Hallam watched and felt the old equivocal feelings run through him: the melancholy, the unreachableness, and the enigmatic fascinations of observation.

He levered his eyes away from the glass. He sat down on the warm lead roof with his back to the skylight and dipped his head, searching for strength. Then he reached over and picked up the roses. He got on his knees and dropped the bouquet on the skylight. Then he sat back cross-legged and waited for when she would open her eyes. Three minutes forty-two seconds later and the skylight window was tipped. The roses slid inwards and fell out of sight. Hallam waited another fifty-eight seconds before he heard her voice, wary, impatient. 'Are you still there?'

Despite his longing to answer, he did not. He could not. He heard the sound of movement below, a bounce of bedsprings and two sets of slim female fingers briefly appeared on the sill. They strained for a moment.

'Help me,' she said, her voice clenched from the effort. Hallam rose, stood astride the window, grabbed each of her wrists and with a straight back lifted her onto the roof.

She rubbed her wrists and looked at him. He had stepped back deferentially and was peering at his feet. He glanced up. She looked around at the view. 'It's beautiful up here.'

Hallam's fears abated slightly and he joined in her admiration of the urban panorama. 'I know.'

They moved to sit on the ridge, feet on the lead tiles keeping them steady in the light breeze which occasionally flicked her long hair forwards and across her face.

'What made you want to watch?'

'It wasn't about sex. Not directly anyway.'

'Then what?'

He thought about this. 'It was about making sense of things. Of people.'

'It must have been some kind of escape.'

'Yes, but . . .'

'I'm trying to understand.'

Hallam tried too. 'I thought that if I could understand how other people lived their lives, then maybe it would help show me how to live my own. I mean private life. Intimacy. Maybe that's what I lacked, and I didn't know how to go about getting it.'

'Love, you mean.'

Hallam shrugged. 'The thing is, I think I was given love. Only I forgot.' He paused. 'I wanted to know how to be normal, but what I saw of normality put me off, and so I ended up . . .' he waved his hand vaguely, 'nowhere.'

She laughed. 'So who was the paragon of normality you studied? Alasdair?' Then she stopped laughing, noticing how he avoided her gaze. He was amazed that she had not seriously considered the possibility of having been under detailed observation until now.

It was a struggle: he could see it in her face. The sense of having been invaded, the pure creepiness of finding that you have been someone's subject.

'You can trust me with everything,' he said. 'You can always trust me.'

She wavered, perched there on the ridge, disgust pushing her one way, understanding the other. She pulled back the hair from her face where the wind had just blown it. She thought hard. 'Some things I don't want to know. About myself, I mean.'

She turned to look at him. 'Your sister told me that when you were only sixteen you saved her from a gang of hooligans in Leicester, and took a punch in the mouth for it.'

'Seventeen,' he corrected, silently blessing Lucy. 'Actually it wasn't quite like that.'

'I didn't know you were chivalrous. But oddly enough I can believe it now. Do you know,' she said after a moment, 'Alasdair's been trying to get hold of me again. That's partly why I wasn't answering the door. I thought it might be him.'

There was a short silence. 'You're still angry with me,' he said.

She looked at him drily. 'Attempting to murder your stepmother is generally regarded as a dumping offence. Not that we were going out anyway.'

'Of course not.'

'Are you talking to your father again?'

'We never did talk. I thought that he was indifferent to me and it pissed me off. I was right, too, but it's OK now. I'm beginning to admire his style. Lucy told me he's asking for planning permission to construct a full steeple for Chanby Church, in steel and glass. The village will go mad when it goes public.'

'What about you?'

'You mean the Carter writ?'

She was irritated. 'No, forget about the writ, that will be sorted out in the end. What I meant was, you're going to have to live your own life now. Apply what you've learnt.'

'Am I alone in that?'

Their eyes met. Her hair blew in her face and back again. She pulled some strands out of the side of her mouth, laughed and pulled out a pack of cigarettes from her tracksuit. She tried to light one but the hair was a problem again. Hallam carefully reached out and pulled it back for her, his fingers lightly touching the nape of her neck. He felt the warm skin cool now that it was exposed to the breeze. A puff of smoke whipped across his face and he let the hair fall back. 'Thanks,' she said, exhaled. Then she turned to face him matter-of-factly. 'No, you're not alone.'

The lights were off and the blind was drawn across the skylight. Some items of clothing had been stuffed behind it to block the last cracks of daylight.

'Tell me your fantasy.'

'In the wardrobe.'

There was a giggle. 'Now that is weird, I was expecting a roof to figure in there somewhere.'

'Too exposed.'

There was a pause as she thought about the request, then a slow intake of breath. 'Whoah, coffins.'

Hallam managed to laugh. A sane laugh. Fairly sane, anyway. 'No. I happen to like the smell of wood.'

'You don't want me to take a cold bath and lie very still?'

'No. I want you to love me.'

The blind had been rolled back once more to let in the afternoon sunshine. Hallam dressed and noticed the disk that had been in the diskman: Afro-Cuban Allstars. Kate lay in bed and was watching him. She smiled lazily and raised an eyebrow as she looked his body up and down. He suddenly felt very self-conscious. He attempted to put on a sock but lost his balance and toppled over onto the discarded roses. He squawked, she laughed.

He got up again, dabbing thorn scratches on his thigh, face burning.

'Are you all right? Let me see.'

He paused, defensive, but then showed her his leg. She ran a finger over his cut and gave it a small kiss.

'I'd better be going,' said Hallam. His voice was strangled and he struggled with his plimsolls. She was smiling at him. He was not used to any of this. He got up on the bed quickly, and with a small bounce caught the lip of the skylight and prepared to lift himself up.

'You can use the door, you know,' she said. He swung gently under the sill, twice, three times, thinking.

'Nah, it's quicker this way.'

He pulled himself up through the panel of light. Then he turned, crouched and looked back down to where she lay, her hair spread out across the pillow, her expression half expectant, inquisitive. He decided that he liked the way she looked at him. He smiled, waved his fingers and made his own way across the city.

BETSY TOBIN

Bone House

'Wonderful! . . . poignant and gripping'
Tracy Chevalier, author of *Girl with a Pearl Earring*

Bone House is the tale of two women. The icy death
of the first, a large, voluptuous and charismatic
prostitute, transforms the lives of all around her: her
giant son, a hunchbacked lord, his decaying mother,
and a painter, whose arrival in the village threatens
them all.

The second is slight and solitary – a servant, whose
investigations into the prostitute's strange death
result in a terrible discovery, and the beginnings of a
future.

Set in 1603, *Bone House* is a novel about bodies and
flesh, desire and murder, medicine, superstition and
mundanity. Elegant, sensual, fiercely compelling, this
is a shockingly assured and modern debut.

'A wonderful and moving novel' Iain Pears, author of
An Instance of the Fingerpost

'Provocative (and) gripping . . . a tale shimmering
with psychological depth' *New York Times Book Review*

'(Tobin) cuts through a tangle of dark and dirty
secrets . . . with pearly clarity . . . A compelling story
of haunted lives' *Time Out*

0 7472 6491 0

review

Now you can buy any of these other
Review titles from your bookshop or
direct from the publisher.

FREE P&P AND UK DELIVERY
(Overseas and Ireland £3.50 per book)

Hens Dancing	Raffaella Barker	£6.99
The Catastrophist	Ronan Bennett	£6.99
Horseman, Pass By	David Crackanthorpe	£6.99
Two Kinds of Wonderful	Isla Dewar	£6.99
Earth and Heaven	Sue Gee	£6.99
Sitting Among the Eskimos	Maggie Graham	£6.99
Tales of Passion, Tales of Woe	Sandra Gulland	£6.99
The Dancers Dancing	Éilís Ní Dhuibhne	£6.99
After You'd Gone	Maggie O'Farrell	£6.99
The Silver River	Ben Richards	£6.99
A History of Insects	Yvonne Roberts	£6.99
Girl in Hyacinth Blue	Susan Vreeland	£6.99
The Long Afternoon	Giles Waterfield	£6.99

TO ORDER SIMPLY CALL THIS NUMBER

01235 400 414

or e-mail orders@bookpoint.co.uk

Prices and availability subject to change without notice.